DEATH TRAIL

Cody couldn't shake what he had seen in that squalid little room. Whoever the killer was, he enjoyed the hell out of his work—and this was the man who was after the Yellow Rose. Whatever the man's motives for wanting to get Rose in his power, the lovely young woman was in more trouble than she realized.

Hardened veteran of the frontier or not, a shudder ran through Cody. This was no ordinary love-struck admirer. He was a ruthless killer, willing to murder one of his own employees just so that no one would be able to follow his trail. Cody was sure that was why the hardcase had been killed. But as for the girl called Lupe . . . that was sheer evil.

The Yellow Rose had been in Del Rio less than twenty-four hours, and already four people were dead. Cody wondered what the hell was going to happen next.

Cody's Law
Ask your bookseller for the books you have missed

Book 1: GUNMETAL JUSTICE
Book 2: DIE LONESOME
Book 3: BORDER SHOWDOWN
Book 4: BOUNTY MAN

CODY'S LAW
Book 5

MANO A MANO

Matthew S. Hart

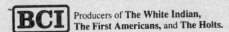 Producers of **The White Indian,
The First Americans,** and **The Holts.**

Book Creations Inc., Canaan, NY • Lyle Kenyon Engel, Founder

BANTAM BOOKS

NEW YORK • TORONTO • LONDON • SYDNEY • AUCKLAND

MANO A MANO

*A Bantam Domain Book / published by arrangement with
Book Creations, Inc.*

Bantam edition / May 1992

*Produced by Book Creations Inc.
Lyle Kenyon Engel, Founder*

*DOMAIN and the portrayal of a boxed "d" are trademarks of
Bantam Books, a division of Bantam Doubleday Dell
Publishing Group, Inc.*

ISBN 0-553-29670-1

Published simultaneously in the United States and Canada

Bantam Books are published by Bantam Books, a division of Bantam
Doubleday Dell Publishing Group, Inc. Its trademark, consisting of
the words "Bantam Books" and the portrayal of a rooster, is Regis-
tered in U.S. Patent and Trademark Office and in other countries.
Marca Registrada. Bantam Books, 666 Fifth Avenue, New York, New
York 10103.

PRINTED IN THE UNITED STATES OF AMERICA

RAD   0 9 8 7 6 5 4 3 2 1

MANO A MANO

CHAPTER
1

It was amazing, Cody thought, how much difference a long soak in a tub of hot water, followed by a few hours of passion with a beautiful woman and then a good night's sleep, could make in a man. He felt damn near human again this morning.

He had ridden into Del Rio just as the sun was going down the day before, bone-tired and covered with dust from two weeks on the trail in pursuit of a desperado with the unlikely name of Florian Ormond—which just went to show that it took all kinds to make up the great state of Texas. He'd finally caught up to Florian in a *taqueteria* in a sleepy little border hamlet. With his mouth still full of tamale, Ormond had knocked his table over and dropped behind it as he grabbed for his gun. Only problem was the flimsy table wasn't thick enough to stop the four .45 slugs that Cody had fired through it in a hurry. Then the *mamacita* who ran the place had come waddling out from the kitchen, cursing and jabbering at Cody for putting those bullets through a bowl of frijoles on their way to their eventual destination in the body of the outlaw and splattering beans all over the place. Cody had just sighed, dropped his revolver back in its holster, and bent over to grab Florian's collar and haul the carcass out of there. He'd paid out of his own pocket to have the desperado planted in the local boneyard, then headed back to Del Rio, the headquarters of Ranger Company C.

The long ride was worth it, because Marie had been waiting for him when he got back.

Now, as he sat in the nearly empty dining room of the Rio Grande Hotel and contemplated his late-morning breakfast of pancakes, steak, and fried eggs—with a pot of black coffee on the side—Cody knew that life was good.

Marie Jermaine sat across the table from him, sipping from her own cup of coffee that was liberally laced with brandy. She studied her rugged-looking, dark-haired companion, her green eyes twinkling with amusement, and said, "You are smiling, Samuel. What are you thinking, *chéri*?"

Cody knew it might sound a little foolish if he said what was really on his mind. Putting down his coffee cup, he wiped his thick mustache with his finger and replied, "I was just noticing how beautiful you are."

"You are noticing this for the first time?" Her eyebrows arched.

"No, I've known it all along."

That was true. It was impossible not to be aware of Marie's beauty. She was a tall, statuesque redhead with lovely features and a spectacular figure. If there was a more attractive woman anywhere west of the Mississippi, Cody had never run into her. There was more to Marie than sheer beauty, though. She was smart, and life had seasoned her without making her hard like so many women in her line of work were. Marie was a hostess here at the Rio Grande, and while it was true that her favors were for sale, she was no common prostitute. She was also Cody's best friend.

He picked up his fork and dug in, attacking the food with all the gusto of the cowboy he'd once been, before the Rangers had beckoned. Anyone who spent much time riding the range knew you had to take advantage of every opportunity to eat; you never knew when you might have to go without food for a while.

The plate was almost clean and Cody was working on his third cup of coffee when a sudden commotion caught his attention. He looked past Marie through the archway that led from the dining room into the lobby of the hotel. Several people had just entered the establishment, and one of them was using his palm to repeatedly ring the bell on the counter. "How about some service here?" the man gruffly called.

The door behind the counter opened, and Ernest Pelletier, the small, gray-haired Frenchman who owned the Rio Grande, appeared, looking somewhat annoyed at the disturbance. His expression changed abruptly when he looked past the man banging on the bell and focused on the woman who was waiting patiently behind him.

Cody was watching her, too, from his place in the dining room. She was a bit above medium height, with skin a little lighter than honey, hair darker than midnight, and large brown eyes revealing a Spanish heritage. An expensive dress of yellow silk hugged the curves of her slender body, and a stylish hat of the same shade, topped by a feather, perched on her luxuriant mass of raven hair. She was strikingly attractive, her beauty rivaling Marie Jermaine's.

"She is very lovely, no?" mused Marie, who looked over her shoulder at the newcomers and knew without having to ask which one had attracted Cody's attention.

"She is lovely, yes," Cody agreed. "I wonder who she is."

The vision in yellow silk was accompanied by three men, including the one whose bell ringing had summoned Ernest Pelletier, and one woman, who was also dark and pretty and well dressed but whose looks and apparel were completely overshadowed by those of her more glamorous companion.

The bell ringer was short but powerfully built, with broad shoulders and long arms. He wore a dark-gray suit that was probably pretty warm in this weather and a derby hat shoved back on his bald head. He had the air of an easterner about him, Cody thought.

The other two men—brothers by the looks of them, the Ranger decided—were Mexicans. They were attired in frilly shirts and short charro jackets and wore their sleek dark hair smoothed straight back.

Deciding he was finished with his meal—and curious about the newcomers—Cody shoved back his chair and tossed his napkin on the table in preparation for standing up. Marie chuckled before the Ranger could get to his feet. "The lure of a beautiful woman is hard for you to resist, Samuel, as I well know," she said. "But in this case, you shall have to be content to look and not touch."

Cody looked at her. "What do you mean by that?"

Marie inclined her head toward the woman. "I heard Ernest speaking about her when he was making the arrangements to have her stop here in Del Rio. That is the Yellow Rose, *chéri*."

"The Yellow Rose," repeated Cody. He frowned and shook his head, not recognizing the name.

With a sigh Marie said, "You Rangers have no appreciation for culture, for the finer things in life."

Cody glanced again at the woman called the Yellow Rose and allowed dryly, "I don't know that I'd say that."

"What I mean is that unless a woman wears petticoats and lace panties that show when she kicks up her heels, you don't pay any attention to her singing."

Cody was beginning to understand what the redhead was getting at. "You're saying this Yellow Rose is a singer."

"One of the best," Marie said with a nod. "She's very well-known, and I'm sure her servants take great pains to see that the common people don't bother her."

"Nothing common about the Rangers," Cody said with a grin. He stood up and took a step around the table toward the lobby, but before he could go any farther, the new arrivals turned away from the counter and swept up the stairs. Ernest Pelletier called after them, promising that he would have their bags brought up immediately.

Cody paused as he passed Marie, leaning over to give her a kiss and murmur, "I'll see you later." Then he went on into the hotel lobby and grinned at Pelletier, who was looking quite harassed and irritated now that his guests had vanished up the stairs.

"I hope I have not made a great mistake," the little Frenchman said as Cody came up beside him and leaned against the counter.

"By hiring the Yellow Rose to sing here, you mean?"

"Ah, you saw her. Well, I am not surprised. You always did have an eye for a beautiful woman, my friend."

"Looked like that bald-headed hombre in the ugly suit was jawing at you pretty good," Cody commented.

Pelletier nodded. "Mr. Barney Gellman. He calls himself the Yellow Rose's manager. A very obnoxious fellow, but one who has to be dealt with if I wish to reap the benefits of the lady's visit to the Rio Grande." He looked at Cody. "You've heard of the Yellow Rose, of course."

"Of course," Cody agreed without hesitation. "I hear she's quite a singer."

"'Quite a singer,' he says." Pelletier cast his eyes heavenward—or maybe just toward the hotel's second floor. "There is not a more famous singer in the world. She has performed in opera houses across the country and all over Europe. I saw her in Paris last year when I was there visiting my brother. *Incroyable!* She packed the house, and everyone was on their feet cheering and applauding when she finished her performance."

"How'd you manage to get her to come here?"

Pelletier gave an eloquent Gallic shrug. "Luck, I suppose. I heard that she was making a rare concert tour through the Southwest and wrote to her, asking her to make an appearance here. She had to come through Del Rio anyway since she is scheduled to perform in both San Antonio and El Paso and we're right on the way. At any rate, she replied that she would be glad to stop. You could have knocked me over with a mesquite bean when I read her letter, Cody. I never dreamed she would even reply, let alone accept my offer."

"Reckon you're a lucky man, all right," Cody said. "You say she doesn't come this way often?"

"To be honest, I don't recall her *ever* performing before in Texas."

"That's a little surprising," Cody said. "You'd think being from Mexico, she'd come through here more often."

Pelletier slowly shook his head. "Actually, no one knows *where* she is from. Mexico, Spain, South America perhaps. It is a mystery."

"Well, what's her real name?"

Again the Frenchman shook his head. "No one knows."

Cody frowned. A lot about this woman called the Yellow Rose seemed to be shrouded in secrecy. He finally said, "Well, I suppose if she can sing as good as she looks, nobody much cares about who she is or where she's from."

"Her singing is even better, my friend," Pelletier assured him.

That was a little hard to believe, considering the lady's beauty, Cody thought.

"But don't take my word for it," Pelletier went on. "You'll come back this evening to hear her, won't you?"

"Her performance is tonight? That's kind of short notice, isn't it? How are you going to let the town know about it?"

"Oh, the town already knows. I found out almost two weeks ago. Handbills are up all over Del Rio advertising the Yellow Rose's performance. It's just that you were gone during that time."

"And too tired to notice them when I got in yesterday, I reckon," Cody said. "If this gal is as popular as you say, you probably don't have any tickets left."

"It just so happens that I have a few," Pelletier said. "Your friends Seth and Alan have already purchased theirs, and I took the liberty of saving the seat next to them, just in case you returned to Del Rio in time."

"Thanks, Ernest. You're a good friend." Cody dug for coins in his pocket. "Now, how much is this ticket?"

"Only ten dollars."

Cody's eyebrows went up. "Ten dollars! Hell, that's a week's wages for a cowhand. Damn near that for a Ranger."

"Ah, but what is a week's wages when you're talking about an experience you will remember for a lifetime?"

Grinning, Cody brought out a gold eagle and shoved it across the counter. "Okay, you've convinced me," he said. "I can't pass up a pretty woman and a song."

"Most of the townspeople seem to agree with you. I'm

going to convert the saloon into a concert hall for tonight, and I expect it to be full."

Heavy footfalls on the stairs made both Cody and Pelletier look in that direction. Barney Gellman was coming downstairs, still sporting his heavy suit and derby. He had added a long cigar, which he rolled unlit from one side of his mouth to the other as he approached the desk.

"I thought you were going to have our things sent up," he snapped at Pelletier, his accent confirming for Cody that he came from somewhere back east.

Pelletier slapped himself on the forehead and let out a soft exclamation in French. "I am so sorry, Mr. Gellman," he said quickly. "I started talking to my friend, here, and I forgot. I will attend to this matter immediately. You have my word on that."

"Just so we get our bags," Gellman grunted. He glanced over at Cody, his small, deep-set eyes dropping for an instant to the silver-star-on-a-silver-circle pinned to the lawman's vest. If he recognized it as the badge of the Texas Rangers, he didn't make any comment about it. Without another word he turned and headed back up the stairs.

Cody followed the man's progress for a moment before looking back at his friend. "I'll see you later, Ernest. I imagine the cap'n's getting a mite impatient to hear my report." With an offhanded wave he exited the hotel and started down the street toward the large adobe building that housed the headquarters of Company C.

Two desks sat just inside the front door of the headquarters building. One of them was unoccupied at the moment; behind the other was a man who seemed to be standing at attention even when he was sitting down. Lieutenant Oliver Whitcomb had dark hair and a closely trimmed spade beard, and he wore his range clothes like a uniform. Frowning in disapproval, he looked up as Cody strolled in.

"I heard you arrived back in Del Rio yesterday afternoon," the officer said without any sort of greeting. "Captain Vickery and I expected your report before now, Cody."

"Well, it was late yesterday afternoon when I rode in," Cody said casually. "And after the last two weeks, I didn't much feel like getting up with the chickens this morning. Sorry, Lieutenant."

Whitcomb snorted. It was obvious that he knew just how sincerely sorry Cody was: not much. Whitcomb was of the opinion that the Rangers should be run with all the polish and discipline of a crack military unit, something that had never set well with lone wolves like Cody. The two men tolerated each other and each respected the other's strengths, but that was about the extent of their relationship.

"Come on," Whitcomb instructed as he stood up. "The captain's in his office."

Cody followed the lieutenant past the desks and down a short corridor to the sanctum of Captain Wallace Vickery, the commander of Company C. Whitcomb rapped on the door and opened it without waiting for a response.

He got one anyway.

"Damnation!" came a gravelly voice. "You interrupted my prayin'!"

"Sorry, Captain," Whitcomb said. "But Ranger Cody has returned from his mission and is here to give us his report."

"All right. Reckon I'll get back to the Almighty later." Vickery gave his subordinate a stern look. "I just hope He understands why I had to quit right in the big middle of things." He switched his gaze to Cody. "You catch up to that son-of-a-buck Ormond?"

Cody nodded. "Sure did, Cap'n."

"And?"

"He didn't much want to be taken into custody. He's buried at a wide place in the trail about sixty miles down the Rio."

Vickery grunted and leaned back in his chair. "This settlement got a name?" he asked.

"If it does, I never heard it," Cody replied.

"Well, I reckon that's good enough," Vickery said with a wave of a big, callused hand.

The captain wore a black suit, a white shirt, and a

string tie. Cody had never seen him in any other outfit, winter or summer. The only thing Vickery added when he went outdoors was a broad-brimmed black hat. He reminded some people of an undertaker, but what he really looked like was a hard-shell Baptist preacher—which was exactly what he was, in addition to being a Ranger leader, an Indian fighter, and an outlaw chaser. He had a ruddy face with skin that had been turned to leather by years of exposure to the elements, a thatch of white hair, and a bristling mustache of the same color. There wasn't a man alive whom Cody respected more.

"Wait a minute," Whitcomb said. "You bring us this unsubstantiated report of Ormond's death and expect us to accept it? Did you at least notify the local authorities in this place with no name?"

"No name, no law," Cody said with a shrug.

"The word of a Ranger's more'n enough," Vickery said firmly. "Always has been, always will be. We'll close the books on this here Ormond."

Whitcomb nodded reluctantly, but Cody knew that it wasn't that the man doubted the truth of the terse account of the matter; it was just his nature to demand more details, more verification. The lieutenant said, "I'll see to it," and left the office.

"Don't mind Oliver," Vickery said when Whitcomb had gone. "You know how he is. Leastways, you ought to by now."

"Sure, Cap'n." Cody snagged one of the ladder-back chairs next to the wall, reversed it, and straddled it. Cuffing back his Stetson, he went on, "Got any more chores for me?"

"Not a blessed thing. This section's got downright law-abidin' of late." The captain sounded almost disappointed. "That feller Ormond was the only one raisin' hell hereabouts, and you took care of him." Vickery shook his head. "Florian Ormond . . . What the hell kind of name is that for a desperado, I ask you?"

"Well, he was a mean one, no matter what you called him," Cody said. "Folks along the border'll sleep a little easier knowing he's gone under."

"You can get some rest, too, I reckon. I'll let you know if anything comes up. Bound to be somethin' poppin' soon. A new gang of owlhoots'll move in, or a bunch of renegade Comanch'll go on the rampage. Never knew things to be this quiet for long."

Cody stood up. "It'll be all right with me," he said. "A man gets tired of helling around all over the place, never knowing when somebody's going to try to kill him."

"Really?" Vickery looked and sounded genuinely surprised.

Cody just grinned, gave the captain a lazy salute, and ambled out of the office.

He had just stepped out the front door of the building onto the porch when two young men reined in their horses and swung down from their saddles at the hitchrack in front of headquarters. "Cody!" the taller one called.

"Hello, Seth," Cody said as the twosome climbed the porch steps. "Where are you and Alan getting in from?"

Seth Williams and Alan Northrup both wore the circled star of the Texas Rangers. Alan was the older of the two, even though he was only in his early twenties. Relative newcomers to the Rangers, they both looked up to Cody and had learned a great deal from him during the short time they had known him.

Chuckling, Seth replied, "We were out ridin' patrol. The cap'n says it's so quiet around here we're goin' to have to start scaring up some lawbreakers instead of waitin' for them to come to us." He carried a Winchester on the shoulder of his fringed buckskin jacket. Blond hair hung down the back of his neck under a flat-crowned tan hat. Seth had a quick smile and at times seemed like hardly more than a boy, but boys in Texas usually grew up in a hurry, and Seth was no exception.

"Of course, we didn't find anything," his companion added. Shorter and stockier than his companion and having a broad, friendly face, Alan looked about as dangerous as a clerk in a general store. But Cody knew he was a competent shot, a good man in a brawl, and the possessor of enough courage for two normal men. He liked both Seth and Alan enormously and hoped they lived long enough to become the Rangers they were capable of being.

"Well, at least you got back in time to hear the Yellow Rose sing tonight," Cody said to his two young friends. "I guess you can be thankful for that."

"You heard about her comin' here?" Seth asked.

"Saw her check into the hotel a little while ago."

Both Seth and Alan stared at him. After a moment, Alan said, "You actually saw her?"

Cody nodded.

"Was she as pretty as everybody says?" Seth asked eagerly. "I've heard she's just about the most beautiful woman anybody's ever laid eyes on."

"She'll make a man take notice, all right," Cody said, thinking that he was understating the case considerably. "I'll be sitting with you boys tonight, just to make sure you don't embarrass yourselves and the Rangers with a lot of hooting and hollering."

"More'n likely it'll be you doing the hootin' and hollerin'," Seth shot back at him.

"We'll see," Cody said with a grin.

"Yeah," said Alan. "Us and practically the whole town besides."

Alan's prediction was accurate. All day long Cody had heard the talk around Del Rio, and it seemed that everybody was eagerly anticipating the performance by the Yellow Rose. So it came as no surprise to him when he, Seth, and Alan arrived at the saloon attached to the Rio Grande Hotel that evening and found the place packed almost to the rafters.

"I told you the Yellow Rose would draw a crowd," Alan said, lifting his voice over the uproar in the saloon.

"Nobody argued with you, did they?" Seth asked.

Both of them were dressed in their Sunday-go-to-meeting finery, which in Seth's case meant that he had added a string tie to his usual outfit and slicked back his hair. Alan had on an actual suit, which, combined with the crowd of people in the room, had him sweating freely.

Cody had put on a suit, too, although he had dispensed with a tie. Weddings and funerals were about the only occasions when he could stand to wear one of the things. But he'd polished his boots and brushed his high-crowned, cream-colored Stetson, and he thought he looked respectable enough.

The usual tables had been carried out of the saloon, replaced with row after row of chairs that were facing the low stage on the right side of the room. The Yellow Rose was not the first singer to perform here at the Rio Grande, but, as Marie had indicated, all of those other songbirds had worn low-cut, spangled dresses and flounced around a lot so that their gowns flew up, whereas the Yellow Rose was the first one to attract a crowd like this primarily because of her vocal abilities.

Cody, Seth, and Alan made their way to their seats, choice ones located in the second row. Not a bad spot, Cody decided, considering that the front row was filled up with local dignitaries. He saw the mayor of Del Rio and Sheriff Christian Burke sitting up there, then had to grin when he noticed who was with them. Captain Wallace Vickery himself had come to take in the show, and Lieutenant Oliver Whitcomb was beside him. It was unusual to see the captain anywhere except Ranger headquarters or one of the local churches, all of which he visited from time to time to deliver a sermon, regardless of their denomination.

As they settled into their seats, Cody nudged Seth in the ribs. "Look over there," he suggested, inclining his head toward Vickery.

Seth followed Cody's gaze, and his mouth dropped open at the sight. He nudged Alan in turn, who said, "Looks like all the law in these parts turned up here tonight."

That comment brought a slight frown to Cody's face. He craned his neck and looked around the room at the rapidly filling seats. Sheriff Burke's deputies were also in attendance, as were quite a few of the other Rangers from

Company C. Any members of the lawless community who wanted to raise a ruckus would have a prime night for it tonight. They could run roughshod over the town with nobody around to stop them.

Cody settled back in his seat and told himself that he was worrying for nothing. After all, hadn't the captain just told him this morning how peaceful things were around here now?

Moments later a signal from Ernest Pelletier sent several men around the room extinguishing the lamps. The only ones they left burning were those over the stage itself. The crowd began to quiet down, knowing that the show was about to begin.

Curtains at the rear of the stage were abruptly brushed aside, and the two swarthy men Cody had seen with the Yellow Rose that morning emerged, each carrying a guitar and a stool. They were bareheaded, and their earlier—and by comparison conservative—suits had been exchanged for fancy charro outfits: wide-bottomed pants with embroidery down the sides, colorful, frilly shirts, and short jackets decorated with all sorts of garish stitchery. They were a sight, Cody thought.

The men placed their stools at the sides of the stage and sat down. Cradling their instruments, their fingers began strumming the guitar strings, and the low-voiced conversations across the room ceased as the first mellow notes floated out.

Having spent years in the border country, Cody had heard plenty of Mexican guitar players, but these two were among the best. Even their tuning up was melodic and in harmony. When they were satisfied with the tones being produced by their instruments, their fingers began to almost fly over the strings, the individual movements lost in a blur.

They played a fast-paced, stirring tune that couldn't help but get the listeners' blood moving, then slowed down for a more mournful piece that invoked a wordless, bittersweet melancholia. Cody glanced over at Seth and Alan and saw by the light from the stage that both of them were swallowing heavily. The ballad touched him, too, making him think of long nights and lost loves. Hell, he thought, these boys were so good with their guitars that you'd think of such things whether you'd ever actually experienced them or not.

When that song was done, the musicians picked up the pace again, their playing becoming faster and more animated until it had reached an almost feverish pitch. Then suddenly, when no one expected it, the curtains parted again, and the Yellow Rose appeared, stepping to the front of the stage and beginning to sing.

She was wearing another yellow gown that hugged her curves as sensuously as had the silk traveling outfit she had worn that morning. Her midnight-dark hair was done up in an elaborate arrangement of curls and was held in place by a red comb and a yellow ribbon that matched the dress. She wore no jewelry, but she didn't need any. She sparkled enough on her own.

But Cody noticed none of that at first. Like everyone else in the room he was immediately entranced by the power of her voice as it blended with the guitars in a fiery tune that spoke of passion, violence, betrayal, redemption. Cody was immersed in the music and carried along by the song—so much so that he felt almost a physical shock when it came to an end and without pause the Yellow Rose launched into a lingering Spanish ballad.

For the next hour Cody had no idea of the passage of time, lost as he was in the voice and beauty of the Yellow Rose. She sang love songs of Mexico and Spain as well as some American ballads and operatic arias. It didn't matter what the songs were or where they came from, though. The Yellow Rose made all of them her own.

Normally an audience would applaud after each number; the people here in the Rio Grande were too absorbed for that. They listened in rapt silence until, at the conclusion of a song, as abruptly as she had entered, the Yellow Rose bowed her head for a second and then faded back through the curtains. The last notes from the guitars trailed away, and then the musicians were gone, too, and the audience was left to slowly realize that the show was over.

When they did, their applause just about lifted the roof off the Rio Grande Hotel.

Men surged to their feet, beating their hands together and cheering at the top of their lungs. Cody was among them, demonstrating his appreciation as exuberantly as everyone else. Del Rio had never before seen a show like the one tonight, and the people made that quite evident.

Though hoping for an encore, the audience was destined to be disappointed. After the applause had gone on for nearly ten minutes, they began to realize that the Yellow Rose was not going to put in another appearance, and the hotel employees relit the lamps. The respectable ladies in the audience who had come to the Rio Grande tonight only because it had been temporarily converted into a concert hall quickly left with their escorts; everyone else headed for the bar, which was now open again.

Cody felt a mixture of emotions as he made his way through the crowd with Seth and Alan. There was a keen sense of loss brought on by the absence of the Yellow Rose's voice, yet at the same time he was filled with excitement, knowing that he had witnessed something very special tonight.

Ernest Pelletier had been right. Memories that a man would carry with him through a lifetime were well worth a week's wages.

"I've never seen or heard anything like that before," Alan said as he and his companions finally reached the bar and signaled for beers to be brought to them.

"Me neither," Seth agreed. "That lady can sure sing. And I don't reckon I've ever seen a prettier woman."

Cody nodded. An idea was playing around in the back of his mind, and after a white-aproned bartender had brought their beers, the big Ranger took a sip of the cool, frothing liquid and announced, "I think I'll go backstage and congratulate the Yellow Rose on her performance."

Seth and Alan both stared at him as if they thought they'd heard him wrong because of the hubbub in the room. After a moment Alan asked, "What'd you say?"

"I think I'll go backstage and congratulate the Yellow Rose," Cody repeated.

"Hah!" Seth exclaimed. "Cody, I reckon you could get into the middle of a Comanche village if you set your mind to it, but not even you are goin' to be able to get close to that woman."

"We'll see," Cody said calmly, then took another swallow of beer.

Alan was shaking his head. "It's impossible. Her servants will stop you."

A sudden bold urge seized Cody. He wasn't sure where all this bravado came from, but he declared, "Boys, I'll not only get to talk to the lady . . . I'll bring back that yellow ribbon from her hair as a souvenir. Just to prove I saw her, you understand."

Seth cackled and slapped his palm down on the bar. "You've been in the locoweed, Cody! I never knew you to act so plain crazy."

Maybe the youngster was right, Cody thought briefly. He *was* usually pretty levelheaded. But seeing the Yellow Rose tonight and listening to her sing had done something to him, made him feel like taking a chance and daring the odds. He drained the rest of the beer, thumped the empty mug down on the bar, and said, "I may be crazy, fellas, but before the night's over, I'll have that hair ribbon."

"Well, don't let us stop you," Alan said with a chuckle.

Grinning, Cody left the bar and headed toward a small door to the right of the stage that he knew opened into a narrow corridor leading to a couple of dressing rooms. Sometimes a touring company of actors would come through town and put on a series of scenes from Shakespeare or some such, and they always used the dressing rooms. Cody had no doubt that the Yellow Rose was back there now.

No one challenged him as he opened the door and stepped into the hallway. He pulled the door shut behind him and looked down the lamplit corridor. Two more doors opened to his left. Cody started toward them.

The nearest one opened before he could reach it, and he suddenly found himself facing the two Mexican guitar players and the brawny, bald-headed man he'd seen that morning in the hotel lobby. Barney Gellman, that was his name, Cody remembered.

"Hold it right there, mister," Gellman growled, his heavy features creased in a frown that made him look like a wrinkled old bulldog. "Where do you think you're going?"

"I want to say hello to the Yellow Rose and congratulate her on her performance," Cody said honestly. "I've never seen anything like it."

"Yeah, you and all the other yokels around here," Gellman gibed. "The Yellow Rose doesn't see any admirers, so you might as well beat it, cowboy."

Cody kept a tight rein on his temper, even though Gellman's high-handed tone put his teeth on edge. He knew what Gellman and the two musicians were seeing: a big, mustached range rider, humbly holding a Stetson in his hands, who was wearing a suit that had seen better days despite its being cleaned and pressed that very day by Ling the Chinaman. To people who had been all over the country, all over the world, for that matter, he probably did look pretty unimpressive.

Well, he had a trump card to play, he thought, and moved the lapel of his coat to the side so that the badge pinned to his vest was visible. "I'm a Texas Ranger," he said. As a reminder to Gellman he went on, "I think you saw me in the hotel lobby this morning."

"If I did, I don't remember," Gellman said. "And I don't care if you're President Grant's ex-bartender, you ain't getting in the Yellow Rose's dressing room."

Obviously the man didn't intend to budge. Cody sized him up for a moment. Gellman would be a pretty even match for him in a fight. They weighed about the same, and while Cody had a height advantage, Gellman's unusually long arms offset that. The Ranger glanced at the two Mexicans. Both of them were watching him with dark, unfriendly eyes. Close up like this, the resemblance between them was strong. Brothers, no doubt, the Ranger thought.

The older of the two—judging by the flecks of gray in

his smooth, dark hair—moved his right arm slightly, and Cody saw the handle of a small knife protruding from the white sleeve of the man's shirt. The weapon would be a throwing knife, Cody decided, snugged into a sheath strapped onto the man's forearm. A glance at the other brother told Cody that he was probably armed in the same manner.

Gellman wouldn't need or want a weapon, unless it was a blackjack. The expression on his face said that he would cheerfully beat Cody to death with his bare hands.

"All right," Cody said slowly, unwilling to cause a scene but loath to think about the unmerciful ribbing he would take from Seth and Alan if he returned without the Yellow Rose's hair ribbon. "I didn't come back here to start a fight, just to tell the lady that I enjoyed her sing—"

A sudden, muffled scream cut off what Cody was saying.

The heads of all four men jerked toward the source of the jarring sound: the second door, the door behind which was the Yellow Rose . . .

Gellman and the two musicians hesitated only an instant, then plunged toward the door. Cody was right behind them. Instinctively, his hand went to the Colt on his hip, fingers closing around the smooth walnut grip.

Another frightened cry came from behind the door.

"Get back, dammit!" Gellman rasped at Cody as the men converged in front of the door. "You can't go in there!"

Cody's revolver slid briskly from its holster. He didn't point it directly at Gellman, but its muzzle was drifting menacingly in the easterner's direction as Cody said, "Gellman, there's trouble in there, and that makes it Ranger business!"

Cursing, Gellman reached for the knob of the door. He twisted it, but the door remained shut. "They've jammed it some way!" he said, anger and despair blending in his voice. "Okay, have it your way, Ranger," he went on. "I'll bust down the door, you be ready!"

Cody nodded grimly as the gun in his fist lifted. He was ready, all right.

Gellman drove his beefy shoulder against the door with a grunt and a crash. The panel shivered but didn't give. His face contorting with the effort, the easterner drew back a couple of steps and hit the door again. This time there was a splintering sound and Gellman lost his balance, pitching forward as the door popped open. He landed half in and half out of the dressing room.

Cody vaulted over him into the room to witness the scene being played out before him: The Yellow Rose was on the far side of the room struggling with two men who were gripping her by the arms and dragging her over to the open window. A split second later the two musicians spilled into the room behind Cody, trampling on the cursing Gellman, who was trying to scramble back to his feet.

The nearer of the would-be kidnappers turned to meet the threat by the rescuers, his free hand reaching for his holstered revolver. From the corner of his eye Cody saw the older musician's arm whip up, back, and then forward with the same blurring speed that his fingers had demonstrated on the strings of the guitar. The throwing knife flicked across the room and sank into the assailant's chest. With a high, thin cry of pain, the man let go of the Yellow Rose's left arm and sank to the floor, pawing at the handle of the knife for a second before he fell forward.

At virtually the same time the other man released the singer's right arm and, spewing an obscenity, reached for his own gun. Cody shouted at the woman, "Get down!" as the kidnapper jerked a long-barreled Remington out of its holster.

Ranger Colt and outlaw Remington roared at almost the same instant, the two explosions blending into one. But Cody's shot came first, the slug driving into the man's chest and knocking him backward. The kidnapper's arm drooped so that his shot went into the floor. As he reeled from the impact of Cody's bullet, the back of his knees hit the windowsill and he toppled through the opening, falling into the alley.

Frantic hoofbeats then sounded from the alley. Cody sprang to the window, leaping past the Yellow Rose lying stunned on the floor where she had fallen. Even though

Cody was fairly certain that the man he had just shot was either dead or unconscious, he still felt a twinge of unease as he stuck his head out the window. The hoofbeats were coming from his right. He looked in that direction, and in the shadows of the alley he saw a man riding a horse and leading two other mounts. Apparently the animals had been spooked by the gunfire, and the man was having trouble controlling them.

He must have seen Cody looking out the window, because he twisted in the saddle and gun flame bloomed orange in the gloom. As the sound of the shot echoed off the walls of the narrow alley, Cody felt the wind of a slug whipping past his ear. He grimaced and triggered a couple of shots, not really expecting to hit anything in such poor light.

And he was right. The fleeing man turned a corner without slowing down, pulling the other horses with him as he vanished. The sound of racing hooves faded away quickly. The Ranger knew that the man'd be long gone before he could catch up to him. Trying would be a waste of time.

Pulling his head back inside, Cody straightened and turned back to the room. The threat seemed to be over, so he pouched his gun. The Mexican who had downed one of the kidnappers with his knife was kneeling beside the fallen man, making certain he was dead. Satisfied, the musician withdrew his blade and wiped the blood from it on the corpse's shirt. The younger Mexican was standing close by, the knife gripped in his hand ready for instant use in case of more trouble.

Barney Gellman was helping the Yellow Rose to her feet, hovering over her with the anxious attitude of a mother hen. "Are you all right, Rose?" he asked, his voice tight with strain and worry.

"I . . . I am fine," she replied in that same husky, vibrant voice that could work wonders with the simplest song. "Those men . . . they came in through the window before I could stop them. . . ."

"There, there," Gellman said, awkwardly patting her

on the back. "Don't you worry about a thing. It's all over now."

"Yes," the singer said with a nod, visibly controlling her emotions. She turned to face Cody then, and her smile made her even more beautiful than he would have thought possible.

"Ma'am," he said, nodding, his mouth suddenly dry.

"I do not know who you are, sir," the Yellow Rose said, "but it seems that you have saved my life. Thank you."

And then, before anybody in the room had a clue as to what she was about to do, she stepped forward and kissed him.

CHAPTER
2

It was only a quick brushing of her lips across his cheek, a gesture of gratitude and nothing more, but the contact still sent a jolt through Cody. This woman's touch, even a light one, packed the same power as her voice.

As she stepped back from him, he saw the looks of disapproval on the faces of Gellman and the two musicians. They didn't like what the Yellow Rose had done, even if Cody had helped prevent three strangers from abducting her.

"We could've taken care of them, Rose," Gellman said.

She turned toward him quickly. "I know you could have, Barney," she assured him. "But you might have gotten hurt. Those men had guns. I would have hated to see any of you come to harm."

"Guns don't matter," Gellman insisted, but he shrugged to indicate that he wouldn't push the matter any further.

With Gellman slightly mollified, the singer shifted her attention back to Cody. "I should know your name, sir, considering what you have done for me."

"It's Cody, ma'am," he said. "Samuel Clayton Woodbine Cody." He smiled. "My ma got a little long-winded sometimes. Most folks just call me Cody."

"I am glad to meet you, Mr. Cody." She waved a slender, long-fingered hand toward Gellman. "This is my business manager, Bernard Gellman."

Cody nodded to the bald-headed man. "We hadn't

been formally introduced, but we've met." He held out his hand. "Pleased to make your acquaintance."

Gellman's grunt and the glare he gave Cody made it clear that the feeling was not mutual, but he shook the Ranger's hand anyway. If the Yellow Rose noticed his surly attitude, she gave no sign of it.

"And these are my accompanists, Alonso and Eduardo Martinez," she continued, indicating the two musicians.

Cody nodded and shook hands with both men. Eduardo, the older one, seemed slightly friendlier than Alonso, who was frowning almost as darkly at Cody as Barney Gellman was.

The Yellow Rose's gaze touched the badge on Cody's vest. "You are a Texas Ranger."

"Yes, ma'am," he confirmed, although her words had been a comment, not a question.

"How is it that I am lucky enough to have a Ranger waiting so close by when trouble came to visit me?"

Cody grinned, intending to take full advantage of this opportunity. "I wasn't looking for trouble," he told her. "I came back here to congratulate you on your performance tonight. You really stood Del Rio on its ear."

"Thank you," she said graciously, adding with a smile, "that was my intention. No matter where I am, a concert hall in London or Paris or the Rio Grande Hotel in Del Rio, I always try to give my very best performance."

"Well, I don't see how you could ever beat tonight's show," Cody said, then looked sharply toward the door as the sound of heavy footfalls came from the corridor.

Several men appeared in the open doorway, among them Sheriff Christian Burke, a middle-aged, heavyset lawman with a drinker's nose. He pointed at Cody and said to his companions, "You see, I told you I heard shots. If Cody's here, there must've been some sort of ruckus."

Captain Wallace Vickery stepped into the room behind Burke, and Lieutenant Oliver Whitcomb followed Vickery. With his white mustache bristling, the captain looked at Cody and demanded, "Well, how about it, son? There some trouble here or not?"

"Not now, Cap'n," Cody replied easily. "Some hombres tried to rustle Miss . . . Rose here." He jerked a thumb toward the dead man on the floor. "There's one of them. You'll find another one out in the alley under the window. A third man got away. Sorry."

"Too bad," Vickery said. He looked at the Yellow Rose with something like awe in his eyes. "Want you to know, ma'am, Del Rio ain't always like this."

"That's right," Sheriff Burke added. "Most of the time it's a real peaceable little town."

"Do not worry, gentlemen," the singer told them with a smile. "I have traveled a great deal and know that evil men can be found everywhere."

Gellman could not resist adding, "But especially in these frontier burgs—"

Cody moved smoothly between Gellman and the local authorities. Sheriff Burke, especially, looked as if he might be on the verge of losing his temper. "Sheriff, why don't you have your deputies take charge of these bodies?" the Ranger suggested. "I imagine the lady would appreciate it if they were gotten out of her vicinity."

"I would indeed," she said.

"Of course, ma'am," Burke said gruffly. "I'll tend to it right away."

As Burke turned toward the door, Captain Vickery nodded to the young woman and told her, "It's sure an honor to meet you, ma'am. I purely enjoyed your singin'."

"Why, thank you, Mr. . . . ?"

"Vickery, ma'am. Cap'n Wallace Vickery of the Texas Rangers." He indicated Cody with a nod of his head. "This young fella's boss."

"Well, your Mr. Cody must be an excellent Ranger. He probably saved my life with his quick actions."

"He's one of our best, all right," Vickery agreed, and Cody saw the slightly pained look that crossed Lieutenant Whitcomb's face at this testimonial. Vickery clapped his hat on his head and went on, "We'll get out of your way now, ma'am. Sorry this had to happen and spoil your evenin'."

"Oh, my evening is not spoiled at all." She cast a look toward Cody that the big Ranger couldn't quite translate. "It is not spoiled at all."

Vickery raised a bushy white eyebrow, then gestured for Whitcomb to precede him out of the dressing room. Cody stood there while his superiors left. No sooner were they out of the room than two of Sheriff Burke's deputies came bustling in. "Sheriff sent us to haul a carcass away," one of them explained bluntly.

Cody indicated the body and stepped back out of the way. He heard noises in the alley that told him more deputies were out there, tending to the other dead man. In a matter of moments the corpses were gone, and Cody was left with the Yellow Rose, Barney Gellman, and Eduardo and Alonso Martinez. The atmosphere in the room, already heavy with tension, thickened even more. The three men seemed to be waiting for him to leave, but he didn't intend to go until he had explained to the singer about why he needed that ribbon in her dark hair. . . .

"Please leave us now," she abruptly told Gellman, putting a hand on the burly man's arm as she spoke. Gellman looked as surprised at the request as Cody felt.

"With this fella, you mean?" Gellman asked, waving a knobby-knuckled hand at Cody.

"I think I will be perfectly safe with a Texas Ranger," the Yellow Rose replied softly. "I wish to speak with Mr. Cody privately."

Alonso moved closer to her and murmured something in Spanish. Cody understood the language, having grown up in Texas, but the words were too soft for him to catch. The Yellow Rose gave a short shake of her head, and Alonso started to say something else, but she silenced him with a touch of her hand on his shoulder.

Eduardo put a hand on his brother's other shoulder and inclined his head toward the door. He might not like it, but he was willing to go along with whatever the Yellow

Rose requested, Cody figured. Alonso went with him, grudgingly.

Before he left, Gellman growled, "I'll be right outside." He took a cigar from his pocket and stuck it in his mouth without lighting it, his strong brown teeth taking out his obvious anger on the tightly rolled cylinder of tobacco.

When they were finally alone, the Yellow Rose strolled slowly to the opposite side of the room and then turned to look at Cody. It was not a long walk; the dressing room was small. She smiled at him and said, "You must wonder why I wished to be alone with you."

Cody shrugged slightly and met her steady gaze. "There are a lot of reasons why a woman might want to be alone with a man," he said. "I reckon you'll get around to telling me which one you've got in mind."

"Do not flatter yourself, Mr. Cody." Her words were rather sharp, but the warmth in her eyes took most of the sting out of them. "This is not a romantic rendezvous. I wanted to . . . thank you again for your help."

"That's not necessary, Miss—"

"Call me Rose," she said. "No Miss. My friends know me by that name, and I am hoping we will be friends, Cody."

"Fine by me," he replied with a nod. "Now I've got a question to ask you."

She looked a bit surprised. "A question?"

"Yes. Can I have that ribbon in your hair?" He pointed to the yellow silk ribbon entwined in the dark curls.

Rose lifted her hand to it. "This ribbon, you mean?"

Cody nodded.

"But why?"

"Because I told a couple of friends of mine that not only would I get to talk to you, I'd get your hair ribbon to prove it," Cody said forthrightly. "They'll really ride me if I come back without the ribbon, so I thought, since I saved your life and all . . ."

Rose threw back her head and laughed as his voice trailed off. It was a good laugh, hearty and honest. "I see you are a man who speaks his mind, Cody," she said after a moment. Her fingers plucked loose the hair ribbon, and it dangled from her hand. "I will be glad to give you this ribbon—"

Cody lifted his hand and reached for it.

"—in return for a special service," she concluded.

Cody's hand stopped where it was. After a moment's silence he said, "I'm not sure I can promise that. What is it you want?"

Suddenly the merriment dancing in Rose's eyes vanished, and her lovely face became solemn. "Come with me," she said. "Come with me on the rest of this tour and protect me. You see, tonight was not the first time someone has tried to abduct me."

A muscle twitched in Cody's cheek. Rose's proposal had taken him completely by surprise. He was not the kind to flatter himself, but he'd had enough luck with the ladies in the past to have believed that something along the lines of a pleasant interlude was what she'd really had in mind, despite her statement to the contrary. Now it seemed he had been dead wrong. Her motive in asking for this private meeting had been practical, not romantic.

He took a deep breath, then said, "That's a mighty tempting offer. But I'm a Texas Ranger, Rose. I can't just up and leave Del Rio to go with you. I've got duties—"

"Such as the protection of the innocent and the apprehension of wrongdoers?"

"Well, yeah, I reckon you could put it like that."

She raised her hand and held up one slender finger. "In New Orleans, there was a man in my hotel room. Barney came when I cried out, and he chased him away." Another finger went up. "When we reached Galveston, two men accosted me backstage at the theater where I was performing. Again someone intervened before the encounter became violent." A third finger. "In San Antonio, my stop prior to this one, men followed me. I am convinced that there would have been an attempt to kidnap me there, if I had not changed hotel rooms in secret. In fact, I heard the next morning that there had been an altercation between one of the guests and a prowler in the man's room—the same room where I was supposed to spend the night." Rose held up the fourth finger. "Now this incident here in Del Rio. Tell me, Cody, am I being a foolish, frightened woman . . . or is someone really after me?"

Cody's expression had become more and more grim during her story. He admitted, "It sounds to me like you've got trouble, all right. But you've also got Gellman, Eduardo, and Alonso to handle it for you. They seem to me like pretty competent hombres."

"They are good men, good friends," she said. "Barney calls himself my manager, but he is actually my bodyguard."

"I figured as much," Cody said.

"He is a hard, capable man. So is Eduardo. Alonso is brave, but he is young and I think he is a bit in love with me. This can be a disadvantage. But you are right, they can handle almost any kind of trouble." Rose stepped closer to him, and the fingers that had ticked off the events of her recent history now brushed Cody's cheek. "Still, I sense that you are special, Cody. I am a good judge of men—"

Cody didn't doubt that for a second.

"—and I think it will take a special man to handle this trouble."

"Well . . ." Cody grimaced. He supposed he could at least discuss the problem with her. "Who do you think is after you, and why?"

She shrugged her elegant shoulders, left bare by the gown she still wore. "It is so simple. I believe that one of my admirers has been hiring these thugs to capture me."

"An admirer?" Cody repeated with a frown. "Why would an admirer do something like that?"

"Why, so that he can have me all to himself. At least, this is what he believes will happen."

"You sound like you've got somebody in particular in mind."

Rose shook her head. "No. There are many men who have wanted me. It sounds immodest of me to say this, but I know it is so. Many have come backstage—as you have tonight—to see me after my performances. Some of them bring flowers or gifts. Some say plainly that they would like to take me away with them." She smiled. "You know, I could have been a princess by now, perhaps even a queen. If that were what I wanted."

Cody's mind was working, going back over everything she had told him during the past few minutes, and another possibility had suggested itself to him. He turned his hat over in his hands, feeling a little awkward about talking to a woman concerning such a subject, but he asked, "You make pretty good money from these singing engagements, don't you?"

She inclined her head negligently. "Money is good only for what it can buy. I pay little attention to it. But, yes, I am well paid. You do not think that could have anything to with the attempts to abduct me, do you?"

"Your associates could probably come up with a pretty healthy ransom if anything happened to you," Cody suggested. "That sounds to me like a good motive for a kidnapping."

"No!" She turned away from him sharply and walked across the room, her anger visible in the stiff set of her shoulders and back. "Someone is obsessed with me, acting out of a cruel, twisted love."

The more he thought about it, the more that sounded to Cody like something out of one of the melodramas the traveling actors staged. Obviously Rose didn't see it that way . . . or didn't want to see it that way.

He hesitated a few seconds, then said, "Look, it really doesn't matter why somebody's after you. The important thing is for you to keep your eyes open and be careful."

"I agree," she said briskly, turning to face him again. "That is why I want you to come with me. You will be my eyes. You will see the danger coming."

"I can't. I'm sorry, but I just can't take off on my own like that—not and stay part of the Rangers."

She regarded him steadily for a long moment, then sighed. "I see that you are telling the truth," she said, a slight bitterness tingeing her voice. "I also see that you are not a man to desert his duty. Very well. As you say, I will keep my eyes open and trust that Barney, Eduardo, and Alonso will protect me."

Cody almost weakened at that moment, but then the

power of the oath he had sworn to the state of Texas came back to him. "I'll tell you what," he said. "I can do this much: I'll try to find out all I can about those two dead men. If I can learn who they are, maybe it'll lead me back to whoever hired them. An investigation like that falls within the scope of my job, I reckon."

Rose nodded. "All right. And thank you, Cody. I know you want to help me all you can." She stepped closer to him again. "We will not be leaving until the next west-bound stagecoach comes through. If you discover anything before then, you will come and tell me?"

"Right away," he promised.

"Gracias." Somehow she'd gotten right in front of him without his really realizing how close she was. She came up on her toes and kissed him again, and this time her lips pressed warmly to his mouth for an instant. "Good night, Cody."

"Good night," he managed to say. He turned toward the door, slightly dazed from her kiss.

"Cody," she called to him, a mocking lilt in her voice.

When he turned, he found her holding up the yellow ribbon from her hair.

"You forgot this."

She released the ribbon, letting it flutter to the floor. Cody's eyes followed it, and when he looked up again, she had disappeared. There was only one place she could have gone, and that was behind a small dressing screen in one corner of the room. He heard the faint noise of slithering fabric as her dress fell to the floor.

Cody didn't push his luck any further. He scooped up the yellow ribbon, put his hat on, and got out of there. Gellman was just outside the door, true to his word, and the Ranger felt the bald-headed man's eyes boring into his back as he went down the hall.

Guitar music floated through the night, and while it was not played with the same expertise as that of Eduardo and Alonso Martinez, it throbbed with the same sort of passion. The notes came from a squatty adobe cantina in a section of Del Rio known for the hardcases who frequented it. Sudden death was common there.

The man who walked toward the cantina looked ready for any kind of trouble. His shoulders, though slumped, were broad and powerful, and his right hand never strayed far from the worn grip of the Colt on his hip. A battered black hat was crammed onto his head above a ratlike face. His name was Al O'Neil, and he had just come from stabling three horses, his own and two that had belonged to his friends—friends who were now dead.

O'Neil lifted a hand, rubbed his jaw, and grimaced. The man who had hired him and his partners had assured them that it would be an easy job. Just grab one woman, he'd said, and bring her back here to the cantina. One particular woman, of course. The Yellow Rose. That singer who had put on a show at the Rio Grande Hotel earlier in the evening. Yeah, easy, O'Neil thought bitterly.

He didn't know exactly what had happened inside the dressing room; he only knew the job had gone wrong. There was shooting, and Sherm came tumbling out the window. O'Neil had known he was dead when he saw the way Sherm fell loose-limbed into the alley. He wasn't sure what had happened to the other man, Keaton, but when that Ranger stuck his head out the window and started firing, O'Neil knew that his other friend wouldn't be coming back, either. He got the horses moving, threw a shot at the Ranger just to rattle him a little, and got the hell out of there.

Now he was back here at the cantina where he was supposed to meet his employer, and O'Neil wasn't sure how the man was going to take the news of failure. But he didn't much give a damn. As far as O'Neil was concerned, the boss hadn't played straight with them. They should have been warned that they might run into trouble—especially Ranger trouble.

The rat-faced hardcase reached the open doorway of the cantina and paused there, looking around the smoky room. Men lounged against the bar, which was nothing more than a few wide planks laid across some barrels. Rickety tables and chairs filled part of the room, and there was an open space for dancing in the rear, along with an arched, curtained doorway that led to a hallway and private rooms. A peon was crouched in one corner, playing the guitar, his sombreroed head tilted forward so that most of his dark face was invisible. The patrons were a mixture of white and Mexican, but all of them had in common the taut features and narrowed eyes of men who had known little in their lives but trouble. Serving girls with brown skin and long, loose raven hair moved about the room on bare feet, their long skirts brushing the hard-packed dirt of the floor. The low-cut blouses they wore barely contained the thrust of their breasts.

In the midst of this sordidness and squalor sat a slender, aristocratic-looking man who seemed as out of place here as would a bishop. He was alone at one of the tables with a bottle in front of him, and he held a glass that he occasionally sipped from. He wore a wide-brimmed, flat-crowned hat, a dark-brown suit, and a cloak, though the night was anything but chilly. His face was narrow and pale, and a neatly trimmed, dark-blond mustache adorned his upper lip above his wide mouth. As if he sensed that O'Neil had entered the cantina, he looked up and met the hardcase's angry gaze with cool blue eyes.

O'Neil strode across the room, jerked out the other chair at the table, and sat down without waiting to be invited. "There's been some trouble," he said harshly.

"I assumed as much," the other man answered, his deep voice calm. "Where are your companions?"

"Dead." The word came out of O'Neil's mouth in a flat, hard tone.

The other man nodded slowly. "I see. You must tell me all about it."

"I want a drink first."

The man lifted a finger, signaling to one of the sluttish serving girls. She came over with a glass and set it on the table, smiling at the man as she did so. He didn't seem to notice. He picked up the bottle and poured tequila into the glass. O'Neil snatched it up, tossed down the drink in one swallow, and shuddered as the fiery liquid coursed down his gullet. He set the empty glass on the table with a *thunk* and said, "Again."

"Of course," the man murmured. "But remember, I want the details of what happened tonight before you get drunk."

"Sure, sure." O'Neil watched impatiently as the man poured him another drink. This time he only swallowed about half of it before he set it down. Abruptly he said, "Sherm's dead. I'm pretty sure Keaton is, too, but I didn't see the body."

"And the woman?"

"We didn't get her." O'Neil glowered at his employer. "A Texas Ranger showed up and ruined everything."

A frown creased the man's high forehead. "A Ranger, you say? How do you know?"

"I got a look at him when he stuck his head out the window and took a shot at me. His name's Cody. I wouldn't have known him if Sherm hadn't seen him earlier today and pointed him out to me. Sherm saw him in action over in San Antonio last year, and somebody told him then that the bastard was a Ranger."

"I see." The man seemed to have forgotten his own drink as he listened to O'Neil's story. "So when the attempt to capture the young woman went awry, you ran."

O'Neil's fingers tightened on his glass and his face contorted angrily, becoming even uglier than it usually was. "There wasn't nothin' else I could do. That room was full of people, and there'd been shootin'. More law was going to show up anytime. Yeah, I got the hell out while I had the chance, and I ain't ashamed to say so."

"Of course not; you were only being prudent," the other man agreed. "Still, I'm disappointed by the outcome of tonight's activities."

O'Neil shrugged. "Sorry." He didn't sound overly sincere in his apology.

The man placed his hands palms down on the table. "Well, there's nothing we can do about the past now. We must look to the future." He stood up. "Come with me."

"Where?" O'Neil asked with a frown.

"I've spoken to the cantina owner, and we have the use of one of the private rooms. There is much we need to discuss."

O'Neil wrapped his grimy fingers around the neck of the tequila bottle. "I'm takin' the booze," he declared.

"Certainly. In fact . . ." The man beckoned to the same serving girl who had brought O'Neil's glass, and she scurried over, smiling provocatively. "Bring us another bottle in a few minutes," he told her. She nodded and moved past him, managing to rub her body lingeringly against his in the process.

Carrying the half-finished bottle, O'Neil followed the man through the curtained doorway and into the gloomy hall beyond. The man opened a door and led the way into a small, square room furnished with a table, a couple of chairs, and a rope bunk with a thin straw mattress on it. The serving girls brought customers to these back rooms to ply their other trade. Ignoring the bunk, the man turned to face O'Neil and asked abruptly, "Who is the most notorious and dangerous bandit in Mexico?"

O'Neil looked at him with a puzzled frown and hesitated for a moment before replying, "From what I've heard, that'd be either Diego Alvarez or Paco Montoya. They're both bad ones, got their own gangs they lead on raids across the border now and then. Why do you want to know about some damn greasers?"

"I have my reasons," the man said softly.

O'Neil figured they had come back here to plan another kidnapping attempt on that Yellow Rose woman. Just because the first one had gone wrong, that didn't mean he couldn't handle the job, the hardcase thought. All he needed was a little time to recruit some more men to side him. Sherm and Keaton had been good partners, but they were dead now, and it was time to move on. There was no room for grief or regrets.

He thumped the bottle down on the table and said, "Look, let's get on with it. I want to get good and drunk tonight after we settle things."

"I'm afraid that will be impossible."

The man stepped around the table, moving closer to

O'Neil. The outlaw's eyes widened. Sometime while
they'd been talking the man who'd hired him had slipped
his hand under that cloak of his without O'Neil noticing,
and now it had emerged holding a dagger. O'Neil's hand
started moving toward his gun, but his dissipated nerves
were no match for the other man's. The man's left hand
closed around O'Neil's wrist, stopping the draw, while
the right plunged the slender blade into the hardcase's
belly.

O'Neil barely felt his wrist breaking as the man twisted
it savagely with surprising strength. There was too much
pain already flooding through him from the wound in his
stomach. The man ripped the dagger from side to side,
then tore it free from O'Neil's flesh. O'Neil opened his
mouth to scream in agony.

The cry never escaped from his lips. Cold steel halted it
by swiping across his throat. O'Neil felt a rush of heat on
his chest and knew it was his life's blood flooding out of
him. He staggered, and a foot shod in an expensive boot
was thrust between his ankles, tripping him. He lived
long enough to feel the impact as his face crashed against
the dirt floor, but that was the last thing Al O'Neil ever
felt.

Looking at his crisp white shirtsleeve, the aristocratic
killer frowned with distaste. He had stepped back as
quickly as possible after cutting O'Neil's throat, but he
had still gotten a little blood on the cuff. That stain would
never come out, he thought. But, of course, he could af-
ford to buy another shirt. Dozens of other shirts. In fact,
he could buy anything he wanted . . . almost.

He still had the knife in his hand when the sound of the
door opening behind him made him turn around quickly.
The serving girl stood there, an unopened bottle of tequila in her hand. Her dark eyes bulged at the sight of the
knife, and they stared even more in horror when she
glanced past the man and saw the gory body on the floor.
The bottle slipped from her fingers and fell with a thump,
but it didn't break and the cork didn't come out of its
neck.

The man stepped forward, caught the girl's arm, and

jerked her into the room. He closed the door, then spun back to her, lifting the blade to her throat as she opened her mouth to scream. "Not a sound," he hissed at her, stopping the outcry. He went on, "You have excellent timing, my dear. I was hoping you'd show up after I'd taken care of this other little problem. Now, you're going to be quiet, aren't you?"

The girl managed to nod jerkily, carefully avoiding the point of the dagger that was only a fraction of an inch from her throat. "*Sí,*" she gasped.

"Pick up that tequila," the man told her. He lowered the knife, but its threat was still there.

She snatched the bottle from the floor and handed it to the man. Carelessly, he put it on the table. "I'll drink it later," he said. "Right now I have more, ah, urgent needs to take care of."

He put his free hand on her bare, trembling shoulder and drew her closer to him. The point of the knife caught the blouse at her waist and began to slice upwards, parting the fabric without touching the skin underneath. When he was finished, he flicked the halves of the garment aside, baring her heavy breasts. The flat of the blade caressed the globes of flesh, lingering on the large brown nipples. He seemed to have forgotten all about the corpse of Al O'Neil, lying nearby on the floor.

"You're not the one I really want," the man whispered to the girl. "But you'll do for tonight. Yes, indeed. You'll do just fine. . . ."

CHAPTER
3

Cody assumed that the two dead would-be kidnappers had been taken down to the undertaker's, so he left the Rio Grande Hotel and strolled in that direction.

There was plenty on his mind. He'd killed a man tonight, and that always led to some mulling over, no matter how justified the killing might have been. Cody hoped he never reached the point where a man's death was something to be taken lightly, to be tossed aside and forgotten. Also there was the matter of the troubles that had been plaguing the Yellow Rose. The pattern of events was too obvious to be ignored or downplayed. Someone was out to grab her. But who? And why?

Sheriff Christian Burke was coming out of Chalmers' Undertaking Establishment as Cody approached the building. "Evening, Sheriff," the Ranger said. "I reckon those bodies are inside?"

"Where else would we put 'em?" Burke grunted. "You come down to take a look?"

Cody nodded. "I thought I might recognize one of 'em, given more time."

"There's no need. I can tell you who they are. Come on in."

Burke turned around and went back into the building, followed by Cody. They went down a hallway past a couple of viewing rooms that were empty at the moment and entered the big chamber at the rear where the real work of the business went on. The bodies were stretched out on a couple of large tables, and the undertaker and his assistant were standing by, ready to get started on their tasks.

"I thought I heard somebody come in again," Oliver Chalmers said. "Forget something, Sheriff?"

"Here? Not likely!" Burke inclined his head toward his companion. "Ranger Cody wants to take a look at the deceased. I figured that'd be all right."

"Oh, certainly," the undertaker said. "We were about to start cleaning them up."

Cody stepped over to one of the tables, and Burke moved alongside him. "That one's Sherm Eggleston," the sheriff said. "The other one's last name is Keaton. Don't know his first name."

Eggleston was the one Cody had shot. Cody looked at him for a moment, then switched his gaze to the second body. Death was never pretty, and it sure as hell wasn't in these two hardcases. "How'd you know who they are?" he asked Burke.

"They've been around town for a while, maybe a week. I knew them by reputation, that's all . . . and it wasn't much of a reputation for either of 'em."

"Outlaws?"

"I suppose they wanted to be. There was no paper out on 'em, though. They were suspected of doing a little widelooping, maybe held up a stage every now and then, but they were strictly small-time. I've been keeping an eye on them. If they'd caused any trouble, I'd've run 'em in right away. As it was, I decided to let it slide as long as they kept their noses clean."

Cody nodded in understanding. To some, Burke's attitude toward lawbreakers might have seemed a mite lackadaisical, but Cody knew what the sheriff meant. Out here on the frontier there were plenty of men whose reps were a bit on the shady side. There had been a time, when Cody himself was a youngster, that some lawmen might have considered *him* the next thing to a desperado. Now he was a Ranger, firmly on the side of law and order. If local authorities like Burke tried to arrest every man in their jurisdiction whose past wasn't lily-white, the jails of Texas would be busting at the seams.

"Was there anybody in particular they ran with?" Cody asked.

"Yep, a fella named Al O'Neil," Burke told him. "As a matter of fact, O'Neil's got a bigger reputation as a gunman than either of these two—not that he's what you'd call a famous desperado. I reckon Eggleston and Keaton here fell in with him hoping they'd get in on some big job."

"Like kidnapping the Yellow Rose," Cody muttered, as much to himself as to Burke.

"That would've been the big time to a trio of losers like that, all right," the sheriff agreed.

Cody and Burke left the undertaker to his work and walked back out to the building's front porch. As he leaned on the railing, glad to be able to draw some clean night air into his lungs again even if it was the warm and muggy kind, Cody said, "I reckon O'Neil must have been the third man, the one in the alley with the horses."

"That's the way I've got it figured."

"You know where I could find him?"

Burke shook his head. "I was about to head back to the office and get a couple of men looking for him."

"I've got a favor to ask. Let me handle the job instead."

Burke frowned. "Well, I don't know . . ." he said slowly. Cody was well aware that the sheriff sometimes resented the presence of the Rangers in Del Rio, feeling that they showed him up too often. He might be reluctant to part with any of his authority in this case.

"I sort of promised the lady I'd look into this for her," Cody explained.

"Oh." A smile that was half leer stretched across Burke's florid face. "Then I can see why you want to handle the investigation yourself." He shrugged. "I'm tired, and I'm not much in the mood to give a damn. If you want this O'Neil hombre, you're welcome to go hunting for him, Cody."

The big Ranger grinned. "Thanks, Sheriff."

"Just let me know what you find out."

"Sure. You have any suggestions where to start?"

"O'Neil's been doing a lot of drinking down in Mex town. I'd try there first." Burke gave him a quick description of the minor outlaw.

Cody nodded his gratitude, settled his hat on his head, and went down the stairs to the dusty street. His steps turned to the section of Del Rio that was primarily Mexican in its population. Across the river was the town of Villa Acuna, but there were plenty of Mexicans on this side of the border, too.

Despite the lateness of the hour, the area was still brightly lit, lantern glow spilling into the street from the cantinas, the whorehouses, and most of the other businesses Cody passed. There were no sidewalks down here, and the riders shared the street with quite a few pedestrians, white and Mexican alike. Competing strains of different songs blended with the laughter of women and the cursing of men to form a unique melody. Cody was thirsty but decided against having a beer. Anything that might muddle the brain even the least bit was probably not a good idea around here.

Still, he stopped in most of the cantinas he came to and took a look around for O'Neil. Even with his coat covering his Ranger badge, most of the denizens of the neighborhood recognized him as a star packer, and a tense silence usually fell whenever he stepped into one of the watering holes. In a few of them, women sidled up to him with invitations that ranged from subtle to blatant. Cody merely smiled and moved on.

As he searched for O'Neil, his brain turned over everything he had already discovered. It'd been a stroke of luck that Sheriff Burke recognized the dead men and was able to name O'Neil as their probable partner. But from what Burke had said about the three hardcases, it was unlikely that any of them had masterminded the kidnapping attempt. No, Cody was sure that someone else had hired O'Neil and his pards to snatch the Yellow Rose.

Now it was just a matter of finding O'Neil and forcing him to reveal who that someone was.

Just looking around wasn't getting him anywhere. He realized he was going to have to start asking questions.

That could lead to trouble, but he didn't see any way around it.

Reaching the next cantina, he stepped inside and headed for the bar. As usual, the drone of voices inside the place died away a little at his entrance. But it didn't fade entirely, and as he came up to the bar, the talk in the cantina increased. The customers noticeably relaxed. Maybe the Ranger had just come in for a drink, some of them must have thought—though the men at the bar, while staying within earshot, moved away from him; nobody wanted to stand too close to a Ranger.

In fact, Cody did say, "Bring me a beer," when a bartender with a prominent belly and a shirt that had once been white came over and stood in front of him. The man drew the beer and slid it across the bar. Cody dropped a coin on the hardwood to pay for the drink, then said, "I'm looking for somebody."

A man several feet away turned to look at Cody. His face was flushed and pouchy from too much drinking, and several days' worth of stubble covered his jowls. He was probably twenty-five, but he looked closer to fifty. He wore range gear, the clothes patched in some places and threadbare in others. The black-butted gun holstered on his hip looked well taken care of, though.

"Lookin' for somebody?" he repeated.

"That's right," Cody said, half turning toward the man. There was a fly-specked mirror behind the bar, and the Ranger could keep an eye on at least part of the place by watching it.

"I don't like that," the man said, squinting.

"You don't even know who I'm looking for," Cody pointed out reasonably.

"Don't matter! Man's got no right to come in here and start houndin' folks! 'Specially not a damn lawman!"

Cody sighed. Drunk or not, the man had sized him up accurately. The Ranger said, "Listen, friend, why don't you just stay out of this? Unless you know a man named Al O'Neil, that is."

"Never heard of him."

"Then it's none of your business, is it?"

The man took a step closer to Cody. "Told you, it don't matter. You got no right to be here. Now, get the hell out!"

Cody was starting to get angry. He hadn't wanted trouble, but sometimes there was no avoiding it. "The state of Texas says I've got every right to be here, mister, so unless you want to go up against the Lone Star, you'd better get back to your drink."

The man just clenched his fists. "Son of a bitchin' lawman!" he snarled, then launched a blow at Cody's head.

The punch was slow and telegraphed by a mile. Cody moved to his left to let it go by, intending to grab the man while he was off balance, shove him against the bar, and try again to talk some sense into him.

That might have worked if somebody else hadn't walloped him from behind.

The unexpected blow made Cody stagger forward, and he collided with the drunk. He felt their feet getting tangled up and tried to pull away. He had no friends in here. If he went down, he might wind up getting stomped half to death.

His hand slapped against the bar and he hung on, pulling himself up while the drunk fell to the floor. A figure loomed in front of Cody, and in the murky light of the cantina he sensed as much as saw the fist streaking toward his face. He dropped into a crouch, weaving to the side so that the punch scraped across his right ear but didn't do any major damage. In close quarters now with his assailant, Cody hooked a hard right to the man's belly. Whiskey breath spewed in his face as his fist sank into a flabby stomach.

Hands pawed at him, and somebody kicked him in the shin. These were low-class toughs swarming around him, but even a pack of mongrels could be dangerous when the bloodlust was on them. For a split second Cody considered reaching for his gun, then discarded the idea. Too easy for somebody innocent to get hurt in a fracas like this once bullets started flying. Instead, he swung his arms in a couple of looping blows that knocked several of his opponents away from him.

That gave him some breathing room. He blocked a punch, then crashed a right to a man's jaw. Someone grappled with him and tried to get an arm around his neck from behind to choke him, but Cody caught the man's arm, pivoted at the waist, bent, and heaved. With a wild yell the attacker flew over Cody's shoulder, knocked down a couple more men, and then crashed into a table that promptly collapsed under him. Cody only barely noticed all that from the corner of his eye as he turned and shot a left jab into the face of another opponent. Blood splashed on Cody's knuckles as the man's nose flattened.

The odds against him were dropping in a hurry as the would-be brawlers discovered that they would have to pay a painful price for bringing him down, even outnumbered as he was. Several men scrambled for the door of the cantina and vanished into the night; others crawled under tables, joining the serving girls who had taken shelter there as soon as the fight broke out.

Cody glanced at the bartender, worried that the man might reach for a greener or pick up a bung starter and deal himself in. But the bartender was merely standing there with a bored look on his moon face. Obviously he had seen plenty of these kinds of fights before.

Cody was taking some punishment. Blood trickled into his left eye from a small cut on his forehead, and he ached from the blows that had thudded into his body. He seemed to be in better shape than any of his opponents, however, and within a few minutes he was facing only two men. The others had all given up and slunk off. One of the two who were left was the drunk who had started the whole thing, and Cody was a little surprised to see the man on his feet again. The other one was a burly, black-bearded bruiser who seemed to be enjoying himself despite the damage that Cody had inflicted on him. With a roar this man threw himself forward, lowering his head and bellowing as he came.

The easiest thing was to step aside and let the man crash headfirst into the bar—which was exactly what Cody did. The bruiser bounced off the hardwood, shook his head a couple of times, then slumped to the sawdust-covered floor and started snoring loudly.

That left the drunk. He held up his hands, palms out, and started backing up. "Hold on," the man choked. "Enough, mister. I don't want no more."

Cody advanced on him, fists balled and held ready, his face taut with anger. "You were full of big talk a few minutes ago about how I had no right to be here," the big Ranger snapped. "What about now? Have I earned the right?"

"S-sure. It was nothin' personal—"

"Do you know Al O'Neil?"

"I . . . I seen him around, I know who he is. I didn't exactly tell the truth about it before." The man swallowed nervously.

Cody was right in his face by now, and he menacingly lowered his right hand to the butt of his Colt. "Where can I find him?"

"Hell, I . . . I wouldn't know that! I don't keep tabs on the guy or noth—"

"Where does he like to drink?" Cody cut in.

"Uh, you could check Ramirez's place, couple of blocks over." The man was blinking his watery eyes quickly. Fear had sobered him up. "I seen O'Neil in there quite a few times."

Cody nodded. He glanced around, aware that he was getting quite a few unfriendly looks. It was time to get out of here before he pushed his luck any further.

He turned around and started looking for his hat, which had gotten knocked off in the first few seconds of the brawl. To his surprise one of the cantina's serving girls had picked it up and knocked the dents out of it, and now she extended it toward him. He took the hat, smiled wearily at the girl, and murmured, *"Gracias."*

People got out of his way as he stalked to the door and out into the night. He'd need eyes in the back of his head for a while, he thought; otherwise somebody might try to settle tonight's score with an ambush from a dark alley. But that was really nothing new. Being a Ranger, there was usually somebody or other who wanted him dead.

He knew the cantina the drunk had called Ramirez's place. Cody straightened his coat as he walked toward it, then wiped away some of the blood from his face. He was pretty disheveled and battered. The Yellow Rose probably wouldn't come within a mile of him, the way he looked now. He slipped his left hand into his pocket and grinned as his fingers touched the yellow hair ribbon. He still had that as payment for his night's work—if he ever got back to Ranger headquarters to show it to Seth Williams and Alan Northrup.

The glow of lanterns up ahead was like a beacon, for Cody knew it came from the Ramirez cantina. He picked up his pace.

That was when the screams started coming from the squatty little adobe building.

Cody broke into a run, sensing that this ruckus had something to do with the reason he was here. He had no way of knowing that for certain—trouble was all too common down here—but he was sure of it anyway.

When he reached the cantina and went inside, he saw that most of the place's occupants were clustered around a doorway in the back of the room. One of the serving girls was sitting at a table, her head slumped down on her crossed arms and her back heaving with sobs, while a man standing next to the table was trying awkwardly to comfort her. Cody had been here before, and he recognized the sallow, gaunt-faced man as the proprietor, Ramirez.

Striding up to the table, the big Ranger nodded at Ramirez. "What's happened here?" he asked.

"There has been trouble," Ramirez replied, stating the obvious. He jerked his head toward the doorway with the crowd around it. "Conchata found a couple of dead bodies in one of the back rooms."

The Ranger felt his spine go icy with foreboding. "Who are they?" he asked grimly.

"One is Lupe, Conchata's little sister. The other . . ." Ramirez shrugged his bony shoulders. "A gringo. I do not know his name, but he came here to drink from time to time."

"Damn!" Cody stalked over to the door, shouldering his way through the morbidly curious crowd, who got out of his way as soon as they realized who he was. There was no doubt which of the tiny back rooms the tragedy had taken place in. Only one had its door open, and some of the cantina's patrons stood just outside, staring in.

Gesturing for them to step back, Cody planted his big frame in the doorway. He stopped, grimacing as he realized that he had almost stepped into the edge of a pool of drying blood.

The dead girl lay closest to the door. Her face was untouched, which meant it was easy to see the look of agony and horror that her features were frozen in. She was nude, and the remnants of her clothes were scattered around her body. From the looks of it, the killer had sliced her at least fifty or sixty times with a sharp blade. Cody felt his stomach clench into a tight ball of sickness, and he had to glance away from the grisly sight.

By contrast the other corpse looked to have been killed rather cleanly. Cody moved carefully around the dead girl to the man's side. With the toe of his boot, Cody hooked the man's shoulder and rolled him over carefully. He fit the description of Al O'Neil, just as Cody had expected. The man's throat was cut, and there was another ugly wound in his midsection. Either of the injuries would have been fatal, Cody judged, though the man would have taken a lot longer to die from just the stomach wound alone.

He turned and left the room. The crowd had dispersed. None of the cantina's patrons wanted to be too close to the scene of violence while a Ranger was investigating. Ramirez was back behind the bar, Cody noted, and the grief-stricken girl called Conchata was nowhere to be seen. Someone had taken her home, he supposed.

Stepping to the bar, Cody motioned Ramirez over. "How did that happen back there without somebody hearing?" he demanded sharply.

Ramirez shrugged again, obviously his favorite answer to most questions. "There is always a great deal of noise here," he said. "One man was playing the guitar, and a woman was singing. Men talk and laugh and argue." The gaunt proprietor frowned. "Still, I too am surprised that there was no noise heard."

The killer could have struck quickly enough in O'Neil's case that there wouldn't have been an outcry, Cody thought. It was different with the girl, though. The knife-wielder must have first terrorized her into silence—and then she was probably unable to cry out.

"What were they doing back there?"

"The other gringo came in first," Ramirez began.

"Wait a minute," Cody snapped. "What other gringo?"

"The one who sat alone, drinking tequila. The dead man came in later and talked to him. Of course, he was not dead then. Neither was the girl."

Cody told himself to be patient. "So O'Neil came in to talk to another man?"

"O'Neil is the dead gringo?" Ramirez paused as Cody nodded, then went on, "*Sí*, that is how it was. The two men talked for a while, then went back to the little room. As they headed back there the other gringo told Lupe to bring them another bottle of tequila in a few minutes. I know this because she got the bottle from me."

Cody had to admit that Ramirez was actually being pretty helpful. What the Ranger had heard so far supported his theory that O'Neil, Eggleston, and Keaton had been working for somebody else when they tried to kidnap the Yellow Rose. That somebody had to be the man O'Neil had reported to here in the cantina.

"What happened then?"

"Lupe took the bottle," Ramirez said. "She did not come back, but I thought nothing of that. I assumed the gringos were enjoying her pleasures."

"This other man," Cody said, placing his palms on the rough plank bar and leaning forward. "What did he look like?"

Ramirez shook his head. "Who pays attention to gringos?"

"You'd better have." Cody's voice hardened. He sensed that Ramirez had reached the end of the information he intended to part with for free. Slipping a coin from his pocket, he laid it on the bar and covered it with his hand.

"I see so many people here in the cantina, and my memory, she is not what she once was—"

"I'm not in the mood to haggle, Ramirez. Now, tell me what the other man looked like."

The cantina owner swallowed, suddenly nervous as he looked into Cody's eyes and obviously realized he had pushed this little game as far as he could. He said, "This other gringo, he was tall, sort of skinny. He wore dark clothes and a big hat. I think he had a mustache, but I never got a good look at his face."

Cody studied Ramirez for a long moment, trying to decide if the Mexican was telling the truth. Finally, he nodded, said, "All right," and took his hand off the coin, which promptly disappeared somewhere on the other side of the bar. "Anything else you can tell me?"

"The tall man seemed upset when the dead one first sat down and began talking to him, like he was hearing bad news. He calmed down quickly, though."

That fit with Cody's thinking. No doubt O'Neil had told his employer about the failed attempt to abduct Rose. "Did this other man come back out later?" Cody asked.

Ramirez shook his head. "There is another door, at the very back of the building. He could have gone out there without coming through here again. This man killed the gringo and Lupe, Ranger?"

"He must've," Cody grunted.

Ramirez didn't ask why or do any speculating on motives. He would feel like it was none of his business, Cody knew. The only thing that really mattered to the man was that he had lost one of his serving girls . . . and they were easily replaced in this part of town.

"If you see that other man again, you come and tell me or one of the other Rangers," Cody instructed him, even though he knew it wouldn't do any good. Ramirez was unlikely to get any more involved than he already was.

The cantina owner nodded and said, "*Sí,* of course."

"The same goes for any of the people working for you."

Once again Ramirez nodded.

Cody sighed and turned away. "I'll send someone to take care of the bodies," he said without looking around.

He could sense the eyes following him as he left the cantina and started back toward the main part of Del Rio, leaving behind this rough district along the river. He couldn't shake what he had seen in that squalid little room. Whoever the killer was, he enjoyed the hell out of his work, Cody thought bleakly—and this was the man who was after the Yellow Rose.

Hardened veteran of the frontier or not, a shudder ran through Cody. Whatever the man's motives for wanting to get Rose in his power, the lovely young woman was in more trouble than she realized. This was no ordinary love-struck admirer she was dealing with. The man was a ruthless killer, willing to murder one of his own employees just so that no one would be able to follow O'Neil's trail back to him. Cody was sure that was why the hardcase had been killed. But as for the girl called Lupe . . . that had been sheer evil.

The Yellow Rose had been in Del Rio less than twenty-four hours, and already four people were dead. Cody wondered what the hell was going to happen next.

CHAPTER

4

Seth Williams and Alan Northrup were lounging on the front porch of Company C headquarters the next morning, their chairs leaned back against the wall and their feet resting on the porch railing. Seth was whittling a chunk of wood with a clasp knife but not doing a very good job. Finally he tossed the wood aside in disgust and closed the knife.

"You get frustrated too easy," Alan said, briefly opening his eyes and looking out from under the brim of his tipped-down Stetson. "You've got to learn to relax, like me."

"Hell, if you were any more relaxed, you'd be snorin'," Seth shot back at him. "Anyway, is my memory playin' tricks on me, or didn't you just get out of your bunk about an hour ago? I recollect eatin' breakfast, and then we moseyed over here and sat down."

"Yeah, I reckon that's about right."

"Then why in blazes are you going back to sleep?" Seth demanded.

"A Ranger's got to take advantage of every opportunity to rest," Alan replied. "You never know when we might have to be in the saddle for forty-eight hours straight."

"Seems to me like you said the same thing about eatin' when you went back for a third helpin' of hash browns and sausages."

"Man's got to keep his strength up . . ." Alan muttered sleepily, then belched and pushed his belt down a little to ease the pressure on his stomach.

"Quite correct, Ranger Northrup."

Both youngsters thumped their chairs on the porch as they hurriedly came upright. Springing to their feet, they turned to face Lieutenant Oliver Whitcomb, who had come out the front door of the building without either of them hearing him.

"It's important for a Ranger to get plenty of rest and healthy food," Whitcomb went on, "so that he'll have the strength and stamina required to perform any task assigned to him by his superior officers. Isn't that correct?"

"Yes, sir," both young men replied smartly.

"And are the two of you well rested and well fed?" As Whitcomb asked the question, it fleetingly seemed as though a ghost of a smile was tugging at his stern mouth. Seth and Alan glanced briefly at each other, their eyes first questioning the notion, then discarding it as impossible.

"Yes, sir," they replied in unison.

"Good. The stables out back are in need of a good cleaning. You'll find pitchforks and shovels already there, as usual. Get to work, gentlemen."

With an effort the young Rangers suppressed the urge to groan in dismay. There were stable hands whose job it was to take care of such unpleasant tasks, but Lieutenant Whitcomb liked to assign the job to some of the newer Rangers from time to time. It helped build discipline—or so he claimed. As far as Seth and Alan were concerned, all the chore built was blisters on the hands and a powerful need to take a bath.

Still, there was no arguing with the lieutenant. Both of them saluted him, said, "Yes, sir," for a third and final time, then turned toward the alley that led to the back of the headquarters building and the stables beyond.

"What a life," Seth muttered as they headed down the alley. "Listenin' to a gal like the Yellow Rose sing one night, then shovelin' horse shit the next mornin'."

"It's downright unfair, that's what it is," Alan agreed.

"I'd rather go fight some Comanches or owlhoots."

"Me, too."

Seth suddenly grinned. "Could be worse," he declared.

"Yeah? I don't see how," Alan groused.

"Well . . . *I* didn't go back for two extra helpin's of sausages and hash browns at breakfast this mornin', like somebody else did."

Alan suddenly turned green and patted his stomach uneasily. The frown on his face almost made the whole thing worthwhile, Seth thought. Almost.

After leaving the cantina the night before, Cody had notified the undertaker that there was more work waiting for him at Ramirez's place, and then he went back to his room at the Rio Grande Hotel. He had considered stopping by Rose's room to let her know what he had found out but decided it could wait until the next day. She was probably tired, and he didn't want to disturb her. Besides, he was in no mood to face the hostile stares of Gellman, Eduardo, and Alonso again, and he knew he wouldn't be able to talk to the singer without going through them first.

Instead, he had gone to bed himself and spent a couple of hours staring up at the ceiling, trying to get the gruesome scene he'd witnessed at the cantina out of his mind. It had helped when Marie Jermaine joined him, her shift down in the saloon over for the night. She had slid into bed beside him, all soft, warm, perfumed flesh, and her mouth had sought his in the darkness. Lovemaking had been the last thing on Cody's mind, but Marie had been insistent and inventive, and he had to give her credit for that. She had succeeded in taking his mind off the problems the Yellow Rose had brought to Del Rio, and—sated and exhausted—Cody had fallen into a deep sleep that lasted until well after daybreak.

After enjoying breakfast with Marie again, just like the day before, Cody once again considered going up to talk to Rose, and once again he postponed it. Instead, he left the hotel and headed for Ranger headquarters, intending to fill Captain Vickery in on what he'd discovered the night before about Al O'Neil and the mysterious man who had employed him—and killed him.

Lieutenant Whitcomb was out of the office on some chore, so Cody was able to go straight to Vickery's office and rap on the door. At the captain's growled summons, Cody went in and tossed his hat on one of the nails in the wall next to the door. Vickery was behind the desk, laboriously scratching out words on a piece of paper with a stub of pencil. "Dadblasted reports," the grizzled Ranger commander muttered without looking up.

"I thought the lieutenant did most of those," Cody said as he reversed one of the chairs facing the desk and straddled it.

"He does. But I got to write one up every now and then so Major Jones won't figure I've died and left Oliver in charge. I want to get this on the eastbound stage to San Antone tomorrow, so I figured I'd better get started on it this mornin'."

Cody grinned. Major John B. Jones was the commander of the Frontier Battalion of the Texas Rangers, which Company C was a part of. The major's office was in San Antonio, and Cody had met him a few times. Jones was a staunch frontiersman much like Captain Vickery himself, so Cody doubted that he cared too much about paperwork. It was really the pencil pushers in Austin who insisted on documentation for everything.

"Dammit!" Vickery threw the pencil down and flexed his fingers. "Those things are instruments of the devil himself!" He looked up at the big Ranger seated across the desk from him. "What's up, Cody? You find out any more about that Rose gal and her troubles?"

"That's why I came to talk to you, Cap'n," Cody said. Quickly, he filled Vickery in on everything that took place after they had parted company at the Rio Grande the night before, including the discovery of the bodies of Al O'Neil and the girl called Lupe at the cantina. Vickery's thick white brows drew down in a ferocious glower.

"Sounds like we got a real bad hombre on our hands," he said when Cody was finished. "*Muy malo,* all right. I ain't surprised you went lookin' for that third gent, the one who was waitin' in the alley, but I didn't reckon you'd find him with his gullet sliced open."

"Neither did I," Cody said. "I'd say Rose is in real trouble, whether she knows it or not." He hesitated a second, then went on, "After you and the lieutenant left last night, she asked me to go with her on her tour."

Vickery clasped his knobby hands together on the scarred desktop. "That don't come as no shock. Looked to me like the two of you was hittin' it off pretty good."

"That's not really it. I think she wanted me to be her bodyguard more than anything else."

"Could be," Vickery said, nodding, "though I had that bald-headed fella pegged for that job."

"His name's Barney Gellman. He claims to be Rose's manager, but she told me he's really there to protect her. Those two guitar players lend a hand, too. It was Eduardo who downed one of those rannies with his knife."

"So you're sayin' the Yellow Rose has already got plenty of protection?"

Cody didn't answer for a moment. Then he said, "You'd think so. But what if one of those three is actually working with the man who wants to kidnap her?"

Vickery frowned again and leaned back in his chair. "Hadn't thought about that," he admitted. "What do you want to do, son?"

"There's not much I can do," Cody said with a sigh. "I've already told Rose I can't abandon my Ranger duties to go with her. I thought maybe I could find the third man and backtrack to whoever hired them, but that's not going to pan out now." Not with Al O'Neil having literally become a dead end, he added to himself.

"Well, I feel right sorry for the gal, but I got to go along with that. The Rangers are already stretched mighty thin. I'm afraid I can't give you permission to take her up on the offer, Cody. It's been pretty quiet around these parts, you know that, but I got a hunch all hell's just waitin' to break loose."

Cody nodded. "You're probably right, Cap'n." He stood up and pulled out his large pocket watch, flipping it open to check the time. "Westbound stage is due through around noon. Rose said she'd be taking it and heading on to El Paso. Reckon I'd better go talk to her before she leaves. I want to be sure she takes all this seriously enough. She's got the idea in her head that these kidnapping attempts are just because some admirer's in love with her."

"Sounds like more than that to me," Vickery mused.

"To me, too," Cody agreed. He snapped the watch shut and slipped it back in his pocket, then snagged his hat from the nail. "Be seeing you, Cap'n."

He left the office and stepped out onto the front porch of the headquarters building, and as he did so, Seth Williams and Alan Northrup came out of the alley to the side of the adobe structure. The two youths looked miserable and smelled worse. Spotting them, Cody paused and didn't bother trying to hide his grin.

"Looks like the lieutenant put you boys to work," he said by way of greeting the younger Rangers.

"Don't you go laughin' at us, Cody," Seth warned ominously. "We ain't in any mood for it. How long's it been since that stable was cleaned, anyway?"

"Too long," Alan said wearily. "I think I'm going to go dunk myself in the nearest horse trough."

"You two aren't a couple of nosegays, that's for sure," Cody said. "Maybe this'll cheer you up." He reached in his pocket and brought out the yellow ribbon that Rose had taken from her hair the night before.

Seth groaned. "Tell me that's not what I think it is," he said.

"'Fraid so. I told you I'd get to see the Yellow Rose. Of course, it wasn't all pleasantries. . . ."

"I heard something about that at breakfast this morning," Alan said. "What happened, Cody? Something about a shooting?"

Cody told them about interrupting the would-be kidnappers at their work, then later finding the trail blocked by the death of Al O'Neil. Both youngsters shook their heads in dismay; then Seth said, "And to think we headed back to the barracks and went to sleep. We should've stayed with you, Cody. We missed all the excitement."

"There wasn't anything you could've done," he told them. "I'm on my way to see Rose now, to let her know this business is more serious than she thinks it is." Despite the gravity of the situation, he couldn't resist adding, "If you fellas smelled a mite better, I'd think about taking you along with me."

"Now just hold on, Cody," Seth said quickly. "We can go take a bath—"

Cody shook his head. "She'll be leaving on the noon stage. I'm afraid there really isn't time to wait for you."

"Dammit!" Seth exclaimed.

"And he called her Rose," Alan added with a sigh. "He could've introduced us. . . ."

Cody gave his friends a grin and turned away, saying over his shoulder, "See you boys later." He could hear Seth and Alan grousing and snapping at each other for almost a block as he walked away.

When he knocked on the door of the Yellow Rose's hotel room a few minutes later, it was opened by the young, attractive Mexican girl he had seen with the group the day before. With everything else that had been going on, he had forgotten about her. Cody took his hat off, gave her a smile, and said, "Hello, señorita. I'm looking for the Yellow Rose."

"It is all right, Estrella." Rose's voice came from inside the room. The girl stepped back and the singer came into view. She was wearing another traveling outfit, this one in a darker shade of yellow, and was holding yet another matching hat. With a smile at her visitor she explained to her companion, "This is Mr. Cody. He is a friend of mine, as well as a Texas Ranger. Estrella is my maid . . . and my friend."

The girl bowed her head and didn't meet Cody's eyes as she murmured a greeting. Then she busied herself closing the bags that were lying on the bed. Whatever packing that needed to be done prior to Rose's departure from Del Rio had obviously been completed.

Rose ushered Cody into the room and shut the door

behind him. He glanced around the room, saw that Rose and Estrella were alone, and asked, "Where are the others?"

"I imagine Eduardo and Alonso are in their room finishing their packing," Rose said. "Barney went downstairs to settle accounts with Mr. Pelletier, I believe."

Cody nodded, wondering just how much Gellman would collect from the hotelkeeper in payment for the Yellow Rose's performance. It wouldn't be polite to ask, he decided, and anyway, he was here for a more important reason.

He glanced at Estrella and hesitated, then thought that if the girl was working as Rose's personal maid, she was bound to know what had been going on. He said, "I told you I'd let you know if I found out anything about those men who tried to abduct you."

Rose leaned closer to him and put her hand on his arm. "You have discovered something about them?" she asked eagerly.

"Well, not much," Cody admitted. "I found out their names, and I'm pretty sure they were working for somebody else. They were really small-time owlhoots, not the kind who'd do something like that on their own."

"This person they were working for—do you have any idea who he is?"

Cody had to shake his head. "I've got a description, but not a very good one. Tall, slender, well dressed. He might have a mustache; the man who saw him wasn't sure about that."

Rose shrugged prettily and said, "That could be almost anyone. I have hundreds—perhaps thousands—of admirers. Many of them try to see me after my performances, as I told you."

"I know. That's why I said the description wasn't going to do us much good."

Rose turned and paced across the room, her face thoughtful, obviously mulling over what Cody had just told her. She spun around to face him again and suggested, "Perhaps the third man can tell you more about him. You said you know that one's name."

"Doesn't do us any good, either," Cody returned bleakly. "He's dead."

Her breath catching in her throat in surprise, Rose stared at him. "Dead?" she repeated after a moment.

"That's right. The man he was working for killed him. I figure the man saw how badly O'Neil and his pards botched things and didn't want to use him anymore. It was safer just to kill him than leave him alive to maybe talk later."

A visible shudder ran through Rose's slender body. "How dreadful."

"It gets worse, Rose." Cody took a deep breath. "This man, whoever he is, killed a girl in one of the cantinas last night, too. Cut her up real bad. This is no admirer, no would-be suitor you're dealing with. This fella's loco."

Rose studied him for a long moment, then shook her head. "No. You cannot know this. There is no proof the one who killed the girl is the same man who wants me." She paled slightly. "Is there?"

"Well, that's the way it looks to me . . . but I reckon there's not any hard evidence," Cody admitted reluctantly. "The cantina where the killings took place is in a rough part of town. It's not unusual for folks to wind up dead down there."

"There, you see." Rose brightened. "You admit it yourself. I am sorry about the girl, and even about this man you say was trying to kidnap me, but they must have been killed by someone else."

Cody felt frustration boiling up inside him. Rose simply refused to see the truth.

Before the Ranger could say anything else, a knock sounded on the door. Estrella hurried over and opened it, and Barney Gellman came into the room, seeming to bull his way in just by the simple act of walking through the doorway. He stopped short when he saw Cody standing there, hat in hand.

"What are you doing here?" he demanded.

"Mr. Cody was kind enough to investigate that kidnapping attempt last night, Barney," Rose said.

Gellman grunted. "Find out anything?"

"Nothing very helpful," Cody replied.

"He thinks a madman is after me," Rose said with a little laugh that didn't sound quite as light as she had probably intended.

"A madman?" Gellman repeated incredulously. "What the devil are you talking about, Cody?"

"The third man, the one who was waiting in the alley, was killed later last night, his gut sliced open," Cody told him. "I figure whoever killed him is the same one who hired him and his pards to snatch Rose."

"But there is no proof of this," the singer added.

Gellman frowned darkly. "I don't much like this," he said heavily.

"Neither do I," agreed Cody. "But I can't seem to convince the lady how serious it is."

"Well, I take it seriously." Gellman glanced at Rose. "From now on, you're not leaving my sight, understand?"

Rose smiled. "That could become a bit awkward, Barney." Her voice took on a slightly cooler tone. "Besides, you must remember that you work for me. That does not give you the right to issue orders to me."

His bulldog face slowly turning brick-red, Gellman controlled his anger with a visible effort and said, "Yeah, I guess you're right. I'm just worried about you, that's all."

"And I know this," Rose said quickly, stepping over to him and putting a placating hand on his shoulder. "Do not be offended, Barney. I know I could not have a better protector."

For her sake Cody hoped she was right. Gellman's reactions had seemed sincere enough, but the Ranger couldn't shake the thought that had occurred to him earlier: Someone close to the Yellow Rose might be working with her enemies. Gellman was the most likely candidate, Cody thought, but he couldn't ignore Eduardo and Alonso, either.

Not that he could do a whole hell of a lot about it, he thought. If the stagecoach was on schedule, Rose and her party would be leaving Del Rio within the hour, and that would be the last Cody ever saw of them. Whatever happened, he would not be involved.

It wasn't a good feeling, and he wished there were some way around the problem. Since joining the Rangers, though, he had always lived up to their proud tradition, a tradition that had been established in part by his own father, Adam Cody, who had been one of the first Rangers along with Jack Hays, Samuel Walker, and the other founders of the organization. Adam Cody was gone now, but his son still wore his silver spurs, a constant reminder of the legacy the elder Cody had left.

"I've got to be going," the Ranger said to the singer. "The cap'n's probably got a job or two for me to do—and, besides, your stage will be here soon."

"Of course." Was that regret he saw in Rose's eyes as she murmured the words, Cody asked himself? She added, "Please, wait a moment," then turned to Gellman and asked, "Barney, will you and Estrella see to the baggage for me?"

Gellman hesitated, no doubt aware of the same thing Cody was: Rose wanted to be alone with the Ranger for a few minutes before she left town. Finally the burly man nodded grudgingly and said, "I'll go downstairs and take care of it. Come on, Estrella."

Eyes still downcast, the maid followed Gellman out of the room. Gently, Rose closed the door behind them and then turned to face Cody once more.

"You have not reconsidered my offer, have you?" she asked.

"I've thought about it a lot," Cody said truthfully. "But I'm afraid the answer's still the same."

"You would be well paid. As you implied last night, I am a wealthy woman."

Cody shrugged and shook his head. "I make enough from my Ranger pay to feed me and my horse and keep me in bullets. That's about all I need."

The same as the night before, she had pulled that same trick of getting right in front of him without his being aware that she had done so. He could smell her perfume as she looked up at him and said softly, "There would be other benefits, as well. . . ."

She rested her hands on his chest, leaned in to him, and kissed him.

Cody's arms went around her, pulling her closer to him. Her body pressed against him as her lips parted. Her tongue speared his, and the moist heat of their duel made his entire body stiffen. Rose writhed her soft belly against his groin, and a hoarse sound of desire came from deep within her. Cody's hands roamed slowly down her back and found her buttocks, cupping them through the dress, lifting her and drawing her tightly against him. . . .

Through the open window of the hotel room, he heard the clatter of wheels, the pounding of hoofbeats, and the unmistakable sound of a jehu calling out to his team as he brought the animals to a stop.

Cody took his mouth away from Rose's, grimaced, and said, "That's the first time that goddamn stagecoach has been here right on schedule in six months!"

She was breathless. The passion she had just demonstrated was no act to get him to change his mind about coming with her. It had been genuine, Cody sensed.

And it was obvious that she saw in his eyes that the answer was still the same. With a faint smile, she sighed. "Ah, well . . . It would have been a good idea, don't you think?"

"A very good idea. If things had been different."

"Yes." She slid smoothly out of his arms. "I must be going now. I enjoyed meeting you, Cody. And I'm glad you have that ribbon of mine to remember me by."

As if he would ever forget her singing—or her kiss. Both would stay burned into his memory. She started to turn away, but he caught her arm. "You will be careful, won't you?"

"Of course. Do not worry, Cody. Whoever is behind my troubles has failed four times now. Surely he will give up soon."

Cody wasn't sure of that at all. The killing of Al O'Neil indicated that the hardcase's employer wasn't in any mood to quit just yet. But the Ranger had done all he could to convince Rose that she was in danger. From here on out it was up to her and Gellman and the Martinez brothers to keep her safe.

He escorted her downstairs, through the hotel lobby, and out to the red-and-yellow Concord coach. Quite a crowd was on hand to bid good-bye to the Yellow Rose, and as Cody glanced at the townspeople, his gaze sweeping over dozens of familiar faces, he couldn't help but wonder if the killer was out there, too, watching and waiting and planning.

He shut the door of the stagecoach, and Rose leaned out the window. "Farewell, Cody," she said, smiling warmly at him. "Perhaps we will meet again someday."

"I hope so," he said honestly. He looked past Rose. Gellman, Eduardo, Alonso, and Estrella were sitting in the coach, as were a couple of other passengers. Rose had a long, dusty, crowded ride in front of her, but she didn't seem to mind. She waved merrily from the window when the coach lurched into motion a few minutes later, rolling away down the main street of Del Rio.

Hearing hurried footfalls, Cody turned to see Seth and Alan running toward him. They had cleaned up and changed clothes, and now they slowly came to a stop and looked at the departing stagecoach with devastated expressions on their faces.

"Doggone it!" Alan said fervently. "We almost got here in time to meet the Yellow Rose! Cody, you've got to tell us all about her."

Cody slipped a hand in his pocket and fingered the hair ribbon, remembering the way she had kissed him. He would try to satisfy the curiosity of his young friends, he thought—but there were some things about the Yellow Rose that he was going to keep to himself, some memories that were his alone.

CHAPTER
5

This was a lonely, desolate land, so blasted by the sun and scoured by the wind that it seemed nothing could possibly live here. The Rio Grande and the ribbon of green that followed its life-giving waters might as well have been a million miles away, rather than fifty miles to the north. Yet even here on the Mexican desert there were small pockets of life, and anyone who knew where he was going could move between them in relative safety, especially if he traveled at night and rested during the heat of the day in whatever meager shade could be found.

Pierre Desmond knew where he was going.

Several days had passed since he had left Del Rio with his saddle horse and a pack animal. Desmond was well aware that pushing his mount too hard would eventually result in his death, so he took it easy, heading steadily toward the mountains that loomed in front of him to the southwest. They never seemed to draw any closer as he rode in the moonlight. But he knew they really did, knew in fact that he would soon reach them.

When the sun came up in the morning, he kept moving rather than stopping for the day. The mountains were close enough now that he believed he would be there before the heat of the day got too bad.

Even after waiting this long—after all the weeks of planning that had come to nothing—he was still impatient. He did not want to unnecessarily postpone his next move even by a matter of hours.

He continued riding toward the upthrust heights, leading the packhorse behind him, and by midmorning, he could feel eyes watching him. . . .

Paco Montoya hated to be interrupted while he was making love. He stalked out of his tent without putting on his shirt; all he had done when Esteban summoned him was to step into his pants, sling a bandolier full of cartridges over his bare shoulder, and pick up a rifle. Glowering fiercely and thinking of the fleshy Indian woman who had been left behind in the tent, he demanded of Esteban, "What is it that is so important you had to disturb me?"

"A rider is coming out of the desert, Paco," Esteban said, a worried frown on his face.

"A rider?" Montoya repeated.

Esteban nodded.

"*One rider?*" Montoya's voice lifted into a shout, and curses spilled fluidly from his mouth. Esteban stood stolidly, accepting the abuse. Paco Montoya in a full rage was a terrifying sight, but Esteban was used to it. He had ridden with Montoya for almost five years now, longer than any of the current members of the bandit gang.

Montoya was tall, broad-shouldered, his deep chest covered with a thick mat of black hair. He was a fine figure of a man—or at least he would have been had he not been so ugly. Nature had given him a beetling brow that shelved out over small, piggish eyes and almost twice as much nose as most men possessed. His mouth was a wide slash, though it was practically hidden by a heavy mustache, and his face was decorated with several reddish ridges, badly healed scars that were permanent reminders of the knife fights he had been in. The Mexican outlaw was ugly, no doubt about that. But he was also respected and, more importantly, feared.

When his outburst of profanity finally ran out, Montoya drew a deep breath into his shaggy chest and said, "Why do you summon me for only one rider?"

Esteban was shorter than his leader, more thickly built. The only member of the band more brutal and dangerous than he was Montoya himself. That was how Esteban had worked himself into the position of second in command. He had been tough enough—and smart enough—to survive that long. "One man is unusual," Esteban said in reply to Montoya's question. "If it had been a troop of Rurales to be killed or some wagons to be robbed, I would not have bothered you, Paco. But I thought you would be curious why one man would approach our camp by himself."

Montoya spat in disgust. "A lunatic, maybe," he said. "Only a madman would do such a thing."

"Or a very brave man," Esteban countered in a voice soft enough to prevent the other men from hearing their leader being contradicted—which would not do.

Montoya supposed Esteban could be right. For a long moment he considered that possibility. The lone rider was very foolhardy or very courageous—or both. Even a stupid man could be brave at times. For that matter Montoya had known some brave men who were as dumb as oxen. . . .

He gave a little shake of his head and brought his thoughts back to the matter of the man riding toward the bandit camp. "What have you told the sentries?" he asked Esteban.

"Nothing yet. I was waiting to see what you wanted to do. I can have them shoot him when he comes close enough, if you wish."

Esteban's tone of voice was mild and agreeable, but Montoya knew his lieutenant well enough to know that he was recommending against such a course of action. Frowning, Montoya shook his head and made a curt gesture with his free hand. "Let the fool come into the camp if that is what he wants," he declared. "Who knows? Maybe he will be amusing. Besides, we can always kill him later."

Esteban nodded in agreement and hurried to pass the word to the sentries guarding the entrance to the camp: They were to let the approaching rider enter unmolested.

Getting out again might be an entirely different story.

Montoya squinted against the glare of the sun as he waited. Not even noon yet and already the heat was hard and brassy. No longer interested in the woman he had left in the tent, Montoya rested the butt of his Winchester on the hard, rocky ground and leaned on the barrel as he surveyed his domain.

It might not look like much to some people, but Montoya was proud of it. Nestled in a valley between two foothills, the camp was shaded in the late afternoon by the crags that vaulted into the sky behind it. A small stream trickled through the middle of the valley, its water flowing from a spring that bubbled out of the mountains somewhere high above. The stream was responsible for the grass that grew along its banks and provided grazing for the horses of Montoya's gang. Deer, mountain lions, and other game came to the stream to drink sometimes, and then the group ate well. He had pitched his tent—the only tent the band possessed—near the stream, and, following his lead, the other men had spread their bedrolls on its banks. The valley's best features as far as Montoya was concerned were its steep sides, the cliff that blocked off the west end, and the narrow gorge that provided an easily defended entrance at the east end. Two men with rifles on the heights to either side of the gorge could stand off an army, as long as their ammunition held out. If there was a more perfect hideout in all of Mexico, Paco Montoya had never seen it.

Esteban came hurrying back up to him. "The man will be here soon. He is a gringo, Ricardo says."

"Of course," grunted Montoya. "Who else would be foolish enough to ride right up to our camp?"

No answer was required.

Montoya kept his eye on the gorge that led out of the valley, and less than five minutes later he saw the man come riding into its shadowy depths, leading a packhorse behind him. The stranger's mount trotted steadily toward the camp.

His arrival was drawing quite a bit of interest. The men who had been lounging around in whatever shade they could find now stood up and gathered near Montoya, bringing their rifles with them. The camp followers, mostly Indian women, were also watching curiously.

Montoya glanced up at the sentry posts and saw both guards on their feet, signaling by waving their rifles over their heads. That was the all-clear, the sign that the gringo was indeed alone and evidently no threat.

As the man rode closer, Montoya saw that he wore a dark, expensive suit, which was now thickly covered with trail dust. He was tall and slender, and a wide-brimmed hat shaded lean features. There was something about him that bothered Montoya, and after a moment, the outlaw figured out what it was: Even though the stranger was a gringo, he had the same aristocratic bearing as the hidalgos who fancied themselves some sort of nobility. The bandits moved to encircle the man as he rode up and reined in, but there was no fear in his blue eyes as he looked around at them. He crossed his hands on the saddle horn and leaned forward, easing tired muscles. His eyes fastened on Montoya and Esteban, who were standing apart from the other *bandidos*. Addressing the larger man, he said in fluent Spanish, "You are Paco Montoya, I take it?"

"What do you wish with the great Montoya?" the bandit leader shot back at him.

Still ignoring the menacing stares of the other men and the weapons in their hands, the man swung down easily from his saddle and strode toward Montoya. "I have invested a great deal of money and effort to locate you, sir," he said calmly. "Now I wish to hire you."

Montoya stared at him. Definitely a crazy man, he decided. But he was curious enough to play along for a little while, and a glance at Esteban told him that his second in command felt the same way.

Montoya extended a hand, palm out in an expansive gesture. "Speak your piece, my friend."

The man took his hat off, revealing a shock of dark-blond hair that matched his neatly trimmed mustache. He took a handkerchief from his breast pocket and wiped sweat from his forehead, somehow making the gesture look elegant. When he had returned the handkerchief to his pocket, he said, "My name is Pierre Desmond. I was a captain in the army that served Emperor Maximilian." There was pride in his voice when he made that statement.

Instantly, all the gang members stiffened and lifted their rifles and pistols, their faces twisted in angry snarls. Once these men had been peasants and farmers, and they and their families had known nothing but grief during the rule of the European-backed dictator. Even now, years after their deaths, the names of Maximilian and his wife, the Empress Carlota, were despised and hated throughout Mexico.

Only a quick gesture from Montoya prevented his men from shooting Pierre Desmond full of holes. The man was a gringo, but Montoya had to admire his brazenness. He stepped closer to Desmond and regarded him with a fierce stare, but the man did not flinch under the bandit leader's scrutiny. Finally Montoya asked, "What is it you want of us?"

A smile tugged fleetingly at the corners of the Frenchman's mouth. "I have returned to Mexico to make amends to the people I formerly helped to oppress."

"Fancy words," Montoya grunted impatiently. "What can a man like you do to help the Mexican people?"

"I can make a select few of you very rich men," Desmond replied solemnly. "All I require is that you perform a certain task for me."

Rich men . . . Montoya liked the sound of that. He didn't trust Desmond, not for a second, but he was willing to listen to anyone who promised to make him rich. He looked at Esteban, and his lieutenant gave a minuscule nod. Esteban was intrigued by this daring stranger, too.

"Come into my tent," Montoya said. "We will talk. Perhaps we can help each other. . . ."

It was not the way of the Yellow Rose to complain, so she would not admit that she was tired. But after several days of bouncing through West Texas in the hot stage-coach, she would be very happy to see El Paso. She and her party were scheduled to spend several days there before journeying on to Santa Fe and Denver, and Rose intended to enjoy that time.

She leaned back against the hard rear seat of the coach

and held a handkerchief over her nose and mouth to filter out some of the ever-present dust that swirled in through the windows of the vehicle. The canvas curtains were rolled down, but the flying grit seeped in around them anyway, so all they really accomplished was to trap even more heat inside the coach.

Even so, this was not the most unpleasant trip she had ever made, Rose reminded herself. Things could always be worse.

Ever since the stagecoach had left Del Rio, she had been thinking about what had happened there and the things Cody had said to her. Could he have been right? Was the man who was after her a dangerous lunatic who would not hesitate to kill if it was convenient for him?

After the incidents in New Orleans, Galveston, and San Antonio, Rose had convinced herself that the man's motives were strictly romantic, that he was obsessed with her beauty or her singing or both. She was well aware of the effect she had on men, and she knew how some of them would go to great lengths to get what they wanted. More than one erstwhile suitor had threatened to kill himself if she withheld her love from him.

But none of them had threatened to kill her.

Rose blinked, her eyes watering from the dust, and looked across at Eduardo and Alonso, who rode in the front seat, facing backward. The older brother was dozing with his head tilted back and his eyes closed. Alonso was watching her, though, and when her eyes met his he looked away quickly, a slightly sheepish expression appearing on his face.

He was definitely in love with her, Rose thought, or at least thoroughly infatuated. Never had he expressed that feeling in words, and Rose doubted that he ever would. He was simply too shy. But what he felt for her was obvious to one who had as much experience in reading men as she did.

Eduardo was different. The passions of youth no longer flowed in his veins. His love was for the music. He looked on Rose almost as he would have a talented younger sister. He was a friend and admirer of her vocal abilities, but he would never seek to be anything more.

Estrella sat beside the singer, coughing delicately into her own handkerchief. Rose felt sorry for her servant, who was becoming more pale and drawn with every day that went by. She was obviously not cut out for this kind of travel. But in the year that Estrella had been working for her, Rose had found her to be an excellent personal maid, and she would not have wanted to make this trip without the girl.

On the other side of Estrella was a bony, derby-hatted gentleman who sold nuts, bolts, and screws to hardware stores. His sample case was at his feet. He had introduced himself as Hector Bagby when he boarded the stage at Sanderson and since then had said very little. Sitting beside Alonso on the front seat was another drummer, one Marcus Dunaway, whose line was ladies' hats. He had stared at Rose when he first boarded the coach, then had made a few mildly suggestive comments before he noticed the icy, menacing stare Alonso was giving him. That had put an end to his flirting, harmless though it had been.

Barney Gellman was riding atop the coach at the moment, along with the driver and the shotgun guard. There would have been room for him inside; the narrow bench that ran through the center of the coach was unoccupied, and it was likely that a glower from Gellman would have been enough to make one of the drummers move and give up his seat. But Gellman had discovered he liked riding on top of the coach. From there he could see everything that was going on around them and would have some extra warning in case of trouble.

The stagecoach had passed through Alpine, Fort Davis, Valentine, Van Horn, and Sierra Blanca. The next major stop was El Paso, and the driver had promised his passengers that morning that they would reach it by nightfall. Rose hoped that proved to be the case. She had kept up with the date as best she could, and if she was correct, her first performance in El Paso was scheduled for the next night. That would give her a day to rest before the show. When need be, she could give a performance on the same day she arrived in a town, but it was easier if she didn't have to.

The stage rolled through Ysleta in midafternoon, following the course of the Rio Grande now, and a short time later the bustling settlement of El Paso came into view. Overlooked by Mount Franklin, El Paso del Norte was a growing community that served as a gateway between the United States and Mexico.

It was said that one could buy virtually anything one's heart desired in El Paso, though Rose knew that wasn't strictly true. Besides, what she wanted wasn't in El Paso, it was back in Del Rio—and it wasn't for sale.

Cody. He was a stubborn man; there were no two ways about it. But he was also quite an appealing man. Rose had first noticed him when she and the other members of her party arrived at the Rio Grande Hotel in Del Rio, though she had made sure that he didn't notice her scrutiny. He had been sitting at a table in the dining room with a lovely redheaded woman, and Rose had felt a surprising pang of envy for that redhead. Cody was a big man, too rugged to be called handsome, but he had a certain air about him. . . . At any rate, he had made enough of an impression on her during that brief glimpse that she would have been gratified when he had shown up at her dressing room that night even if his entrance hadn't been timed so that he could gun down one of the men trying to abduct her. His cool bravery under fire had told her that here was a very special man indeed.

She sighed and wished that he were with her now.

"El Paso, folks!" the driver sang out from the box. "Comin' into El Paso!"

Rose felt the coach slowing down. It would be a wonderful relief to stand up and stretch, she thought. The stage roads across Texas were not noted for their smooth surfaces, and the constant bouncing and jolting were hard on the spine.

Beside her, Estrella muttered a prayer of thanksgiving in Spanish. Rose smiled slightly in sympathy, hiding the expression behind her handkerchief.

The coach came to a stop in front of the stage station in the center of town. Barney Gellman dropped down from the roof and opened the door, and everyone waited for Rose to get off first. She took Barney's hand and stepped down, glancing as she did so toward the crowd on the sidewalk. The arrival of a stagecoach was always an event of interest in these frontier towns, and it was even more so when the coach carried someone famous like the Yellow Rose. She gave the crowd a gracious smile, hiding her weariness behind the expression.

A slender older man in a gray suit stepped forward to meet her. His goatee and thinning hair matched the color of his clothes. In one hand he carried a soft felt hat and a silver-headed walking stick; the other he used to take the hand Rose extended to him and lift it to his lips. "Pleased to meet you, ma'am," he said after he had kissed her hand. "I'm Wilbur MacInnes, the owner of the El Paso Opera House."

"But of course, Mr. MacInnes," Rose said brightly. "I enjoyed your letters. You were so very kind."

"Only telling the truth, ma'am. You are a star of brighter magnitude than any that has ever graced my humble stage."

The impresario was a smooth one, all right, Rose thought. But, then, Rose had expected no less. Anyone who could build a concert hall in a rough-and-tumble frontier town like El Paso and then make a success of it had to be shrewd, daring, and charming all at the same time. She sensed that Wilbur MacInnes fitted that description perfectly, and she instinctively liked him right away.

"And you must be Mr. Gellman," MacInnes continued, pumping the hand of the bald-headed manager and bodyguard. "So nice to meet you at last."

"Same here," Gellman grunted, and Rose thought that he could probably take lessons from MacInnes in proper behavior. Of course, she had not hired Gellman for his manners. He was rough and aggressive and didn't care who knew it. He was also devoted to his employer.

Estrella, Eduardo, and Alonso climbed down from the

coach as MacInnes turned back to Rose and said briskly, "I'll have your baggage taken care of right away."

"You will see that it is taken to the hotel?" Rose asked.

MacInnes shook his head.

Rose frowned. "I do not understand."

"No hotel," MacInnes declared firmly. "You and your party will be staying at my house."

"Oh, no," Rose began. "We could not impose—"

"No imposition at all," MacInnes insisted. "I've got plenty of room. It's one of the biggest houses in El Paso, you know," he added, allowing some pride to creep into his voice. "I must say, ma'am—"

"Please, call me Rose."

MacInnes beamed with pleasure. "I must say, Rose, you're a refreshing change from most of the performers I've brought to El Paso. Many of them have been quite arrogant and unpleasant."

"I am here to bring pleasure to those who would hear me sing and those who make it possible. And I am grateful for that opportunity."

The impresario was obviously quite taken with her and offered her his arm. "My carriage is right over here," he said. "If you and Mr. Gellman and your other friends will come with me . . . ?"

Rose was aware of the excited whispers coming from the crowd as she slipped her arm through MacInnes's, and the two of them led the small procession to an impressive carriage that was hitched to a team of six magnificent, finely matched black horses. This was a sight that the townspeople of El Paso would not soon forget. Even tired and dusty from traveling, the Yellow Rose brought a touch of glamour to the often difficult lives these pioneers led.

Gellman rode on the front seat with MacInnes's driver, while Rose, MacInnes, and the others settled down on the padded benches inside the carriage. This was a far cry from the stagecoach, Rose thought. In a luxuriously appointed vehicle like this, one could almost travel across Texas in comfort—if not for the dust, of course. And that was less of a problem here in El Paso, where some of the streets were actually paved with bricks and cobblestones. As the carriage rolled along the avenues of the town, Rose looked out and saw that most of the businesses they passed seemed to be doing a brisk trade. El Paso was a center for ranching, mining, and commerce between the United States and Mexico. She expected that there would be a large, enthusiastic crowd on hand at the opera house the following evening.

Wilbur MacInnes's estate was on the outskirts of town, near the river. The carriage entered the property through a gate in a high stone wall and proceeded up a driveway made of crushed rock. This lane led to a sprawling adobe house patterned after the haciendas of Mexico, complete with a red-tiled roof and a large courtyard with a fountain in the center of it. The carriage came to a stop in front of a wrought-iron gate that opened into that courtyard.

Rose felt a sudden pang deep within her as she looked at the house in the late afternoon light. It was beautiful. Live oaks arched over the courtyard, and she could hear water tinkling in the fountain. Birds flitted from branch to branch in the trees, warbling what might have been a song of greeting. The scene brought back a flood of memories for Rose, memories that at first were warm and happy. . . .

Memories that turned ugly without warning.

She thrust those thoughts from her mind and put a smile back on her face as Wilbur MacInnes hopped down from the carriage and then turned to assist her. "You have a lovely home, Mr. MacInnes," she said as she stepped down to the ground in front of the gate.

"Thank you. I rattle around in it a little since I'm all by myself except for the servants. By the way, I'd appreciate it if you'd call me Wilbur."

"Of course, Wilbur." She smiled brightly at him, knowing that he was impressed by the attention being paid to him by a beautiful young woman less than half his age. None of it was serious, of course, and both of them knew it, but it was still pleasant.

"Your bags will be along presently, and I'll have them taken to your rooms. Until then, I have a bottle of fine

wine waiting for us inside." After opening the gate he
linked arms with Rose, and the two of them strolled into
the courtyard, trailed by the others. Rose glanced over
her shoulder and saw that Barney Gellman was looking
around suspiciously, as usual, his eyes darting to every
corner of the courtyard.

She felt safe with Gellman close by, as well as Eduardo
and Alonso, of course. Ensconsed here in this lovely
house, surrounded by her friends and employees, surely
nothing would happen to spoil this stop on her tour. But
still, she would have felt better if a Texas Ranger named
Cody were with her right now. . . .

Cody lifted the mug of beer to his lips and took a long,
thirsty swallow. The cool liquid cut the dust in his throat,
and when he lowered the mug to the counter, he sighed.

"Tired, Cody?" asked the white-aproned man behind
the bar here in the saloon in the Rio Grande Hotel.

"A mite," Cody admitted. "Of course, I don't know
why. Haven't been doing anything except riding around
looking for trouble that's not there."

He picked up his beer again and then turned around to
lean back against the bar, resting the elbow of his free arm
on the hardwood. His Stetson was cuffed to the back of
his head, and he wore a blue bib-front shirt with the
sleeves rolled up a couple of turns. He'd spent the day out
on patrol and hadn't run into a single episode of law-
lessness. The border country was still as quiet as he had
ever seen it.

He didn't like it. Not one damned bit. It reminded him
of a hot, still, cloudless day that suddenly turns ugly and
spawns one hell of a storm. That was the feeling that was
in the air: violence just waiting to erupt.

Instead, the only thing that came to pass was Seth
Williams and Alan Northrup strolling into the saloon,
bickering about something as usual. They broke off their
argument when they saw Cody standing there and came
over to him.

"Run into any problems?" Alan asked as they gestured for the bartender to bring them beers.

Cody shook his head. "Not hardly." He grinned. "About the most exciting thing I did all day was help a farmer find a goat that'd strayed off."

Seth shrugged. "That beats what we've been doin' lately."

Cody grinned, then turned his attention back to his beer. Ever since the Yellow Rose had left Del Rio, the big Ranger had spent his spare time trying to find out more about Al O'Neil and his two confederates and who might have hired them. So far, he might as well have been butting his head against a stone wall. That, combined with the lack of activity on behalf of the Rangers, had him good and frustrated.

Suddenly the sound of galloping hoofbeats came floating into the saloon. Somebody was riding in a big hurry down Del Rio's main avenue. Cody set his nearly empty mug on the bar and started toward the street door. Instinct was setting off warning bells inside him—or maybe he was just tired of hanging around and doing nothing.

Seth and Alan exchanged a quick glance, then hurried after him, leaving their beers untouched on the bar. "What is it, Cody?" Seth asked.

The big Ranger thrust the batwings aside and stepped out onto the sidewalk just as a man raced past on horseback. Cody caught a glimpse of a frightened, bloody face. The rider was hatless, and he was pushing his mount to the limit. Cody's gaze followed the man's progress down the street; the frantic rider jerked his horse to an abrupt stop in front of Ranger headquarters.

"Something's going on," Cody muttered as the horseman half fell, half slid from his saddle and staggered into the building. Breaking into a trot, Cody started toward headquarters with an eager Seth and Alan right behind him.

By the time they reached the outer office, the man who had come flogging hell-for-leather into town was seated in one of the straight-backed chairs, his head drooping onto his chest in exhaustion and his hands hanging loosely between his knees. Lieutenant Whitcomb had a wet cloth in his hands, and he lifted the man's head to clean away some of the blood that had dried on his face—blood that came from a long scratch on his forehead. Cody recognized a bullet crease and knew that a couple of inches had meant the difference between life and death for the man.

Captain Vickery stood nearby, his hands clasped behind his back and his bushy brows drawn down in an ominous frown. "You say rustlers hit your folks' ranch, boy?" he asked.

The rider looked up, and for the first time Cody realized how young he was—sixteen or seventeen at the most. He nodded and said in a choked voice, "They shot my brother, and I reckon they thought they killed me, too, when that bullet grazed me. My ma and pa and my sisters were holed up in the house, and I knew I had to get help for 'em. You got to get out there, Captain! I don't know how long they can hold out! I got here as fast as I could from Lobo Canyon—"

"Take it easy, son, we're on our way right now," Vickery said. "Your family'll be all right, Lord willin'." He glanced up and saw Cody, Seth, and Alan standing just inside the door. "You men—" he began.

"On our way, Cap'n," Cody said before Vickery could finish. He wheeled around and headed out the door, hurrying toward the corral out back. His horse, a rangy lineback dun with a bad disposition and enough sand for two normal horses, was probably a little tired from the day's patrol, but Cody would still bet on its being able to cover ground faster than any other mount he might use.

"I knew somethin' was going to happen!" Seth said excitedly as he and Alan hustled along behind Cody. "I just knew it!"

"Well, you were right," Alan said.

Cody just hoped they were in time to save the rest of the youngster's family from the raiders. The boredom and frustration of the previous days' inactivity had vanished. All that mattered was reaching the ranch in Lobo Canyon before it was too late.

And for the first time in quite a while, Cody realized, he wasn't worrying about the Yellow Rose.

CHAPTER
6
▬▬▬▬▬▬▬▬▬▬

After all she had been through in her life, the Yellow Rose would not have thought that the simple act of stepping out onto a stage and singing would provoke such fear inside her. And yet it always did. Without fail a rush of sheer terror always went through her as she stood waiting for the curtains to part. Tonight was no exception.

Eduardo and Alonso stood to either side of her, here backstage at the El Paso Opera House. Eduardo gave her a calm, reassuring smile, knowing that her nerves were stretched almost to the breaking point. As for Alonso, he shared her stage fright, so he looked nervous, too, as he always did.

Rose managed to smile at both men. Soon they would step out through the curtains with their guitars and begin playing, settling down the talkative audience and getting them involved with the music before Rose made her entrance. As the threesome waited, Wilbur MacInnes came bustling up to them, rubbing his hands together with a Scotsman's glee at the prospect of a healthy profit.

"There's a full house, just as we expected," he said. "And they're all going to be completely thrilled to hear you, my dear."

"I hope you are correct, Wilbur," Rose said with a smile.

"I know I am. All of El Paso is clamoring to see and hear the famous Yellow Rose. There were stories in the newspaper today about your arrival and about the performance tonight, and it seems that no one in town is talking about anything else. I've heard that people have come from as far away as Sweetwater just to hear you, Rose."

"Hopefully none of them will be disappointed."

MacInnes chuckled. "I doubt very much that you have to worry about that." He patted Rose's shoulder, left bare by the elegant yellow gown. "Just a few moments, and then you can begin." With that, he hurried away to attend to more of the details of the evening's performance.

"The little man is right," Eduardo said softly. "Everything will be fine, Rose."

She nodded. "I know. But thank you for telling me, Eduardo. It always helps."

Drawing a deep breath, Rose felt her jitters ease somewhat. The confidence and determination that had brought her to her present position swelled within her. She had no control over her talent and her beauty; God had given her those. But as for what she did with those assets . . . ah, that was entirely up to her.

She had enjoyed her stay so far in El Paso. Wilbur MacInnes was a charming host. They had dined well at his house the night before, enjoyed a bottle of fine wine, and spent the evening in pleasant conversation. Following that, one of MacInnes's servants had drawn a tub of hot water for her, and she had soaked in it for a long time, bathing away not only the dust of travel, but its aches and pains as well. The room that she had been given for the duration of her stay was furnished with a huge four-poster bed with a soft, downy mattress. Rose had slept deeply and well, not rising until nearly ten o'clock that morning.

After that she had spent part of the day being shown around El Paso by MacInnes. She had been introduced to the mayor and also to the alcalde of Juarez, El Paso's sister city across the border river, and then the group had dined at a fine restaurant. Barney Gellman, Eduardo, and Alonso had stayed close to her at all times, protecting her without being intrusive.

This afternoon there had been a nap—not that she really needed it—and a light dinner at MacInnes's house. Following the performance, the impresario had informed her, there would be a party at his estate for El Paso's social elite, complete with music, dancing, and barbecue—a party with the Yellow Rose as the guest of honor. Rose was less enthusiastic about that, knowing that she would be exhausted after the concert, but she had masked her lack of enthusiasm. MacInnes was doing his very best to make her stay here special, and she had not wanted to be the one to disappoint him.

Now, Eduardo and Alonso each gave her another smile, Eduardo's confident and his younger brother's a bit more shy, and then they gripped their guitars and stepped out through the curtains. Rose heard the hubbub from the audience begin to die away, and the crowd became ever more silent as the brothers began to play, working their magic with the strings of their guitars.

The last of Rose's worries faded away, too. At every performance when the music began she found herself so swept up in it she no longer even thought about the people watching her from the other side of the footlights. The only things in her mind were the songs she would sing. All thoughts of trouble vanished, even on a trip like this that had been plagued with problems from the start. As she had told Cody, she always tried to give her very best performance, no matter where she was or what the circumstances.

Thinking about Cody made her hesitate slightly. This would be the first time she had sung since that night in Del Rio. It would have been nice if the Ranger were in the audience tonight to hear her songs and to wrap his strong arms around her afterward.

But that was not to be, and Rose thrust the thought out of her mind. Then Eduardo and Alonso reached a specific passage in the tune they were playing. Taking her cue, she stepped forward and brushed the curtains aside, making her way to her place on the stage between the brothers. She immediately lifted her voice in song, clasping her hands in front of her and swaying slightly back and forth in time to the music of the twin guitars.

When she was finished, the audience erupted in thunderous applause, and she beamed out at them for a mo-

ment before launching into the next song. No matter
where she traveled, she had only one real home, and that
was the stage.

Tonight Rose had come home again.

If any performer had ever been given a longer, louder
ovation than the one the Yellow Rose received when her
performance was over, no one could remember when it
was. Backstage afterward, flushed with success, Rose ac-
cepted the congratulations of Wilbur MacInnes.

The impresario was ecstatic. "I've never seen anything
like it," he bubbled to Rose after he had kissed her hand
several times. "El Paso is yours, dear lady!"

"Thank you, Wilbur," she said graciously. "I am glad to
be able to bring so much enjoyment to so many people."

"You have indeed done that. Now, if you'll allow me to
escort you to your dressing room . . ."

The dressing rooms here at the opera house were larger
and a great deal more opulent than the chamber she had
used at the Rio Grande Hotel in Del Rio. As she linked
arms with MacInnes and headed down the hall toward her
dressing room, Barney Gellman hurried ahead to open
the door and make sure everything was all right inside.

Once he had taken a quick look around, he stepped
back from the entrance and crossed his arms over his barrel chest, nodding his approval to Rose. She swept into
the room on MacInnes's arm.

Estrella was waiting there to help her mistress change
clothes. "Was it a good performance, Señorita Rose?"
the girl asked.

"Very good," MacInnes answered for her. "Excellent,
in fact!" He lifted Rose's hand to his lips for one final
kiss—for the time being. "I'll be back shortly to escort
you to the gala."

"I'll be ready," Rose promised. As the door shut behind the impresario, she caught a glimpse of Gellman, Eduardo, and Alonso standing in the hall outside. Gellman
would stay there by the door, guarding it, while the Mar-

tinez brothers went to their own dressing room to change
from their flashy stage clothes into more subdued outfits.

Earlier in the day Rose had picked out a gown to wear
to MacInnes's party, and Estrella had it ready for her now.
She slipped out of the dress in which she had performed
and stood there in her corset and petticoats. Estrella
picked up the new gown, this one a more subtle shade of
yellow than the brightly colored garment she wore during
the show, and brought it over to her.

Rose lifted her arms and wriggled into the tight-fitting
dress. As Estrella stepped behind her to fasten the tiny
buttons that ran up the back, Rose said, "You will come
to the party, too, won't you, Estrella?"

"Oh, no," the servant said quickly. "This fiesta is for
your important friends, señorita, not for lowly ones such
as myself."

Rose turned around to face her. "But you are my
friend, too, Estrella. I would be lost without your help. I
think you should go." She paused for a moment, then
added, "Besides, I think Alonso would like it if you were
there."

"Alonso?" Estrella repeated in surprise. "But why
should Alonso care— Oh!"

Rose just smiled meaningfully. She was stretching the
truth a bit; she had never seen Alonso look at Estrella
with anything more than companionable regard. But the
servant girl was quite attractive when she took the time to
put on a pretty dress and use cosmetics, as she had done
tonight. Perhaps what Alonso needed so that he would
quit mooning over Rose was to have his attentions pointed
in a more suitable direction.

"Very well, I . . . I will go," Estrella said. "If you are
sure it is all right. I would not want to offend Señor Mac-
Innes."

"I will see to it that he is not offended," Rose said,
completely sure of herself when it came to Wilbur Mac-
Innes. He would not deny her anything she wanted.

The singer sat down in front of the dressing table and
touched up the makeup on her own face, then tucked up
several strands of hair that had escaped from the elabo-

rate arrangement of raven curls on her head. Only someone who knew her very, very well would notice the hint of
weariness in her eyes, she thought as she studied her reflection. She was satisfied.

A few minutes later a knock sounded on the door, and
Estrella opened it. MacInnes stepped in and smiled
across the room at the singer's reflection in the mirror,
asking, "Ready to go, my dear?"

"Yes, I'm ready," Rose said, standing up and turning to
face him. She took the arm he offered, and he led her out
into the hall. Gellman, Eduardo, and Alonso were waiting
there, as was a crowd of well-dressed men.

Rose had been through dozens of scenes like this before, drawing admiring men backstage after every performance, and though the faces might change, the things
they said never did. At the sight of the Yellow Rose, the
men clamored for her attention and tried to press bou-
quets of flowers on her, most of them shouting about how
lovely she was and how they adored her. If not for the trio
of Gellman, Eduardo, and Alonso moving them steadily
back, she and MacInnes might not have been able to get
through the press of people. Estrella followed closely behind, looking for all the world like a cornered rabbit.

MacInnes was beaming with pride, obviously thrilled
to have on his arm a woman desired by so many men.
Rose gave him a smile, then darted a glance at the crowd
as she walked toward the rear door of the opera house.
Suddenly she felt an icy touch of fear in her middle. Was
he one of that throng of admirers—the man who had hired
kidnappers, the man who, according to Cody, was
ruthless enough to kill his own employees and enjoy it?
She tried to repress the shudder she felt running through
her and hoped that MacInnes wouldn't notice it. There
was no way she could explain her reaction to him. She
couldn't tell him that she was afraid one of these men was
really a vicious murderer. He would think *she* was the
insane one.

With Gellman and the two Mexican musicians clearing
a pathway, Rose and MacInnes made their way quickly to

the exit and left the massive redbrick building that housed the concert hall.

More people were waiting outside to cheer her, but MacInnes's driver joined the other three men in keeping them back, and she and the Scotsman were soon ensconced in the carriage. The others boarded quickly, and the carriage rolled away from the curb, bound for MacInnes's estate on the edge of town.

They soon reached the estate and turned into the driveway, the wheels of the carriage making a crunching sound on the gravel-covered lane. Minutes later the driver braked to a stop, and MacInnes helped Rose down from the carriage and escorted her through the wrought-iron gate and into the courtyard.

Rose smiled with pleasure at the sight. The house was brightly lit, as was the courtyard in front. Multicolored lanterns hung from the trees, their glow reflecting brilliantly in the fountain's rippling water. Tables set up under the trees appeared to be groaning from the weight of the food stacked upon them. Huge platters were loaded with everything from barbecued beef to mounds of vegetables to pies and cakes of every description. From the looks of it, there was enough food here to feed all of El Paso. There seemed to be something almost shameful about such excess, but Rose had to admit that it was no worse than what she had seen in the capitals of Europe. In fact, the parties she had attended there had usually been even more lavish. Still, for a place like El Paso, MacInnes had put together quite an impressive gala.

The center of the courtyard had been left clear for dancing, and a mariachi band was off to one side preparing to play. Eduardo and Alonso looked on with interest, and Rose could tell that both of them were thinking about joining in if the band leader would allow it. Any musician would have to be a fool not to want those two playing alongside him, she mused.

"I hope you enjoy yourself, Rose," MacInnes said. He gestured around the as-yet-unpeopled courtyard. "I did all of this just for you."

"Thank you, Wilbur," she told him quietly. "You have made me feel very welcome here."

"No more welcome than you deserve to be. You've brightened this old man's life immensely." He chuckled. "Not to mention enriched it a little, too." He stopped and turned to face her. "Now, if you'll be so kind . . . May I have the first dance?"

"But of course." Rose smiled at him, taking the hands he held out to her.

MacInnes nodded to the musicians, who began to play a waltz, and he and Rose started swirling around the courtyard as other guests began arriving.

MacInnes's vehicle had been merely the first of a long procession of carriages and wagons that stretched back to the center of the city. As the guests arrived, they drove through the gate in the outer wall and then parked their vehicles along the gravel driveway. They were entering the courtyard in a steady stream now, and some couples immediately joined Rose and MacInnes in the dancing, while others headed for the food first thing.

As Rose was whirled around by MacInnes—and she found him surprisingly light on his feet for a man of his age—she lost track of Gellman and Estrella, Eduardo and Alonso. All of them were still around close by, she supposed, but their exact whereabouts were of no consequence. The fear that had touched her earlier had disappeared. No one, no matter how insane, would dare to bother her at a celebration like this one. Why, half of El Paso must be here, she thought. For tonight, at any rate, she was safe, and so she was determined to put all the worries out of her mind and simply enjoy herself.

Her tiredness had vanished, too, despite the late hour. As far as she was concerned, the band could play all night. Because she intended to keep dancing. . . .

The Rio Grande was only perhaps two hundred yards south of the outer wall surrounding Wilbur MacInnes's home, so the music from the party carried that far without any trouble. In turn, that music drowned out the sound of hooves splashing through water as thirty men rode in the moonlight across the shallow, slow-moving river.

All of the men were heavily armed, and black bandannas tied across their noses concealed the lower halves of their faces beneath their wide-brimmed sombreros. The big man in the lead reined in and held up his hand, signaling for his followers to stop. "We will wait here," Paco Montoya said harshly in Spanish.

Two men had been sent across the river earlier to scout the group's destination. One of them was Esteban, and Montoya hoped that nothing had happened to his loyal lieutenant. The bandit chief didn't figure they would have any trouble tonight, but he was not going to risk his entire gang without knowing for certain what they were riding into. Esteban and the other scout, Jorge, would be back soon, Montoya told himself, and then they could get on with the job that had brought them here across the border, into the hated land of the gringos.

A few more tense minutes had passed when Montoya heard the soft *clip-clop* of approaching hoofbeats. He stiffened in the saddle and stared out into the night. Enough illumination came from the moon and stars so that he was able to discern two shadowy figures riding toward the waiting *bandidos*. He relaxed when he recognized Esteban and Jorge.

Esteban called out a quiet greeting as he and his companion rode up to Montoya. "Good news, Paco," he said. "Everything is as we had hoped, perhaps even better."

Montoya grunted. "What about guards?"

"There were only two, both of them posted at the rear gate where supply wagons enter." Esteban's teeth gleamed whitely in his brown face when he grinned. "Both of them are dead now, and the open gate awaits us. I would strike soon, before anyone notices what has happened."

His brutal face tightening a little under the black mask, Montoya nodded. He would have to have a talk with Esteban later. The second in command sounded almost as if he was giving orders rather than merely suggesting, as was his place. Still, Esteban had done well by killing the sentries and opening the gate, so Montoya would not be too harsh with him.

The bandit leader slipped one of his matched Colts from its holster and lifted it as he tightened his grip on the horse's reins with his other hand. Twisting halfway around in the saddle, he raised the pistol in the air and called in a savagely exultant tone, "We ride, *hermanos*!"

Then the pistol slashed down and the long silver rowels of Montoya's spurs dug cruelly into the flanks of his horse. The animal bounded forward, breaking into a gallop as Montoya steered it toward the glimmering oasis of lights that marked the location of MacInnes's estate. The other bandits followed, restraining the urge to shout and fire their guns in the air. Montoya's orders had been plain: Do not give the gringos too much warning.

The gang swept on through the night toward the house, like a tide of death.

Rose had almost forgotten what it was like to relax and enjoy herself this much. All the men at the party were eager to dance with her, so she found herself switching from partner to partner every time the band finished one tune and started another. She caught a glimpse of Eduardo and Alonso sitting with the other musicians, strumming their ever-present guitars.

Barney Gellman had a plate piled high with food in his hands, and he seemed to be enjoying himself as well. Rose didn't know where Estrella was, but she assumed the maid was also having a good time. Before the night was over, Rose thought, Estrella would probably be flirting with Alonso, hopefully with some success.

Finding herself in MacInnes's arms again just as the band began a fast, fiery Mexican song, Rose let herself be carried away by the ringing notes. After only a few moments, MacInnes stopped and said with a smile, "I'm going to have to sit this one out, Rose. It's just too fast for an old man like me."

"Oh, Wilbur, you are not old!" Rose cried, a little disappointed.

He stepped back and regarded her with admiring eyes. "Dance for me," he suggested. "I'd love to watch you."

Rose smiled and nodded, allowing herself to be caught up again in the infectious rhythm. Her feet moved faster and faster as she twirled around, her skirts fanning out around her slim brown legs. Her hair had worked itself partly loose, so she pulled out her high comb and, with a shake of her head, did away with the rest of the elaborate hairstyle, letting the raven curls tumble freely to her shoulders. MacInnes was clapping in time with the music now, a broad smile on his face as he watched her.

For the first time in perhaps years Rose truly let herself go, and without her even being aware of it, a circle of spectators formed around her, watching this beautiful young woman dance with hoydenish abandon. She might have been a serving wench in some cantina far south of the border, judging from the way she was behaving.

All Rose knew was that it felt good, so very good.

She spun around, clapping her hands over her head and kicking high her slipper-shod feet. Her head was thrown back, her eyes half closed. She felt a familiar warmth deep in the pit of her belly and used it to fuel her smooth, sensuous movements. Finally the song came to an end, and the Yellow Rose sank into a crouch, lowering her arms and letting her head fall forward so that her long dark hair screened her face. She had not danced so hard in ages, and her breasts rose and fell rapidly as she replenished the air in her spent body.

All eyes were on her now. All the other dancers had ceased earlier, stopping so that they could watch her. No one applauded; that would have seemed somehow inappropriate. What they had just witnessed was too personal, too moving, for mere applause. The whole group seemed to draw a deep, collective breath.

That was when the shooting started.

Rose's head jerked up as the rumble of gunfire blasted the night. Mixed with the shots was the pounding of dozens of hooves. Men cried out in surprise, and women began to scream. People ran crazily through the courtyard, not knowing where the danger was coming from, just running because every instinct in their bodies commanded them to flee.

As Rose came to her feet, a group of men on horseback surged around the corner of the house, coming from the rear of the estate. In the lantern light she could see that they were all masked and had guns in their hands. Those guns spat noise and flame and death, and the horses trampled brutally over anyone unlucky enough to be in their path.

Standing still in the middle of the sudden chaos, Rose looked around for some means of escape. Old instincts had come to the fore inside her, and while a small part of her felt the fear that gripped the rest of the guests, on the surface she was cool and calm. She caught a fleeting glimpse of Barney Gellman trying to force his way through the crowd toward her. His only concern right now, she knew, would be reaching her side. A glance in the other direction showed her Eduardo and Alonso attempting to do the same thing.

The raiders seemed to be shooting indiscriminately, though there was little resistance from the partygoers. A few of the men had been armed, but when they jerked their guns out, they were chopped down by the deadly fire of the invaders. Rose felt sick as she saw the bodies already littering the courtyard.

Then Wilbur MacInnes was beside her, catching hold of her arm and tugging frantically at her. "Come with me!" he cried over the tumult. "I'll get you to safety!"

Rose began to run with him toward the house, but they had gone only a few steps when one of the raiders, a huge man on a black horse, burst through the crowd and raced madly toward them. A harsh shout came from him, and then he cried in accented English, "Get away from the girl, old man!"

MacInnes thrust Rose behind him. "Keep going!" he told her. "I'll stop this—"

Before he could finish his bold statement, the gun in the big man's hand boomed, and MacInnes was lifted off his feet by the slug tearing through his body. The bullet punched completely through his slender frame, exploding from his back. He dropped onto the flagstones of the courtyard, stained now with blood, and gasped a couple of times before he died.

The rider never slowed down. Ignoring the impresario's corpse, he galloped straight toward Rose.

Her eyes widened in terror as the horse loomed in front of her, and then the animal suddenly veered to the side as the rider leaned over from his saddle. He had holstered his gun, leaving his hand free, and his long arm looped around her, grabbing her and jerking her off her feet. Rose cried out in fear and shock, then gasped for air as her captor flung her facedown across the saddle in front of him, the saddle horn driving into her stomach and knocking the breath out of her.

The horse reared up and wheeled around as the big man hauled back on the reins. He shifted his grip on Rose, now lifting her so that she was sitting in front of him with his arm clamped tightly around her. When the horse dropped its front legs back to the ground with a jolt, the rider shouted in English through the chaos, "Tell all of Texas that Diego Alvarez has returned! Only Alvarez would be bold enough to take the Yellow Rose!" With his cries ringing in Rose's ears, the man kicked his mount into a gallop again.

They rode toward the rear of the estate, where the marauders had first appeared. The few partygoers who had not scattered for cover now leapt to get out of the way as the big man led his raiders around the house. All except one man, that is. Rose saw Eduardo racing to intercept them, knife in hand.

"No, Eduardo, no!" she screamed, knowing that he could not stand up to these killers alone. He ignored her, though, and lunged to meet them, reaching up to grab at her and slash at the man holding her.

The man drove a booted foot into Eduardo's chest, knocking him away. Then he reined in and turned his horse in a tight circle. Rose screamed again as the animal's cruel hooves thudded into the fallen Eduardo. The musician cried out once, and then one of the hooves struck his head with a brittle, cracking sound. He slumped back, silent and motionless.

"Such is the fate of all who defy Diego Alvarez!" bellowed Rose's captor as he tightened his grip on her. An exultant shout went up from the men following him.

Rose felt sick. Eduardo was dead, and it was all her fault.

The band of raiders headed for the rear gate, pounding through it at a dead run. Rose sagged forward in the leader's iron grip, the wind of their passage blowing her hair into her face. She didn't care. She was numb, stunned into silence and immobility by the horrors of the past few minutes. What had been a lovely, carefree evening had turned without warning into a hellish nightmare, and the worst thing was that Rose knew it was far from over.

With a last volley of gunfire back toward the house, the bandits thundered off into the night, disappearing in the shadows across the Rio Grande.

CHAPTER
7

Slowly, the Yellow Rose's wits returned to her. She lifted her head and let the wind whip the long strands of raven hair out of her eyes. Light from the moon and stars enabled her to see the flat, sandy, mesquite-dotted terrain in front of the band of marauders.

They had covered several miles since crossing the border river, she estimated. The leader's arm was still around her, pressing her tightly against him as he rode. He had said nothing else after his boastful shouts back at the estate of poor Wilbur MacInnes. The whole gang rode in well-disciplined silence.

Now that the confusion and initial terror of the raid were behind her, Rose's brain was beginning to function again. The first question she asked herself was whether this attack was related to the previous attempts to abduct her. If that was the case, the mysterious mastermind behind those attempts had certainly changed his tactics! But it was possible. The man could have grown tired of hiring a few men at a time to kidnap her and having them fail.

But to hire a whole gang of Mexican bandits? If that was indeed the case, the man was far more desperate—or crazier—than she had ever dreamed.

Cody had warned her, she remembered grimly, that she was dealing with a very dangerous man. She had chosen to take that warning lightly, preferring to dwell instead on more romantic scenarios. Now she was confronted with grim reality . . . and she knew that she was in terrible trouble.

Of course, there was a possibility that this raid had no connection with all the other problems she had encountered on this southwestern performance tour. Even if that were the case, though, her immediate future still looked bleak. She could expect no mercy from these *bandidos*. That she would be repeatedly raped and then probably murdered seemed a foregone conclusion.

The riders reached a range of low hills and climbed into them, barely slowing their horses as they ascended the slopes. Rose heard the leader's harsh breathing, felt the warmth of it on the back of her neck. His grip was so tight that she knew there was no chance of her wriggling out of it. All she could do was wait until they came to a stop and hope for some miracle to occur then that would give her a chance to escape.

That halt was not long in coming. A few minutes later the riders topped a rise and started down into a small valley. At the base of the slope was a campfire, a brilliant orange eye winking in the darkness. A lone man was crouched next to the flames, and he stood up as the riders thundered down toward him. In the garish light of the fire Rose could discern only a tall, slender figure enveloped in a capelike coat and wearing a wide-brimmed hat.

The man did not flinch as the bandits rode up and surrounded him. The leader brought his mount to a stop directly in front of the waiting man, and, jerking down the black mask that had hidden his features, he growled, "Here she is."

"I can see that," the waiting man said with a nod. "Was there any trouble?"

A harsh laugh burst out from the leader of the gang. "Trouble? From a bunch of gringos and their women? No, señor, there was no trouble."

He threw a leg over the saddle and slid to the ground, taking Rose with him. She sagged in his grip, her head drooping forward again. Let them think she was senseless, she decided. Such a ruse could do no harm and might somehow help her.

The tall, slender man stepped closer to her, and there was an anxious edge to his voice as he asked, "Is she all right?"

"Fainted, perhaps," grunted the bandit who held her. "She was unharmed when we left the estate, and nothing has happened to her since then."

"Very well. Take her to my tent."

Rose felt herself being lifted. She kept her eyes closed as she was carried through the night. Canvas brushed against her cheek as the man who held her went through the opening of a tent. A moment later she was lowered, none too gently, onto a cot.

She opened her eyes imperceptibly, just enough to be able to see the big man looming above her as the other one came into the tent and lit a match. She heard the scrape of the lucifer and smelled sulphur; a second later a yellow glow filled the tent as the match was held to the wick of a lantern. The slender man lowered the chimney on the lamp, and the glow brightened even more.

Now Rose could see the features of the man who had spearheaded the attack on MacInnes's party, and she understood why he wore a mask. He was probably the ugliest man she had ever seen, and his face was most memorable. Glowering, he turned to the other man, then snapped, "I did not like pretending to be that jackal, Alvarez. His name tasted like dung in my mouth when I shouted it."

"The masquerade was necessary, my friend," murmured the other man. "You did a good job, Paco. Thank you."

"Do not bother thanking me. Just make me a rich man, as you promised."

"Be patient. When the right people find out we have the Yellow Rose, our price for her safe return will be met. You have my word on that."

The bandit called Paco just grunted in response to the pledge, and Rose thought that he sounded rather doubtful. Still, he didn't continue arguing with the other man but instead turned on his heel and stalked out of the tent, leaving her alone with the individual who had obviously hired the bandits to snatch her.

She remembered that Cody had also told her that the man's motivation might be financial, but she hadn't put much stock in *that* notion, either. Now it looked as if the Ranger was going to be proven right about everything.

Not that that would do her any good now.

Rose feigned a moan and turned halfway onto her side to get a better look at her captor. He took off his cape and then his hat, revealing a handsome, aristocratic man in his forties with dark-blond hair and a neat mustache of the same shade. Something about him was vaguely familiar to Rose, but she couldn't place him or put a name with the face. He came closer and dropped to one knee beside the cot, leaning over her and regarding her with an unreadable expression on his face.

"Are you awake, my dear?" he asked softly.

Letting her eyelids flutter rapidly, Rose stirred slightly and then finally looked up at him. She caught her breath and drew back from him, because that was the reaction he would be expecting.

"Don't be afraid," he assured her. "None of those savages will lay a hand on you. I give you my word on that."

"Wh-who are you?" she gasped.

A faint, ironic smile tugged at his wide mouth. "You don't remember me, do you?"

Rose shook her head in small, jerky movements.

"Well, I'm not surprised. You had no real reason to recall me—even though I've never forgotten you."

She pushed herself into a sitting position. He didn't seem to mind, and she felt less threatened without him looming over her like that. He sat back on his heels and continued to smile at her.

"You must have come to one of my performances," she ventured. "I'm sorry I can't remember everyone who comes backstage—"

"I never came backstage," he cut in, his voice hardening a bit. "I did see you perform, that's true. It was last year, at a concert hall in Paris. But I didn't need to go backstage to know that I had found you again at last."

At last . . . What did he mean by that? Who *was* this man?

Evidently seeing the confusion in her eyes, he said, "Think back, my dear Rose. Think back to the days when your father was a crony of the Emperor Maximilian. There were many visitors from Europe at your family's hacienda in those days, true?"

Rose nodded hesitantly, a frown furrowing her smooth brow. There had indeed been many Europeans who came to her father's ranch during the time Maximilian had held the reins of power in Mexico. This man apparently had been one of them, she realized. But for the life of her she did not remember him.

He stood up and tented his fingers, staring intensely at her over them. "Let me give you a name," he said. "Do you remember a young captain in Maximilian's army called Pierre Desmond?"

Licking dry lips, Rose shook her head. She could have lied, but she sensed somehow that following such a course now would be even more dangerous than telling the truth.

"You were only a young girl then," the man continued. "Fourteen, perhaps fifteen years old. But already you were a great beauty, one of the most beautiful girls in all of Mexico. Captain Desmond was greatly taken with your beauty, and he ran certain risks to see you alone, to pledge the love he felt for you." The man's smile disappeared and his voice began to tremble as he continued, "But you spurned his love. You laughed at him and rejected him. Oh, yes, you were quite the coquette, even then! You enjoyed leading men on and then having your amusement at their expense." He took a deep breath and controlled his obviously raging emotions with a visible effort. "Well, those days are long since gone, aren't they?"

From the man's reactions it was clear that he was talking about himself. He was this Captain Pierre Desmond, late of Emperor Maximilian's army. That army had been routed and broken up when the Mexican people finally found a leader in Benito Juárez and revolted against the European-backed rule of the emperor. Most of the mercenaries who had been employed in the army had been put to death when Maximilian was overthrown and his reign cut short. Most—but not all.

"Captain Desmond . . ." she began tentatively.

He cut her off with a sharp shake of his head. "Captain no more. The rank is meaningless now. You may call me Pierre."

"P-Pierre." The name came awkwardly off her tongue. "I am sorry I do not remember you. I am sorry about the things that happened in the past."

"Sorry, are you?" He clasped his hands together behind him and began to pace back and forth as much as the close confines of the tent would allow. "I barely escaped with my life from Juárez's hordes. As soldiers, we didn't have as much influence as the landowners who were forced to flee with their wealth. But I never forgot you, Rose . . . or the way you laughed as you spurned me." He drew a deep, ragged breath into his chest and watched her with eyes that glowed with an unholy fire. "I would have savored having my revenge on you then, but I assumed you had perished during the chaos following the revolution. I went back to Paris and made another life for myself. I even thought I was a happy man—until I went into that concert hall in Paris and saw a beautiful young woman calling herself the Yellow Rose. Then I knew I could not really live again until the past was well and truly buried."

Rose watched him closely—the strangely glowing eyes, the eager stance as he leaned forward, staring at her. Cody had warned her that the person behind her problems might be insane. She could see now that the Texas Ranger had been all too right.

Some of her unquenchable spirit—a determination that had enabled her to live through the chaotic times Desmond had been talking about—came back to her now. "What is it you want of me?" she demanded. "Why have you been after me ever since New Orleans?"

"Oh, you've put that together, have you?" Desmond murmured. "It is true, I was responsible for those other abortive attempts to kidnap you. You see, you hold the key to justice, my dear. Not only have I brought you here to have my revenge on you for rejecting me, but in the process you will make me and all of my friends rich men." He lifted a hand and clenched it into a fist. "For years your father and the other landowners squeezed every bit of riches out of Mexico they could, and they took that wealth with them when they were forced to leave. It will cost your father a fortune to ransom you now!"

"My . . . father . . ." Rose repeated slowly.

"I know he must have financed your career as a singer," Desmond snapped. "Now he will pay handsomely to have you returned safely."

Rose just stared at her captor for a moment longer, then tipped her head back and began to laugh.

Desmond gaped at her, wide-eyed with surprise at her reaction. Rose leaned over on the cot, hugging herself as her laughter rang out. Finally, obviously unable to stand it any longer, Desmond demanded, "What is wrong with you? Have you lost your mind?"

"Lost my mind? No," Rose managed to say between bursts of nearly hysterical laughing. "But you must have, to think that you will get a dead man to pay ransom!"

His lean face turning pale, Desmond asked sharply, "What do you mean?"

"My father is dead!" Rose told him, and now her laughs turned into half sobs. "He died along with my mother, my brothers, and my sisters. I was the only one who escaped the Juaristas, and that was only because a couple of them smuggled me out of the hacienda before it became a slaughterhouse."

"But your father's fortune . . . ?"

"Gone, you fool!"

A shiver ran through Desmond, as if he had just been struck a physical blow. "That is impossible," he insisted. "Your career as a singer, the money you spend on clothes and travel—"

Rose sat up straight on the cot and interrupted him. "I earn the money I spend," she said firmly. "My own talents have brought me success."

Desmond sank to his knees in the dirt. "Then how did you . . . how did you become the Yellow Rose?"

Slowly drawing a deep breath, Rose asked, "Are you sure you want to know?"

"I *must* know!"

"All right . . . Well, as I told you, a couple of the Juaristas got me away from the hacienda. I thought they had taken pity on me and were trying to help me. But, of course, all they really wanted was a camp follower, a slut of their own. They took turns using me as the rebellion made its way to Mexico City. I walked barefooted through the mountains, I cooked and cleaned for them, I satisfied their lust every night. You know what my life had been like—pampered, protected, never even alone with a man. There was always a duenna nearby." Rose shuddered. "I learned things during those weeks that I never would have dreamed existed. But the main thing I learned was how to hate."

Desmond, still pale and trembling a little, watched her closely, clearly fascinated by her awful story.

"Finally I decided I had to get away from them or go crazy. One night, outside of Mexico City—when they were through with me for the night—I got a knife and I cut their throats while they slept." Rose laughed again, but it was a hollow sound. "They must not have thought that a fragile little flower like me would be capable of such a thing and so they were not too careful. But it was easy."

She stood up and paced a step back and forth, her lovely face tightening into a mask as the memories came flooding back.

"Mexico was falling apart around me. Everything I had known, everyone I cared about, were gone. I knew I had to get out. I had been to Vera Cruz once as a child, and I started for there. I had the knife I had used on the men and a pistol and a little food. It took me three weeks, but I got to Vera Cruz. By then I was so skinny and dirty that no one paid any attention to me. There were not many boats leaving then, but I managed to hide on one of them. It was bound for New Orleans. We were at sea two days before one of the crew found me and turned me over to the captain."

She took another deep breath and then continued her tale. "As I said, I was skinny and dirty, but the captain cleaned me up and decided he liked what he saw. He kept me in his cabin, and by this time I did not care what he did to me when he came to his bunk at night. I was alive and I was out of Mexico, and that was all that mattered to me. When we got to New Orleans, he would have kept me with him—"

"But you killed him, too," Desmond guessed.

Rose shook her head. "No. He was really rather gentle and tried not to hurt me. I might have killed him, if he had forced me to, but I was able to slip away from the ship and get away from the docks. I had received a good education before the uprising; I spoke both English and French as well as Spanish. I found a house in the French Quarter, and the woman who ran the place was willing to take me on and let me live there."

"You became a harlot." Desmond sounded vaguely offended.

"That sounds too . . . biblical." Rose smiled at him. "I was a whore."

Desmond came to his feet, breath hissing sharply between his teeth. In a voice that was almost a groan, he said, "That beautiful young girl—"

"—had at least a score of men every night," Rose finished for him. "I was very good at what I did, Captain Desmond. I was forced to be."

Desmond turned his back to her for a long moment, then swung around and said, "This is insane! How could you have gone from that life to . . . to being what you are now?"

"A woman in that line of work meets a great many men," Rose said wryly. "Some are important and influential, even wealthy. And sometimes they become enamored of one of the girls. They take her under their wing and help her escape from the sordid life she is leading. It makes them feel charitable, I suppose. And I don't want to sound bitter, because that is exactly what happened to me. I was rescued by a kind, generous man. He moved me into a place of my own—"

"Made you his mistress, you mean!"

Rose shrugged. "Call it what you will. All I know is that I was no longer a plaything for any man who had the necessary coins. This man clothed me, groomed me, made me into a whole person again. Then one day he heard me singing, and he said the sound moved him so much that he decided the whole world should hear me." She looked into Desmond's eyes. "That is how the Yellow Rose was born."

"Is this story true?" he asked after a moment, his voice harsh.

"Every word of it."

"Then this man, the one who rescued you—he will pay the ransom for your freedom!"

Rose shook her head. "He died three years ago. His fortune went to his wife and children. I received nothing from him . . . except my sanity."

"Sanity?" Desmond stared wonderingly at her. "You tell me you were a whore and a murderess, and now you speak of sanity?"

"Call it murder if you will. I killed to save my own life, and I would do it again. As for being a whore, that was for survival, too, and what could be saner than that?" She laughed again. "Besides, why am I debating such things with a murdering kidnapper? Or had you forgotten how I came to be here, Captain?"

The tables had turned, Rose sensed. Desmond was clearly on the defensive now and uncertain what to do next. She wanted to keep him that way. She had already looked around the tent and saw nothing suitable to use as a weapon. Besides, even if she got away from him, she would still be in the middle of a bandit camp. Her best chance, she decided, was to keep Desmond off balance. As long as he was undecided what to do with her, at least he would keep her alive.

Wearily, he massaged his temples and said, "I have not forgotten. Do you know who brought you here?"

Not letting on that she had heard anything to the contrary, she replied, "He said his name was Diego Alvarez."

Desmond shook his head. "That was only a ruse, to throw off pursuit. His name is really Paco Montoya. He is perhaps the most ruthless man in Mexico. And I have promised him a fortune in return for bringing you to me."

"My family is dead, my lover is dead," Rose reminded him. "Who will pay this ransom?"

The gleam of a new hope began to show in Desmond's eyes. "You have money of your own," he said. "I know the high fees you command for your performances. Your manager can bring the payment—"

He stopped short as Rose began to shake her head.

"If you want to kill me, go ahead and do it," she told him coolly, knowing full well that he could do no such thing. "I will be damned if I will pay you a penny to secure my freedom, Captain."

He looked around nervously. "Keep your voice down," he warned. "If Montoya hears you—"

"You mean if Montoya discovers you have no way of paying him the money you promised?" Rose threw back her head and laughed again, and this time there was genuine amusement in the sound. "You see now why I acted the way I did when you first mentioned my father's wealth. You begin to understand, Captain: You are as much my prisoner as I am yours, because if I tell Montoya that he risked his men and his own life for nothing, he will certainly kill you."

Desmond lifted his hands to his ears, as if trying to shut out what she was saying. He grimaced, then said, "You are still in my power. I can kill you or have you killed anytime I want."

Rose nodded. "Yes, you can. But it will not profit you a thing."

"Damn you, woman!" the Frenchman grated. He stalked back and forth for a moment, then whirled on her and said, "This place was merely a temporary campsite, a place where I could have our little reunion all the sooner. We will go now to Montoya's permanent encampment. Once we are there, I will think of something to do with you. Until then, I would advise you to keep your mouth shut about everything."

"And why should I do that?"

Desmond grinned wolfishly. "Because if Montoya kills me, there will be nothing holding him back from doing whatever he wants to you. I do not think it would be a long or pleasant life for you under those circumstances."

He was right, Rose realized. She had lived through a hellish nightmare in her youth, and she had no wish to see if she could endure such a thing again. "I will not say anything to Montoya," she promised softly.

"Good," grunted Desmond. He moved in front of her, then grasped her bare arms, pulling her to him. "Besides, there is still the matter of how you treated my advances all those years ago."

With that, he brought his mouth down ruthlessly on hers.

Rose tried to squirm away, but his grip was too tight. After a moment, he broke the kiss and grinned down at her. "We may both be prisoners," he told her in a whisper, "but I still have the upper hand. In the days to come I am sure we will . . . talk about many old memories."

Rose repressed the shudder that ran through her. Desmond could do pretty much whatever he wanted with her, as long as he kept her alive.

Still tightly holding one arm, he abruptly pulled her over to the entrance of the tent and thrust the canvas flap aside. They stepped out into the night, and he led her to the campfire. The bandits had gathered around the flames, hunkering there and passing around several jugs of tequila. Montoya lifted himself to his full height as Desmond and Rose approached.

"Take her to the small tent that was prepared for her," Desmond ordered, his voice firm and showing no sign of how his plans had gone awry. "Remember, no one is to touch her."

"*Sí*, I remember," Montoya said. He leered at Rose.

"This will be a difficult thing, but we will abide by your wishes, Capitán . . . for now." The bandit leader reached out and grasped Rose's other arm.

Desmond released her and Montoya began to lead her away, but a figure detached itself from the group around the fire and suddenly stepped in front of them. "Señorita Rose," a familiar voice said, although the tone was harsher than usual.

"Estrella?" Rose gasped, barely recognizing the servant girl. Estrella wore a gaudy dress, and her long hair hung loosely down her back. For an instant, Rose thought that the girl had been captured during the raid on MacInnes's estate, too, but then she saw how one of the raiders came up to her side, slipped an arm around her waist, and began to nuzzle her shoulder. Estrella laughed, twisting her head so that she could kiss the bandit, her lips open and her tongue working hotly in the man's mouth.

"Not so much the great lady now, are you?" Estrella asked viciously as she looked back at the stunned Rose. "Now you are no better than the lowest *puta*!"

She spat in Rose's face.

Rose was too shocked to draw away. She barely heard Desmond saying beside her, "Yes, Estrella here has been working with me all along, letting me know about your schedule. When she found out what I had planned, she insisted on being brought along when Paco and his men crossed the border. I imagine in all the confusion you just didn't notice her."

This betrayal by Estrella hit Rose harder than anything else that had happened. She had thought that she and the girl were friends; she had liked Estrella and had tried to help her. Now—

Now, as Estrella had said, she was once again no better than a whore.

Montoya jerked her into motion, half dragging her toward a tiny tent nearby. As she went, Rose said to herself under her breath, "Oh, Cody, I wish I had listened to you. And I wish you were here. . . ."

*   *   *

Cody would just as soon have been anywhere else right about now. Anyplace had to be better than crouching behind a rock in the hot sun and listening to bullets whining around your head. A lull came in the firing, so he jacked a shell into the chamber of his Winchester, raised up in a hurry, and snapped off a shot toward the mouth of the canyon where the rustlers were holed up before quickly ducking back down.

"Hell of a mess, ain't it?" Seth Williams called over to him from one of the other boulders.

"Bad enough," Cody replied. "Maybe when Alan gets in position, we can roust those boys out of there." He looked off at an angle to his right, where about a hundred yards away Alan Northrup was slowly working his way up the rugged bluff that the canyon sliced through like a knife wound. Once Alan reached the top, he'd be able to fire down into the rustlers' hiding place, which theoretically would drive them out under Cody's and Seth's guns.

Cody now wished that job had fallen to him; he could tell even from this distance that Alan was struggling to make his way up the steep slope. If he slipped and fell, he could be badly hurt. But when the rustlers had laid their ambush for the trio of Rangers who'd been trailing them for the past several days, Cody and his companions had split up, and Alan was the one who wound up closest to the bluff. Cody had gotten Alan's attention and indicated by gestures what the young Ranger was supposed to do; then Cody and Seth had covered him while he mounted up and raced to the base of the bluff.

Cody figured the rustlers hadn't known that the canyon was a dead end when they selected it for the site of their bushwhack attempt. True enough, there was good cover over there just inside the mouth of the canyon. A jumble of large boulders provided plenty of hiding places. And it was also true that here in the broad, sandy wash where the Rangers had been riding there was very little cover, just these small rocks where Cody and Seth were crouched. But with no back door in that canyon the rustlers were just as pinned down as the Rangers were.

Squinting against the glare of the sun, Cody leaned over just enough so that he could see Alan without exposing himself to the outlaws' fire. Alan was nearly at the top of the bluff now. When he got there, the momentum of this fight was going to swing dramatically. If all went well.

Cody wanted those sons of bitches, wanted them bad. By the time he and his young friends had reached Lobo Canyon, they suspected the worst. A plume of smoke reaching into the sky had told them that the ranch house had undoubtedly been set on fire. Sure enough, when the Rangers arrived at the property a few minutes later they found that the house and all the outbuildings had been burned, and the rest of the family was dead, sprawled on the ground where they had been shot down after being driven from cover by the flames.

Faces grim and hard, the Rangers had paused only long enough to give the victims a decent burial, then started out on the killers' trail. The rustlers had tried to cover their tracks, but that wasn't easy to do when you were driving a good-sized bunch of cattle and horses. Besides, Cody was one of the best trackers on the frontier, and he'd had no trouble following the trail. The bastards might as well have left road signs.

Once the Rangers caught up to them and traded lead with them, the rustlers had abandoned their booty, stampeding the stolen stock back toward Cody, Seth, and Alan to slow them down. That had worked for a little while, but once again the lawmen had picked up the trail, determined to catch up with the marauders even if it meant letting the horses and cattle scatter. The animals could always be rounded up on the way back to Del Rio. Most of them, anyway.

Then, tired of being hounded, the rustlers had set the trap, thinking that they would rid themselves of their pursuers once and for all. But their plan had completely backfired, and now both sides found themselves in a standoff.

A standoff that was about to end, Cody saw, for Alan had reached the top of the bluff. The stocky young Ranger unslung the Winchester that he had strapped to his back with his belt and crept up to the canyon rim.

"Get ready," Cody called over to Seth. "Alan's in position."

"I'm more'n ready!" Seth called back.

A moment later Alan's rifle began cracking, and Cody saw puffs of smoke coming from the Winchester's muzzle. Startled shouts and curses came from inside the canyon as Ranger lead began peppering the rustlers behind what they had thought was impenetrable cover. Alan ducked back away from the rimrock as a few of the outlaws managed to return his fire. From their position, though, their bullets couldn't touch him as long as he stayed back.

With the attention of the rustlers diverted, both Cody and Seth opened fire on them again. Cody spotted a shoulder that had been carelessly brought into view, and he put a slug through it without hesitation. The shot was rewarded with a screech of pain.

Alan emptied his rifle down into the canyon, then rolled away from the edge again and began reloading. Finished with his chore, he came back up on his knees, but after a moment he waved the rifle at his fellow Rangers down in the wash. "They're pulling back!" he shouted, pointing farther down the canyon.

"Come on," Cody snapped as he came to his feet. "We've got 'em on the run, but they're going to come smack up against that dead end in a minute!"

Cody's dun and Seth's buckskin pony had had the good sense to clear out when the shooting started, pulling well back from the spot where Cody and Seth had taken cover, but they came bounding forward now as their masters stood up and called them. The two Rangers swung into their saddles and then sent the horses galloping toward the canyon mouth, guiding the animals with their knees while they tightly gripped their rifles.

They raced from bright sunshine into the cool shadows of the canyon. Cody glanced up and saw that Alan was running along the rimrock as fast as he could. From up ahead came the sound of pounding hoofbeats. Cody reined in and motioned for Seth to follow suit. The rustlers must have discovered that there was no way out of this gash in the earth, because they came boiling around a bend in the canyon wall.

There were four of them left, Cody saw, yelling and firing as they charged the Rangers. Coolly, Cody lifted his Winchester and pressed the trigger. The rifle bucked against his shoulder as it blasted, and one of the rustlers went pinwheeling out of his saddle. Alongside Cody, Seth opened fire just as calmly and downed another of the men. From the rimrock Alan emptied another saddle, and that left the fourth man. Remembering what had been done to those settlers back at the ranch, Cody was in no mood to wait around and see if the owlhoot wanted to surrender.

He fired again, and the bullet drove the last man backward as hard as if he had run into a stone wall.

Even with all the rustlers down, the next few minutes were busy ones. While Alan clambered down the bluff, Cody and Seth checked the bodies. Every one of the rustlers was dead, including three more scattered behind the boulders near the mouth of the canyon. Seth took off his hat, sleeved sweat from his forehead, and asked Cody, "We goin' to bury 'em?"

"Be a waste of time and effort," Cody grunted. He frowned as he looked around the canyon. Something was bothering him all of a sudden. He felt more edgy than he had when he and Seth were pinned down behind the rocks. Maybe it was being out here in the middle of nowhere with seven corpses, he thought. But whatever the reason, he wanted to head out fast and get back to town.

"Let's ride," he said. "We're going to have some bad news to break to that youngster when we get back to Del Rio."

CHAPTER
8
‖‖‖‖‖‖‖‖‖‖‖‖‖‖‖‖‖‖‖‖‖‖‖‖‖‖‖‖

As it turned out, the boy already knew the grim fate that had befallen his family. A troop of Rangers led by Lieutenant Oliver Whitcomb and accompanied by the youngster had gone out to the ranch later the same day that Cody, Seth, and Alan had gone after the rustlers. One look at the fresh graves was enough to tell a story that had been played out all too many times here on the frontier. The troop had taken the lad back to Del Rio and turned him over to one of the local preachers. The minister and his wife had a good-sized family of their own and insisted that taking in one more wouldn't put a burden on them.

Cody was told all this by Whitcomb after he had delivered his own report on the battle with the outlaw gang. He and Seth and Alan had proceeded to Ranger headquarters after gathering up and driving back the rustled livestock and leaving the animals in one of the large public corrals on the edge of Del Rio.

"The cap'n said all hell was due to break loose when it was so quiet around here," Cody remarked wearily. "I reckon he was right."

"Well, it's over now, and that band of miscreants won't be wreaking any more havoc," Whitcomb said.

"The lieutenant means we killed all those hombres," Seth said to Alan. The two younger Rangers were leaning on one of the empty desks in the headquarters' anteroom.

"I know what he means," Alan said irritably. "I've had more schooling than you, you know."

"Well, excuse me all to hell! Just tryin' to be help-ful. . . . ."

Cody ignored the bickering going on behind him. "Where's the cap'n? I figured he'd want to hear that re-port."

"Captain Vickery is in his office," Whitcomb replied. "He instructed me to take your report on this rustling business, then bring you in to see him. By the way, Ranger Cody, you and Ranger Williams and Ranger Northrup did a good job," the officer added grudgingly.

"Thanks, Lieutenant," Cody said, too tired and ner-vous to give Whitcomb any of his usual gibes. That feel-ing of extreme uneasiness he'd felt in the canyon had stayed with him all the way back to Del Rio. He and his companions had made good time, traversing in a day and a half the ground it had taken them several days to cover while they were following the winding trail of the killers. Cody had expected the uneasy feeling to go away during that time, but it was still with him, like the ache in a bad tooth.

Whitcomb slid his chair back and stood up. "Come along," he said, turning toward the hallway that led to Vickery's office. Cody stood up and followed him, and when Seth and Alan started to come, too, the lieutenant said sharply over his shoulder, "The captain's orders were strictly for me to bring Ranger Cody to him, not the two of you as well."

Seth and Alan stopped and exchanged a surprised glance. Cody told them, "It's all right. You boys go over to the Rio Grande and get something to eat."

"Sounds good to me," Alan agreed. He and Seth went out the front door of the building while Whitcomb and Cody entered the corridor.

There was nothing that unusual about Captain Vickery ordering one of his men to appear before him, but today it only added to Cody's disquiet. All of his instincts were screaming at him that something was wrong, something that concerned him personally.

He suddenly thought of his mother and his sisters, still living on the family's spread up close to Bandera. Could something have happened to them? Cody's sun-bronzed face was grim as he entered the captain's office with Whitcomb.

Vickery was sitting at his old, scarred desk with the usual black leather Bible and sheathed bowie knife lying atop it. The captain was seldom without either of those items. In addition to them, however, a yellow telegraph flimsy was lying on the desk, and Cody noticed it immediately. It hadn't been very many years since the telegraph wires had reached into this part of the country, but Cody had quickly learned that such messages seldom contained good news.

Looking up from beneath bushy white eyebrows, Vickery said, "Glad to see you're back, Cody. Have a seat."

Tensely, Cody lowered himself onto one of the ladder-back chairs. "What's going on here, Cap'n?" he asked bluntly.

"You clean up that bunch of wideloopers?" Vickery asked in turn, ignoring Cody's question for the moment.

The big Ranger nodded. "I gave my report to Lieutenant Whitcomb."

"*Bueno*. Figured as much." Vickery reached out and tapped the telegram with a blunt, knobby-knuckled finger. "Got some news here. This wire came from El Paso this mornin'. It ain't addressed to you in particular, but I reckoned you'd want to know about it."

Cody's impatience had grown to an intolerable level. Without waiting for permission, he reached across the desk, picked up the telegraph flimsy, and began to read. His already taut face grew even more grim as the message sank into his brain.

Some of the words stood out more than others: Yellow Rose kidnapped . . . many killed in raid . . . Diego Alvarez responsible . . .

Cody looked up, his eyes meeting those of the grizzled old-timer across the desk. "Is this true?" he demanded.

"Don't reckon the sheriff out yonder in El Paso would've sent it if it wasn't," Vickery replied. "He must've notified us 'cause he knew we've had dealin's with Alvarez in the past—'specially you."

Cody glowered at the memory. He'd had dealings with Diego Alvarez, all right—and the notorious bandit chieftain had come out on top in the end.

Close to a year earlier, Cody had captured Alvarez in San Antonio when the Mexican had been daring enough to venture over the Texas border in order to visit a favorite soiled dove in a San Antonio cathouse. A few days later, when faced by a band of renegade Comanches, Cody and Alvarez had fought side by side as allies, the Ranger being forced by circumstances to free his prisoner and give him a gun.

Alvarez could have tried to escape then, but his peculiar code of honor prevented him from doing so, and Cody had brought him on to Del Rio as a prisoner. Another mission for the Rangers had taken Cody immediately out of town again, and while he was gone, Diego Alvarez had escaped from jail and vanished. Cody had spent nearly a month trying to track him down, to no avail, and that failure had left a bitter taste in the Ranger's mouth whenever he thought about it too much.

And now the authorities were saying Alvarez had kidnapped the Yellow Rose.

Cody shook his head sharply. "No," he said. "I don't believe it."

"Don't believe what, son?" Vickery asked with a frown.

Cody slapped the telegram down on the desk. "Alvarez wouldn't do that. He's a *bandido* through and through, Cap'n, but I don't believe he's low enough to kidnap a woman like that."

"Surely you don't mean it," Whitcomb put in. "The man's a desperado. Nothing is beyond him."

"You're wrong, Lieutenant," Cody insisted. "I fought next to him. I reckon I know him about as well as anybody on this side of the border."

Whitcomb snorted. "You sound almost as if you respect him."

"Maybe I do, a little," Cody admitted. He stood up and looked across the desk again at Vickery. "Doesn't really matter either way, I suppose. There's only one thing I can do. I'm going after them."

"Whoever was leadin' 'em, the raiders went across into Mexico," Vickery pointed out. "We got no jurisdiction across the Rio, Cody; you know that."

"Jurisdiction be damned!" The heated exclamation came from Cody even before he knew what he was going to say. "Rose asked me to come with her and protect her, and I turned her down."

"A perfectly proper response," Whitcomb said. "The Rangers are not a private protection agency."

"Maybe not, but look what happened. She wound up being dragged into Mexico by a bunch of marauders." Cody's voice lowered, and it showed the strain he was feeling. "You know what's likely to happen to her over there, Cap'n."

Vickery sighed heavily. "I know. And I'm mighty sorry things turned out this way, son."

"Sorry enough to send me to El Paso?" Cody demanded.

"The sheriff didn't ask for any Rangers—"

Cody unpinned the circled star from his vest and tossed it on the desk, next to the telegram. "Then I reckon I won't be a Ranger anymore," he said.

The ultimatum cost him a great effort. The Texas Rangers were in his blood, a legacy passed down from his father and strengthened by his own service in this unique frontier legion. But he wouldn't let anything stand in the way of his helping Rose if he could, not even the Rangers.

"Dammit, boy, pick up that badge," Vickery growled. "The kidnappin' took place on Texas soil, so I reckon I'm justified in sendin' somebody to investigate it."

Cody took a deep breath, some of his tension easing. He let his fingers close around the badge, and he seemed to draw strength from it as his grip tightened. "Thanks, Cap'n," he said quietly.

Vickery said to the lieutenant, "Oliver, you go out to the cashbox and get Cody a little travelin' money." Whitcomb nodded and left the room, and when he was gone,

Vickery eyed Cody shrewdly and went on in a quiet voice, "I didn't much want Oliver to hear this, since he's a mite peculiar 'bout rules and such. But I just want you to know, Cody, I never once watched over another fella's shoulder whilst he was followin' a trail. I reckon most of the time a fella's got to take it where it leads."

Cody grinned, knowing that Vickery was giving him unofficial sanction to cross over into Mexico to rescue the Yellow Rose. "I understand, Cap'n," he said. "And I appreciate it."

With a gruff cough Vickery pulled some papers in front of him and said, "I'll get in touch with the Mexican government, since this here kidnappin' is what you call an international incident, and see if they'd like a little official help with it. If they say *sí*, you'll already be there."

"Sounds good to me," Cody said.

"When will you be ready to ride?"

"Soon as I throw some supplies together."

Vickery stood up and extended his hand across the desk. "Good luck, son."

And as Cody shook the old frontiersman's hand, he reflected that since he was going into the wilds of Mexico after as dangerous a man as he had ever encountered, he was likely to need all the luck he could get.

Even riding hard and pushing the seemingly tireless dun for all it was worth, the journey from Del Rio to El Paso still took a number of days. Cody had plenty of time to think along the way.

Seth and Alan hadn't liked the fact that he was riding on this mission alone. They'd been eager to go along and had kicked up a fuss about being left behind until Captain Vickery informed them in a roar that their presence was needed in Del Rio. There'd been no arguing with that. Cody knew that Vickery was already stretching things by dispatching him to El Paso; adding two more Rangers to the mission would just make the situation shakier as far as jurisdiction was concerned. Technically, the Rangers could operate at their own discretion anywhere in Texas, but local lawmen had been known to raise a fuss in Austin when their own authority was overridden.

Cody didn't really give a damn about that. All he wanted to do was find out if Rose was alive, and if she was, to rescue her from her captors.

Sitting beside his campfire each night, he pondered the message that had come from El Paso. It was still hard for him to believe that Diego Alvarez would kidnap a woman, but maybe he was giving the bandit too much credit. After all, Cody had known him only briefly, and, for that matter, people could change in a year's time. One thing was certain: Alvarez was the only starting point he had in trying to track down the Yellow Rose.

Finally, one evening as the shadows of dusk were settling in, El Paso loomed on the horizon ahead of him, more and more of its lights winking on as he rode nearer. It had been a long time since he'd been to this city, and it held a mixture of good and bad memories for him. For a while before joining the Rangers he had been a deputy sheriff here, but before that he had tracked down some of the men who had murdered his father and caught up with them in El Paso.

Cody thrust those dark and bloody thoughts out of his brain as he nudged his horse into a canter, eager to reach his destination. That part of his life was over and done with, and he was here on a mission that was equally important.

The sheriff's office was downtown on Stanton Street. Reaching it, Cody reined in and swung down from his saddle in front of the hitchrack. As he looped the dun's reins over the rail, a man who had been leaning back in a chair on the porch straightened up. He stared at the Ranger in the twilight and said, "Sam Cody?"

Cody grinned and stepped up onto the porch. "Hello, Asa," he said. "I see they haven't been able to get rid of you yet."

The man was past middle age, with leathery skin and a white handlebar mustache. A deputy sheriff's badge was pinned to his shirt. Asa Colfax had been a deputy here at the same time as Cody, and obviously the old-timer still

held the same position. Asa pumped Cody's hand for a
moment, then took off his floppy-brimmed hat and ran a
hand over his bald pate. "So you're a Ranger now," he
said proudly, gesturing at the badge on Cody's vest.

"That's right. Company C, out of Del Rio."

"Del Rio? Say, the sheriff sent a wire down there not
long back, about that singin' gal who was kidnapped by
Diego Alvarez. That why you're up here?"

"That's right," Cody admitted to his old friend and
mentor. Asa Colfax was one of the men who had convinced him to give up a life devoted to vengeance and ride
on the right side of the law.

"Sheriff Tinsley know you're comin'?"

Cody shook his head. "Nope, not unless my captain
wired him after I left Del Rio. Why, does it matter?"

Asa's gaunt face twisted in a grimace. "The sheriff, he
don't like gettin' his toes stepped on. He ain't happy
'bout what happened. The whole town's in an uproar,
matter of fact. Mr. Wilbur MacInnes was one of the folks
who got killed when them bandits came raidin' across the
border, and he was a mighty important man hereabouts.
Been over a week since it happened, you understand, and
the mayor and the town council and the newspapers are
still howlin' for the sheriff to do somethin'. Only there
ain't a whole hell of a lot he can do, on account of the way
the bandits went back into Mexico."

"Sounds like the man wouldn't mind having a little
help, then," Cody reasoned.

"Well, there's some that might look at it that way. But
Sheriff Tinsley, he's liable to think the Rangers're tryin' to
steal his thunder." Asa's voice dropped to a confidential
level. "He ain't an easy man to get along with—or to
like."

"Then why are you still wearing a deputy's badge?"

Asa grinned and shrugged his skinny shoulders. "What
the hell else is an old mossback like me goin' to do? I
been totin' a badge so long I reckon I'd fall over slanch-
wise if I didn't have one to balance me."

Cody laughed and slapped his old friend on the back.

"Come on," he said. "Let's go see this Sheriff Tinsley of yours."

Frank Tinsley must have come to El Paso after Cody left, the Ranger decided when Asa had led him into the office and introduced him to the sheriff. He had no memory of Tinsley, a stocky, florid-faced man who wore a checked suit and struck Cody as more of a politician than a lawman.

Cody felt an instinctive dislike for Sheriff Tinsley, but he told himself that he had to keep that feeling in check. He needed to find out exactly what had happened during the kidnapping raid, and Tinsley's telegram had been rather skimpy on details.

"Ranger, eh?" Tinsley said as he slipped a long, fat cigar from his vest pocket and then waved Cody into a seat on the other side of the big desk. "I must admit, I didn't expect your captain to send a man up here. I sent telegrams to practically every law enforcement agency up and down the Rio Grande, advising them to keep an eye out for that brigand Alvarez."

Cody cuffed his Stetson to the back of his head as he sat down. "Is that so? Cap'n Vickery figured you got in touch with us because you knew we had a run-in with Alvarez last year."

Tinsley smiled, but the expression lacked any real warmth. "No, I'm afraid I wasn't aware of that. And I'm sorry you've made this ride for nothing, Mr. Cody. I've conducted a full investigation of the matter, and I've passed along the details of the raid to the Mexican government. It's up to their authorities to do something now since the outlaws crossed the border after staging their despicable raid."

Cody tightened the rein on his temper. Sheriff Tinsley was a pompous ass, but it wouldn't do any good to tell him so. Instead he asked, "What exactly happened? How do you know Diego Alvarez was responsible?"

Lighting his cigar with a kitchen match, Tinsley puffed on the fat cylinder of tobacco for a second, then said, "Why, the man announced his identity for the whole world to hear! You know how those Mexicans are—half grease, half chili peppers, and all pride. Alvarez didn't want anyone else getting credit for his raid; no, sir."

Tinsley filled in a few more details of the attack, including the fact that Estrella, the Yellow Rose's maid, was missing, too. That was the first Cody had heard of anyone else besides Rose possibly being kidnapped. Then Tinsley drew deeply on the cigar, blew out a cloud of smoke, glowered fiercely, and intoned sternly, "Damned murderers!"

Restraining the impulse to point out that there were no newspaper reporters in the room to witness and record the sheriff's demonstration of outrage, Cody said, "So the gang rode across the river, raided a party being given by this man MacInnes, then rode off with the Yellow Rose and maybe another young woman?"

"After wantonly killing nearly a dozen of El Paso's finest citizens," Tinsley snapped. "By God, I'd like to see Alvarez swinging from my gallows!"

This was a waste of time, Cody realized. It was clear that Tinsley had already told him everything he knew about what had happened. Anything he said from here on would just be posturing. Cody stood up and said, "Well, thanks for the information, Sheriff."

"Wait a minute," Tinsley said quickly, getting to his feet as well. "What are you going to do?"

"Not much I can do," Cody replied with a shrug. "The bandits are across the line. Like you said, I reckon I had a long ride for nothing." He kept his voice mild.

Tinsley seemed a little mollified. "I'm sorry about that. Feel like it's my fault for misleading you into thinking I was requesting aid from the Rangers. Tell you what. Why don't you get a room over at the hotel tonight and tell the clerk it's on me?"

"Why, thank you, Sheriff. I'll do that." Cody straightened his hat, touched a finger to the brim in a casual salute, and turned to leave the sheriff's office.

Asa Colfax, who had listened to the conversation in silence, followed Cody out. Night had fallen now, and as Cody stepped off the porch and grasped the reins of his horse, the old deputy chuckled and said, "You ain't foolin' me for a minute, you know."

"Fooling you about what, Asa?" Cody asked innocently.

"You know damn well you ain't ridin' back to Del Rio just like that."

Cody hesitated, then grinned and said, "Why don't you walk down the street with me for a ways, Asa?"

"Sure, I'll do that. Just don't go too fast. These ol' bones of mine are gettin' kind of brittle."

The two lawmen strolled down Stanton Street, Cody leading the dun. When they were well out of earshot of the sheriff's office, Asa said, "You're goin' into Mexico after Alvarez, ain't you?"

"One of those ladies who was kidnapped is special to me, Asa."

"Sweet on her, are you?"

Cody hesitated. He remembered vividly the kiss he had shared with the Yellow Rose. There was plenty of passion and attraction there, but it was more than that. Maybe it was her singing. Maybe any man who heard her felt that she was singing to him alone. He couldn't explain it, so he said, "Something like that."

"Well, you got a hell of a job cut out for you. Mexico's a big place. And even if you happen to find 'em, that Alvarez is supposed to be a mean son of a bitch."

"I know him," Cody said.

Asa glanced over at him in surprise as they walked along. "You mean he won't kill you?"

"I didn't say that," Cody replied. To tell the truth, he didn't know what the bandit leader might do once he caught up to him.

After a moment of silence, Asa said, "If you're goin' on the other side of the Rio Grande, you'd better do somethin' 'bout that badge. It ain't real welcome over there, 'specially amongst the Federales."

"I know." They had reached the hitchrack in front of the hotel. Cody paused and said, "Look." He reached into his jeans pocket and slipped out his watch, one of the kind of pocket watch called a turnip and large even for that sort. Cody opened it, revealing a photograph of a beautiful young girl on the left-hand side. Twisting the gold ring that held the picture in place, he lifted the photograph, revealing a hollow inside the watch case. Deftly, he unpinned his badge and stowed it away in the secret hiding place. Another quick movement had the picture firmly back in place with no telltale sign of the compartment.

Asa Colfax let out a low whistle. "That's mighty slick," he said admiringly. "Just about as slick as this old man's noggin." He pointed at the photograph. "Who's the gal? Another sweetheart of yours?"

Cody shook his head. "Hell if I know. The picture was in the watch when I bought it and had a silversmith down in Corpus Christi fix up that hiding place. It's come in damn handy more than once. This vest turns around, too, so that you can't see the pinholes from the badge."

The old man chuckled. "You always was a smart one, Cody. Too smart to head off into Mexico by yourself on a fool's errand."

"I didn't know you were going to try to talk me out of it, Asa," Cody said, his tone hardening a little. "We're friends, aren't we?"

"Damn right." Asa sighed. "And I can see you're just as hardheaded as ever. You startin' out in the mornin'?"

"At first light," Cody answered. He trusted Asa with the truth. The old man might not like what the Ranger was doing, but he wouldn't betray him to Sheriff Tinsley, either. Cody was sure of that.

Asa nodded. "Then you'd best get a good night's sleep. You're liable to need it over there. You're goin' to need all the help you can get, too." With that, he gave a casual wave and sauntered off into the night, and Cody watched him go with faint misgivings. What had the old man meant by that last statement?

Cody had a feeling that before he left El Paso, he was going to find out.

He slept surprisingly well. Maybe it was the weariness brought on by the long ride from Del Rio, and maybe it was the fact that Sheriff Tinsley was paying for the pillow under his head. Whatever the reason, Cody woke up about an hour before dawn feeling refreshed.

By first light he had shaved and gotten himself a good-sized breakfast in a diner near the hotel. Leaving the eatery, he headed toward the stable where he had left the dun the night before. There weren't many people on the streets yet. El Paso was just beginning to wake up for the new day.

Two men were waiting in front of the stable, and Cody slowed his step when he saw them. He recognized them immediately: Barney Gellman and Alonso Martinez. They saw him coming, and both of them seemed to tense in anticipation.

"Morning," Cody said curtly as he came up to them. "I didn't expect to run into the two of you."

"I didn't think we'd ever see you again, either," Gellman said, shifting the unlit cigar in his mouth to one side. "Some old geezer wearing a deputy's badge hunted us up last night and said you were going across the border after Rose."

Cody glanced around and said sharply, "Keep it down, Gellman. I don't want that information spread all over town."

"Sorry," the bodyguard grunted. "Anyway, we want to go with you."

That came as no surprise to the Ranger. As soon as he'd seen the two men waiting for him he'd figured that was what they were up to. He wondered where Eduardo was. The older musician might be able to talk some sense into his brother's head.

Cody looked at Alonso, who was regarding him with his usual sullen expression, and asked, "Where's your brother?"

"Dead," Alonso answered harshly. "He was killed when those *cabrones* stole the Yellow Rose and Estrella."

Cody frowned; no one had told him that Eduardo Martinez had been among the victims of the raid. "Sorry," he said gently. "I didn't know."

"That is one more reason we must go with you," Alonso said. "My brother's death must be avenged."

"And we've got to save the ladies if we can," Gellman added.

Cody could sympathize with them. No doubt they were feeling the same guilt and anger and frustration that'd been plaguing him ever since he'd heard that Rose had been kidnapped. But he planned to move fast once he was across the Rio Grande, and he didn't want to be burdened with a couple of amateurs.

"Look, I'm sorry," he began, "but I don't think it'd be a good idea for you to go along. It's going to be real dangerous—"

"You think we give a damn about that?" Gellman snapped. "Both of us would die to save Rose; you know that."

Cody shrugged. "Maybe so. But I still think I can handle this job better alone. And I'm wasting time by standing around here jawing about it."

"That's right, time's wasting. But we're not giving you a choice, mister. We're going, and that's final."

Brushing past them, Cody said flatly, "I don't think so."

"Then I guess I'll have to tell Sheriff Tinsley that you're going off on your own into Mexico. Seems to me like that's probably illegal."

Cody stopped short and turned slowly to face Gellman, who was looking a little smug. The Ranger's first impulse was to plant a hard fist in the middle of the man's bulldoglike face, but that wouldn't accomplish anything. The easterner had Sheriff Tinsley sized up pretty well; if the sheriff knew what Cody was planning to do, he'd surely try to stop him. And Cody didn't need any other complications right now.

"Keep up and keep out of the way," he growled. "And I'm not responsible if you get your damned-fool heads shot off. Understand?"

Gellman nodded curtly. "Sure. That all right with you, Alonso?"

"*Sí.* All I want is a chance to kill the man who murdered my brother. I want Diego Alvarez."

"You ever get him, you may wish you hadn't," Cody

muttered as he turned to go into the stable. Gellman and Alonso followed closely behind him.

Less than ten minutes later Cody had the dun saddled and ready to go. Gellman and Alonso had already rented mounts from the stable keeper, and Cody felt a faint flush of irritation. They'd been pretty damned sure of themselves, he thought as they left the stable. Stopping at an early-opening general store, the three men stocked up on supplies. That done, they headed for the river.

"Are we going across on the ferry?" Gellman asked as the horses trotted down the street.

Cody shook his head. "The river's plenty shallow this time of year. We'll follow it back south a ways, then ford it. No need to announce too loudly what we're doing."

"Makes sense," Gellman said, nodding.

They left El Paso behind, and to anyone watching them, it would have seemed that they were simply heading downriver. When they had covered three or four miles, however, Cody pointed to a shallow depression in the bank that would lead them right down to the water. Gellman and Alonso were right behind him as he sent the dun splashing across the shallow, slow-moving stream.

"Well, we're in Mexico now," Cody said as they climbed the opposite bank.

"Doesn't feel any different than Texas," Gellman commented, summoning up a grin.

Cody glanced over at him. "Wait and see," he warned. "Mexico is a world of its own. Isn't that right, Alonso?"

The musician merely grunted.

And with that the three men rode on, leaving the border behind them.

CHAPTER
9

A week in Mexico sure could make a difference in a man, Cody thought as he looked over at Barney Gellman, studying the man intently. He wasn't sure whether the easterner was going to make it or not.

Gellman's face had sunburned badly the first day on the trail. His bowler hat simply hadn't provided enough protection against the searing rays of the sun. Gellman's heavy features had first turned bright red and then started to peel, and he'd been miserable. Cody with his Stetson and Alonso with his wide-brimmed sombrero had been all right. Besides, both of them were accustomed to the sun.

On the third day Cody had bought a battered straw hat from a farmer whose *jacal* they had stopped at. Plucking the derby off Gellman's head, he had tossed it away and replaced it with the sombrero. "Try that instead," Cody had suggested. Gellman had glowered at him but left the straw hat where it was, clearly grateful for the shade it provided.

Then there were the cold nights on the desert, nights that'd had Gellman shivering and his teeth chattering so hard that he hadn't been able to sleep, especially since his bed was nothing but a hollow in the hard ground. As the three men rode along during the daytime, Gellman had swayed in his saddle in exhaustion. The bodyguard might be as tough as whang leather in a city, Cody had thought, but out here in the wilderness he'd have been totally lost without his two companions to help him.

Alonso had proven to be a good enough trail partner.

He still wasn't what you'd call friendly, Cody had mused, but his sullen attitude seemed to have eased a little. He knew what he was doing and he didn't complain. The Ranger had begun to feel that perhaps bringing him along wasn't a mistake after all.

Now if they could just find a lead that might take them to Diego Alvarez and the Yellow Rose . . .

During the days they'd spent riding from village to village, Cody had asked everyone they encountered for news of Alvarez. The responses had always been similiar: The peasant farmers and their families knew the name of the fierce *bandido,* and a few had even caught a glimpse of him at one time or another, but no one knew where he might be found now.

"You think they were telling the truth?" Cody had asked Alonso on leaving yet another village in the foothills on the edge of the desert.

Alonso had shrugged. "*Quien sabe?* If I were one of these peons, I would think twice before answering the questions of a gringo, especially one who was asking about Diego Alvarez. Men like Alvarez have many eyes and ears and a long reach. The people fear his anger and his vengeance."

"Are you saying nobody will tell us where to find him?" Gellman had asked hoarsely.

"Someone will know," Alonso had replied, his tone resolute. "And they will not be afraid to tell us. I am sure of it."

Cody had wished he could be as certain. Still, he'd known before he ever started across the border that the task he had set for himself wouldn't be easy. He'd be on Alvarez's home ground, and he'd have to play by the bandit's rules.

They had pushed on, gradually working their way southwest, and now El Paso was a week behind them, and they had finally left the desert behind for good. But that wouldn't make their trek any easier.

Cody glanced over at Barney Gellman, wondering again if the man was going to make it. Gellman was over the worst of his sunburn by now, but his once-full face was becoming almost gaunt. The rugged journey was all too clearly taking its toll on him.

Suddenly Gellman moaned and clutched at his saddle horn but missed. He slid off the back of the rented horse and fell heavily to the ground. Cody reined his dun around. "Gellman!" he said sharply. "Are you all right?"

There was no reply from the motionless form on the ground.

"Dammit!" Cody looked over at Alonso and saw that the Mexican was torn by this development, too. From the first Cody had made it clear to his companions that they'd have to keep up, have to be responsible for themselves. There simply wasn't time to wet-nurse anybody—not if they wanted to have a chance of finding the Yellow Rose alive. But Cody knew he couldn't ride off and leave Gellman here to die. It just wasn't in the Ranger to do a thing like that.

Swinging down from the saddle, he knelt beside the easterner and rolled him over on his back. Gellman was breathing, but the sound was harsh and irregular. Cody pressed the back of his hand to Gellman's cheek and grimaced. "He's picked up a fever somewhere," he said, looking up at Alonso.

"What are we going to do?" asked the musician.

"Reckon we'd better find a farm, someplace we can leave him where he'll be taken care of until we can come back for him," Cody decided. He got his canteen from his horse and forced a few drops of water into the unconscious man's mouth, then said to Alonso, "Give me a hand. We've got to get him back on his horse."

Working together, they lifted the senseless Gellman into his saddle, and then Cody lashed him in place with a short length of rope. That was the best they could do. He caught up the reins of Gellman's horse to lead it.

They pushed on into the hills, and less than an hour later Cody spotted a tendril of smoke. Guided by it, they were led to a small adobe cottage with a thatched roof and a tiny garden patch behind it. As they rode up, an old, white-bearded man in a dirty serape stepped out of the squalid dwelling. A scrawny dog stood beside him and yapped at the strangers.

"Greetings, my friends." The old man surprised Cody by speaking in good English.

"Howdy," Cody said, nodding. "We've got a sick man here and wonder if you could help us."

"I can see this. Bring him in. Hush, *perro!*"

Cody untied Gellman and let the man's weight sag onto him. With Alonso's help he got Gellman into the cool, welcome shadows of the hut's interior. The old man gestured toward a rope bunk in one corner of the room, and Cody and Alonso lowered Gellman onto it.

The old man felt Gellman's forehead and muttered, "A fever, *sí*. I thought as much. I have some herbs that may help him."

Cody glanced around the room, and his eyes widened in shock when he spotted a couple of human skulls sitting on a shelf, seeming to grin leeringly at him. Alonso, too, had obviously noticed the skulls, and he caught Cody's eye and jerked his head toward the doorway. Both of them eased back to the entrance, and Alonso pointed to an earthen bowl sitting on a table. It was full of a thick, red liquid, and Alonso mouthed the word *blood*. Cody's eyes narrowed. He didn't know what to make of this, but he knew it made him uneasy.

The old man rummaged among several boxes and vials on the same shelf as the two skulls. He took a pinch of some sort of powder from a small, intricately carved wooden box and said, "This will help your friend's fever." With practiced ease, he abruptly pinched Gellman's nose, waited until the man's mouth reflexively popped open, and dropped the powder onto his tongue.

"Cody . . ." Alonso said warningly.

The old man's actions had taken Cody by surprise, and it was too late now to do anything about the stuff Gellman had been given. But the Ranger asked anyway, "What was that?"

"Merely a medicinal herb, as I said," the old man replied, turning to face them. He frowned a little at the anxious looks on their faces, then followed their glances toward the skulls and the bowl of blood, if that was what it was. Suddenly a laugh burst out of him.

"Don't reckon I see what's so funny," Cody said tensely.

"Oh, but *I* do, my friends. You think I am a *brujo*—a witch man. I assure you, nothing could be further from the truth." He stepped closer to Cody and extended his hand. "Allow me to introduce myself. I'm Dr. Cyril Mortimer, from Philadelphia."

Cody couldn't help but stare. After a moment, he took the old man's hand and said, "We thought—"

"That I was a Mexican peasant, I know." Dr. Mortimer smiled. "I've lived here for so long that my skin is burned to the same shade as my Mexican neighbors', and the language comes naturally to me now. But believe me, I'm as much an American as you."

Cody still wasn't sure of the man. He asked, "What are you doing down here south of the border?"

"I migrated down here many years ago to study the ways of these people. They're quite fascinating, you know. As a doctor, I was interested in their remedies and their medicines. Many of their so-called cures are worthless, of course; I expected that. But some of the herbs I've discovered are surprisingly efficacious."

A grin tugged at Cody's mouth. He was glad Seth and Alan weren't here to squabble over the doctor's vocabulary. He said to Mortimer, "My name's Cody, and this is Alonso Martinez. The fella on the bunk is Barney Gellman."

The old man regarded him shrewdly. "One might inquire as to the reasons *you* three are down here, as well," he said. "By the way, would you like some soup?" He gestured toward the earthen bowl on the table.

"Ah, thanks anyway, but I reckon we'll pass," Cody replied. He hesitated, wondering if he could trust this strange old man, then decided that Mortimer was unlikely to betray them. He said, "We're looking for a man named Diego Alvarez."

"The famous bandit? Oh, yes, I know him well."

Cody and Alonso both stared. "You know Diego Alvarez?" the Ranger asked incredulously.

"Yes, of course. He rides through this way from time to time. I've attended to several of his men who had bullet wounds. Suffered no doubt in battles with the Federales."

"You sound like you don't have much use for the troops," Cody ventured.

Mortimer grimaced. "Sometimes it's difficult to tell who are the worse outlaws, men like Alvarez or the government forces. I prefer to stay friends with both so that neither will bother me. I've come to enjoy the simple life I've found here."

Alonso could not restrain his eagerness. He asked, "Where can we find Alvarez?"

The old man tugged on his closely trimmed beard and pursed his lips. "Now, I'm not sure I should tell you that. As I said, I want to stay on the good side of Señor Alvarez."

"It's important," Cody said. "We're looking for a couple of women, and we think they might be with Alvarez."

"Women, eh?" Mortimer rubbed his nose. "Well, as long as you don't tell Alvarez where you heard this, I don't suppose it will do any harm to tell you. I don't think the three of you can do much damage against all of Alvarez's men."

"There'll just be two of us," Cody reminded him, growing a little impatient. "We're going to leave Gellman with you."

Mortimer waved a hand. "Oh, there's no need of that. I'll give him a couple more doses of that herb tonight, and he should be much better by morning. Once the fever breaks, his strength will come back to him quickly."

Alonso began, "We have already been looking for Alvarez for a week—"

"And so you are anxious to locate him. Your quest won't take much longer, I can assure you. Less than a day's ride from here there is a small valley that's always green because of the stream that runs through it. Alvarez can often be found there."

Cody felt his heart thud with anticipation. "We'll ride out now," he said. "Just tell us how to get there."

"You'll never find the place at night," Mortimer said with a shake of his head. "Please, wait until morning. Mr. Gellman should be able to travel by then, and you'll find the going much easier by daylight." He smiled faintly. "Besides, I get very few visitors out here . . . and I wouldn't mind hearing a little about what's going on back in my native country."

That was the real reason Mortimer wanted them to delay, Cody suspected. He was lonely here in the middle of nowhere, even though he stayed by his own choice. Besides, the doctor had a point: It would be easier to follow the trail without nightfall interfering.

"All right," Cody agreed, abruptly making up his mind. "We'll stay until morning. I don't see how Gellman can possibly be well enough to travel by then, though. You've got to promise you'll take care of him if he's not, Doctor."

"Of course. I'm not going to turn away a patient. But I think you'll be surprised by his recovery, Mr. Cody. These herbs are wonderful things. Good for what ails you, as the old saying goes."

"We'll see," Cody said flatly. In the meantime, he was going to keep a close eye on this bizarre old man.

Dr. Mortimer was proved right. By nightfall Gellman woke, his fever broken. Thirsty and hungry, he asked for water and food. He was introduced to Mortimer, who gave him more of the herb, then fed him some freshly made thick stew. Cody could almost see the strength flowing back into Gellman.

Mortimer went outside and came back with several leaves that he'd broken off a plant growing behind the hut. He squeezed a thick, sticky juice from the leaves onto his fingers, then spread it on Gellman's face. "That will take care of the last of your sunburn," the doctor told the easterner. "And the infection that caused the fever was a mild one. You were really rather lucky, my friend."

"I know," croaked Gellman. "Thanks, Doc."

"You're quite welcome."

Cody and Alonso shared some of their supplies with Mortimer, giving him some sugar and salt and beans. The old man was grateful, but he was even more impressed by the small bag of coffee Cody placed on his table. "Arbuckle's," he breathed in a hushed voice, sounding as awed as if he were gazing upon the Holy Grail.

By the next morning Gellman declared himself fit enough to travel. "This is the best I've felt since we left El Paso," he insisted. "And if Alvarez is as close as the doc says, I don't want to wait any longer to catch up to him."

"Remember, you didn't hear anything from me about where to find Señor Alvarez," Mortimer cautioned as his three visitors mounted up.

"Don't worry, Doctor. We owe you," Cody said. "We won't let you down."

They headed west through the foothills, following the directions Mortimer had given them. The doctor had assured them that the valley Alvarez used for a hideout was less than a day's ride away. Cody didn't set too fast a pace, concerned that Gellman might still be feeling the effects from his brief illness.

However, as they put the miles behind them, all three men began to feel more anxious. Knowing that they were probably getting closer to the Yellow Rose and her maid with each passing minute, they gradually pushed their mounts harder and harder. Cody was aware of what was happening, but he didn't want to force a slowdown. Not now.

They ate jerked beef and stale biscuits in the saddle, washing down the simple fare with water from their canteens. Pushing on to the west, Cody kept a sharp eye out for the landmarks Mortimer had mentioned when telling them how to find the valley. There was a needle-sharp pinnacle, the old man had said, and then a couple of flat-topped hills. . . .

"There," Cody said in the middle of the afternoon, suddenly reining in and pointing to the mouth of a small valley between two ridges about a mile away. Even from this distance they could see the green within the valley, standing out in sharp contrast to the brown and gray and tan of the surrounding foothills.

"That's got to be it, all right," Gellman said.

Alonso asked, "What do we do now? Ride right in there as if we had been invited?"

Cody had to grin. "I think that's what Alvarez would do, if the situation was reversed." He heeled his dun into a trot. "Come on."

Despite his answer to Alonso's question, he intended to approach the valley carefully. After coming this far and enduring the arduous journey through Mexico, it wouldn't do to ride into an ambush and get themselves killed. Cody's keen eyes searched the landscape intently as they rode toward the mouth of the valley.

"I don't see anybody," Gellman said quietly.

"If Alvarez has sentries out, chances are you won't see them," Cody told him. "Just keep your eyes open and follow my lead."

They rode into the valley, the horses increasing the pace on their own once they smelled water. Then Cody spotted a building up ahead, an adobe structure with what seemed to be the remains of a bell tower at one end of it.

Gellman had seen it, too. "What the devil's that?" he asked.

"Looks like the ruins of an old mission," Cody said. "There were plenty of them scattered through this part of the country. Some of them failed, and in some of them the priests were killed by Indians. No telling what happened here."

The dilapidated building was indeed what was left of a mission, Cody saw as they drew nearer. There was no doubt about it. The priests were long gone, and there was probably nothing in those ruins but a few rattlesnakes.

"I still don't see anybody around," Gellman complained. "I think that crazy old man was lying to us."

"That crazy old man probably saved your life," Cody reminded him. "Don't get impatient. Alvarez will show himself when he gets good and ready."

The words were hardly out of his mouth when a rifle cracked and a bullet kicked up dust at the dun's feet. The horse reared back, whinnying angrily. The dun had always had a mean disposition, and it wasn't afraid now, just mad. Cody hauled down on the reins and motioned for Gellman and Alonso to stay back.

The shot had come from the ruins. Now Cody saw the muzzle of a rifle protruding from the gaping mouth of what had once been a stained-glass window. It was then joined by a couple more weapons.

"Just sit still," Cody cautioned his companions in a low voice. He looked back at the old mission and called in Spanish, "We're looking for Diego Alvarez!"

The rifle muzzles sticking out the window didn't move, but three men emerged from the door of the ancient building. All of them wore wide-brimmed, high-crowned sombreros, coarsely woven serapes, and the loose-fitting white shirts and pants common here south of the border. Their faces were bearded and hard-featured, and there wasn't a trace of warmth or welcome in their gazes as they walked toward the three interlopers with rifles held ready for instant use in their brown hands.

Stopping some ten feet away from Cody and his companions, the delegation stood in silence for a few seconds; then one of them said, "We know no Diego Alvarez. Turn and ride away if you wish to live."

"Sorry, *amigo*," Cody said. "We've come a long way to talk to Alvarez, and we're not leaving until we do."

"Then you will not leave at all!" the man ground out, and he slowly started to bring his rifle up.

Cody's hand streaked to his Colt, and as the gun came smoothly out of its holster, the Ranger yelled, "Light out!" From the corner of his eye, he saw Gellman and Alonso wheeling their horses around to flee. Then the gun in Cody's hand boomed, and the Mexican who had challenged him cried out and staggered backward, dropping his rifle and clutching a hand with a bloody bullet hole through it.

"Cody!" Gellman shouted.

The other two guards weren't firing but were attending to their wounded compadre instead. Cody jerked his head around to see what the easterner was yelling about, and he felt a sudden cold emptiness in his belly. Gellman and Alonso had galloped off a few yards, then stopped when they saw that retreat was hopeless. More than a dozen armed men on horseback had appeared from somewhere. They were scattered in a ragged line across the trail, completely blocking escape from the valley.

Cody spurred up beside Gellman and Alonso, both of whom had drawn their guns. "Sit tight," he ordered them. "Nobody else is trying to kill us—yet."

Indeed, though plenty of rifles and pistols were pointed in their general direction, nobody seemed interested in shooting them. If this whole crew of bandits had opened up at once, Cody and the others would've been cut to ribbons by now. Instead, the men seemed content to simply hold them here.

"Put your guns away," Cody said.

Gellman licked dry lips. "You sure that's a good idea?" he asked nervously.

"Just do it." Cody slid his own revolver back in its holster. Reluctantly, Gellman and Alonso followed suit.

Suddenly the line of men across the trail parted, and another rider trotted through the gap, coming toward Cody, Gellman, and Alonso at a leisurely pace. He was short and stocky, his build confirming his Mexican-Cherokee parentage, and since his sombrero was pushed off his head, dangling on his back by its neck cord, it was easy to see his face. Close-set dark eyes like bullet holes on either side of his beaklike nose studied Cody, Gellman, and Alonso, and a straggly mustache hanging like twisted strands of wire from the corners of his mouth only added to his savage appearance. He looked every inch a ruthless, cold-blooded killer—

Until he pulled his horse to a stop in front of Cody, grinned hugely, and exclaimed, "Señor Silver Spurs! Is it really you? What are you doing in Mexico?"

"Howdy, Alvarez," Cody said. He ignored the bandit's question for the moment, commenting instead, "You haven't changed much since the last time I saw you."

Alvarez shrugged. "Nor have you." He nodded to the

spurs on Cody's boots. "You still wear the spurs of your father. But I do not see the badge of the Rangers."

"I'm not here as a Ranger, just as a man looking for a couple of friends."

"And who might these friends of yours be?" Alvarez asked.

Cody glanced at Gellman and Alonso, aware from their expressions that they were getting impatient with this conversation. He said to Alvarez, "One is known as the Yellow Rose and the other is her maid."

Alvarez grinned wider and raised his eyebrows. "Ah, women," he exclaimed. "I should have known. Unfortunately, I cannot help you. I know nothing of this Yellow Rose, lovely though her name may be, or of her maid."

"You're a damned liar!" Gellman burst out before Cody could stop him.

The Ranger gripped Gellman's arm tightly and barked, "Shut up!" but the damage was already done. Alvarez's eyes narrowed, and his men tensed.

"Oh, so I am a liar, am I?" he said softly.

"You'll have to excuse my companion," Cody replied. "He is very fond of one of the women we're searching for, and he's naturally a little upset because we haven't found her."

"I see. And you are fond of her, too, I suppose. This is why you shoot holes in the hand of one of my men. Poor Pablo will never be the same."

Cody glanced at the man he had wounded, who was still nursing his injured hand and glowering fiercely at him. "I shot Pablo before he could do his damnedest to shoot me," Cody said bluntly. "I reckon you can understand that, Alvarez."

The bandit chieftain's stern expression did not alter, but Cody thought he saw a flash of amusement in Alvarez's dark eyes. Still keeping his voice serious, Alvarez said, "Come. We will go to my camp."

With a wave of his brown hand, Alvarez sent his men forward. They formed a loose circle around Cody, Gellman, and Alonso, and then the whole group rode

around the old mission. Surrounded as they were, Cody
and his companions had no choice but to go along.

On the other side of the mission was a trail heading
deeper into the valley. Alvarez led the group along this
trail for a quarter of a mile before reaching a large clearing
where more men were in the process of setting up tents.
As he reined in, Cody looked around, searching intently
for any sign of Rose or Estrella. He didn't see them or any
indication that they were here.

Alvarez swung down from his horse and motioned for
Cody and the others to dismount. Their weapons hadn't
been taken from them, but here in the middle of this bandit camp only a lunatic would have tried to force answers
from Alvarez at gunpoint. Alvarez indicated a freshly
built campfire in front of a large tent and said, "Sit down,
mis amigos. Welcome to my humble home."

Cody sank onto one of the large rocks that had been
rolled up to serve as seats around the campfire and nodded for Gellman and Alonso to do the same. Alvarez sat
on the other side of the fire, which certainly wasn't necessary for heat on a day like this. Several rabbits were roast-
ing on a spit over the flames, however, and Alvarez now
turned them so that they could cook on the other side.
Most of the other bandits went about their business, but
some of them stayed nearby, rifles in hand, in case their
leader needed help.

"You have caught us doing our housekeeping chores,"
Alvarez said. "We arrived back from the south only earlier today, and we are still in the process of setting up
camp again."

"Been down south, eh?" Cody asked.

"*Sí*. It is good to change one's surroundings from time
to time, especially in the line of work my men and I en-
gage in."

"Banditry," Cody said.

Alvarez grinned again. "I have never denied it."

"But you deny knowing anything about the Yellow
Rose or her maid."

"I told you, we just came back to the border country."

"Well, that's a mite strange," Cody mused, "since a

heap of witnesses claim to have seen you kidnap a couple of innocent women in El Paso two weeks ago."

Alvarez bristled. "I do not make war on women," he said with a frown. "You should know this about me, Señor Silver Spurs."

"Goddammit, we all saw you!" Gellman said. "You grabbed Rose up off the ground and said that only Diego Alvarez would be daring enough to do such a thing." The easterner spat into the fire in disgust.

Alonso added, "This is not daring. Instead, it is to be as low as the snake that crawls on the ground."

Alvarez's features darkened with anger. "Tell your friends to hold their tongues, Cody," he warned. "I am a patient man, but I am not without my limits."

"All of you take it easy," Cody said. He looked intently at Alvarez. "You swear you didn't have anything to do with Rose or Estrella being kidnapped?"

"On my honor, I did not. Today is the first time I have heard of such a thing. Someone is spreading base lies about Diego Alvarez."

Cody took a deep breath. "I believe you," he said.

"What?" Gellman exploded. "Blast it, Cody, I was there when this bastard grabbed Rose!"

Alvarez came angrily to his feet, but before he could say anything, Cody asked quickly, "Are you sure, Gellman? Look closely at Alvarez. Could it have been somebody else you saw? What about the voice?"

Gellman glared at the Ranger, obviously reluctant to do as Cody asked, but Alonso, a troubled frown on his face, admitted, "Now I am not sure, Cody. It seemed that the man I saw was . . . bigger, perhaps. But everything was so confused. . . ."

"That's it," Cody said. "We've hit on the explanation. Somebody else was pretending to be Alvarez."

"Impersonating me?" Alvarez said. "Who would dare?"

"Think about it," Cody said, looking at the bandit. "That's why the hombre made sure he announced who he was. He wanted us to come looking for you while he was off somewhere else, getting away with the ladies."

Gellman said grudgingly, "Yeah, I guess it could have worked that way. But I'm still not sure—"

"I am," Cody broke in. He stood up and extended his hand to Alvarez. "Sorry we caused you some trouble. We were just going by the information we had."

Alvarez took Cody's hand and nodded. "*Sí,* I understand. And I think I know the man you want. The only one who would have the arrogance to pass himself off as the great Diego Alvarez is that dog and son of a dog, Paco Montoya."

Cody felt his pulse quicken. He had heard of Montoya, who was supposed to be about as ruthless a *bandido* as Alvarez himself.

"For months now," Alvarez continued, "I have heard that Montoya has been claiming he is the fiercest bandit in all of Mexico. This is a lie, of course. It would be just like such a base coward to steal women. This Yellow Rose, she is pretty?"

"As beautiful as her name," Cody assured him.

Alvarez grimaced. "To think of such a lovely flower in the hands of a man like Montoya." He shook his head. "This should not be."

"That's why we've got to get them back," Cody said. "I don't reckon you've got any idea where we could find this Paco Montoya, do you?"

Alvarez regarded him shrewdly. "And if I do, how will you rescue the women? There are only three of you, and Montoya has many men. They are nothing but curs, of course, but even the lowliest cur can still bite."

"Well . . ."—Cody smiled—"I was thinking that after the way Montoya insulted you by using your name, you might want to help us go after him."

Gellman and Alonso stared at the Ranger, as did Alvarez. What Cody was suggesting was a bold move. But under the circumstances, an alliance with Alvarez and his men might be their best chance of rescuing Rose and Estrella.

After a moment Alvarez threw back his head and laughed heartily. "You have not changed, Señor Silver Spurs," he said. "Always you do the unexpected. And it is true. I *would* like to have revenge on Montoya for sullying my good name."

"But?" Cody asked, sensing that there was a problem.

Alvarez shrugged eloquently. "You came into my valley uninvited. You wounded one of my men. Both of these things are against our rules. And any society, even one of thieves, must have its rules. If I ignored what you have done, my men would lose their respect for me. The only way I can help you is if you prove your courage and demonstrate your worthiness."

Cody squared his shoulders and said, "Whatever you come up with, I'm game for it."

"As I knew you would be." Alvarez looked around at his men—their faces grim and angry—who had been following the conversation with great interest and asked, "What test would you have Señor Silver Spurs face?"

The answer came back in one shouted word.

"Lobo!"

CHAPTER

██████████████ **10** ██████████████

Cody wasn't sure what they meant, but he sensed he'd let himself in for more trouble than he had expected. Then the crowd of men in front of the large tent behind the campfire parted as a tall, heavyset bandit easily pushed his way through in response to the excited cry. The width of his shoulders was astounding, and his arms were long and packed with muscle. He tossed his sombrero aside, revealing a bald head at odds with the crop of bushy black whiskers on his face. He shrugged out of his serape, then took off the fully loaded bandoliers of ammunition that crisscrossed his barrel chest. Flexing long, blunt fingers, he looked at Cody and grinned broadly. His smile was jagged, with several sections of teeth missing. One eye was milky and cocked off at a strange angle, while the other was narrowed down to a mean slit.

Cody glanced at Alvarez. "Lobo?"

"Lobo," Alvarez confirmed, nodding.

Cody took a deep breath. The big bruiser looked like a homicidal maniac, like he would cheerfully dismember Cody and laugh all the while. But the Ranger had no choice. He had said he'd submit to whatever test Alvarez wished, and now there was no backing out.

"Lobo!" Alvarez said sharply. "Do not kill this man. Understand?"

Lobo nodded ponderously. "Hurt him?" he asked.

"You will fight," Alvarez said with a shrug. "What will happen will happen. Are you ready, Cody?"

Gellman said urgently to the Ranger, "Don't be crazy, man. That . . . that *thing* will tear you limb from limb."

"*Sí*," Alonso agreed, "you must not fight him."

"Don't have any choice," Cody told them. He took off his hat and handed it to Alonso, then unbuckled his gun belt, which also supported his sheathed bowie knife, and passed it to Gellman. "Just hang on to those things for me."

Then he turned to face Lobo, his hands balling into loose fists as he did so.

Alvarez turned to tend to the rabbits cooking on the spit, saying offhandedly as he did so, "Whenever you are ready." Cody was willing to bet he was a lot more interested in the outcome of the fight than he was letting on.

The shout that went up from the group of *bandidos* made Cody jerk his attention away from Alvarez and back to Lobo. The huge Mexican was charging him, arms extended to sweep him into a bear hug that would end the fight almost as soon as it began—if Cody let himself be caught. Instead, the Ranger ducked to the side and let Lobo lumber past. Whirling around, Cody clubbed his hands together and smashed them into the back of the giant's neck. Lobo staggered a little but didn't go down, and he was still grinning when he caught his balance and turned ponderously toward Cody again.

It was obvious to Cody that Lobo was slow—there'd been ample demonstration of that already—but he was also extremely powerful. The Ranger crouched and let a looping punch sail over him, a blow that would have taken his head off his shoulders if it had connected. Before Lobo could get away, Cody stepped inside his reach and snapped a couple of punches to his belly, short, hard blows that packed plenty of power behind them even though they didn't travel a long distance.

If Lobo even felt those jabs, Cody couldn't see any sign of it. The man didn't so much as flinch or grunt. He brought a hand up and caught Cody's neck.

Cody was trying to move back out of range of Lobo's grip, but he was too late. That's what he got for underestimating his opponent's speed, he thought bitterly as the long fingers closed around his throat. His air was cut off immediately, and he felt the bones and muscles in his neck strain as Lobo lifted him off the ground. He had only seconds to get free.

With movements so fast that they were nothing but a blur to the eager spectators, Cody brought both hands up and smashed his cupped palms against Lobo's ears. For the first time he got a reaction. Lobo cried out in pain, and the grip on Cody's throat loosened as Lobo took a step back. Cody took advantage of the added room to bring up a sharp kick to Lobo's groin.

That turned the Mexican pale under his sun-burnished skin. Cody tore completely free and staggered back several steps as he drew much-needed air through his aching throat. The punishment Lobo had taken had slowed him down for a moment, but more than anything else it appeared to have made him angry. With an even more menacing scowl he lunged at Cody again.

Was it his imagination, Cody wondered, or was Lobo getting faster as the fight went on? Usually, it was the other way around. Big, heavy men often tired quickly. Not in this case, though. Cody dodged another roundhouse blow and slammed a hard right of his own to Lobo's jaw.

That caused Lobo to shake his head a little, and Cody finally felt he might be getting to his opponent. But he was getting a little slow-footed himself. The rugged, week-long ride through Mexico plus the heat of the day were taking a toll on him. Also, there was the strain of trying to overcome the imbalance of this competition: He had to avoid Lobo's reach at all times because if just one of the huge man's punches connected, it would probably end the fight; but, on the other hand, he'd have to somehow land plenty of blows of his own in order to wear down Lobo. It just wasn't fair, goddammit.

But then, nobody'd ever told him he could expect fairness from a bandit like Alvarez.

For long moments the fierce, brutal, hand-to-hand battle went on. Cody's arms and legs felt like lead, but he had to keep moving, had to keep punching. His heart was hammering wildly in his chest, and the roar of blood in his head was so loud that he could no longer hear the raucous cheers of the bandits or the anxious shouts coming from Gellman and Alonso. So far the only punches of Lobo's that had landed were grazing ones, but that couldn't continue forever, Cody knew. Sooner or later he'd be a split second too slow, and then the fight would be over.

He had to do something that would take Lobo by surprise and swing the momentum of the fight decisively his way. Otherwise he had no chance of winning, and a defeat meant not only that Alvarez wouldn't help him, Gellman, and Alonso rescue Estrella and the Yellow Rose, but also that the other bandits might well kill all three of them, and Alvarez would do nothing to stop it.

Suddenly Cody lowered his head and charged. Lobo was unable to get out of the way of the unexpected maneuver, and the Ranger crashed into him with pile-driving force. Cody's head caught Lobo in the solar plexus, driving the air out of the big man's lungs. With all of Cody's weight behind the charge, the impact was enough to send Lobo stumbling backward, and Cody kept his legs moving, forcing his opponent more and more off balance. He wrapped his arms around Lobo's waist and hung on for dear life as Lobo's weight sagged onto him. As incredible as it seemed, Cody had lifted the giant off the ground.

But only for a split second. Then Lobo crashed down on his back with Cody on top of him. The Ranger clubbed his hands together again and smashed them back and forth across Lobo's jaw. The blows probably would've killed a normal man. In Lobo all they did was make his good eye go glassy. He shuddered and then lay there, still and stunned.

That was enough. Cody pushed himself to his feet and swayed back and forth with exhaustion as he drew great gulps of air into his body. Gellman and Alonso were both shouting in triumph, but the bandits had fallen menacingly silent at the sight of their champion having been defeated. Even Diego Alvarez was watching Cody with a grim, unreadable expression on his face.

"Well?" Cody demanded after a moment, when he

could speak again. He glowered at Alvarez and leveled a finger at the limp form of Lobo. "What about it?"

Abruptly Alvarez grinned, and his callused palms beat together in applause. "Bravo," he said dryly. Then he strode forward and clapped Cody on the back. "The only other man I have ever seen who could defeat Lobo with his bare hands . . . is me. I will help you any way I can, Silver Spurs."

Relief flooded through Cody. Alvarez intended to honor his bargain. That was what Cody had expected all along, but the Mexican was just unpredictable enough to make for a couple of anxious moments.

The other bandits relaxed as well, and when Alvarez turned toward them and asked, "Will you let these men go free?" they nodded and a few even cheered. Cody might be an outsider, but they respected the strength and courage he had demonstrated by not only taking on Lobo, but defeating him.

Cody retrieved his hat and gun belt, and as he was putting them on, Alvarez said, "I have heard that Montoya has a stronghold to the west of here, a valley somewhat like this one but not nearly as beautiful, of course. I am certain we can find it."

"Bueno," Cody grunted.

"However, you must be satisfied with my help alone in this matter."

Cody glanced sharply at him. "I thought your men—"

Alvarez shook his head. "This is a personal matter, my friend," he said. "Once I have given you my word, I will fight at your side to the ends of the earth, Silver Spurs. You know this. But I will not risk the lives of my men."

Cody shrugged and then grinned a little. "We started out as three, and now we're four. Not only that, but we've probably also figured out who really has the ladies. I'll take that . . . for now."

"For now, you and your amigos will share our meal and our wine," Alvarez said, awkwardly throwing an arm around Cody's shoulders despite the fact that the Ranger was a head taller than he was. "Tonight we celebrate. Tomorrow we go find that dog of a Montoya, eh?"

"Sounds good to me," Cody said.

He just hoped that when they found Paco Montoya, Rose was still alive.

Rose almost wished she were dead. Almost. If she had known for certain that her entire world from now on would be this valley and the hellish tortures it contained, then death would be preferable.

But she had learned as a girl not to give up hope. As long as she was alive, there was a chance she could escape from this imprisonment. Even more importantly, there was a chance she could have her revenge on Pierre Desmond.

She knelt on a flat rock beside the stream that ran through the middle of the valley. A pile of dirty clothes belonging to several of the bandits was bundled beside her, and she was washing the soiled garments in the creek. Several Indian women, all camp followers, were doing the same thing. Only Estrella, who was thriving in her new role as a plaything for the bandits, was exempt from this drudgery.

She herself was nothing but a camp follower, Rose thought. During the day, she cooked, cleaned, and did laundry like the other women. And the backbreaking labor of the day was followed by degradation at night as Desmond used her like a common slut. At least she was not passed around among the entire band, like the other women. Her fear of that was Desmond's only real hold on her.

The standoff could not continue forever, though. Montoya was already getting impatient. The bandit leader wanted the huge ransom Desmond had promised him, and the Frenchman was having a more and more difficult time stalling him. Soon Montoya was going to demand either that he be paid—or that the Yellow Rose be turned over to him and his men.

Before that happened, Rose vowed, she would kill herself. She had lived through such things in the past, but she had been younger, more resilient, then. Now she had doubts that she could survive such treatment.

The sound of a heavy footfall behind her made her turn her head. A man loomed over her, his bulky form blocking out the sun and rendering him in silhouette. But even though she couldn't see his features, from the size of him she knew him to be Paco Montoya, and a moment later his harsh rumble of a voice confirmed his identity. "Come with me," he growled. "Desmond wants you."

"I am busy," Rose retorted, turning her attention back to her wash. "That French pig can wait." She was fairly confident that Montoya would not repeat what she said to Desmond. From what she had seen, the burly bandit disliked Desmond almost as much as she did and wished that he'd never become involved with the Frenchman.

Montoya bent over and grasped her arm, then jerked her roughly to her feet. The other women crouched beside the stream pointedly ignored what was going on. Montoya spun Rose around to face him and snarled, "No woman talks to me like that. When I tell you to do something, you will do it! Understand?"

Rose suppressed the fear generated in her by Montoya's anger and gave him a haughty look. "I am not just any woman," she said, making her voice firm. "I am the Yellow Rose."

Scowling, Montoya turned his head and spat. "That is what I think of the Yellow Rose," he said. "What good is a beautiful woman when she has a head like iron and a heart like stone? Desmond is a fool!" A calculating look appeared on Montoya's craggy features. "You would be better off with a man like me. I do not believe Desmond will ever get the money he says you are worth. I should kill him and take you for my own. Then at least someone would get some good out of you." He sneered as he watched Rose for a reaction to his words.

She just stared at him coldly and after a moment said, "I believe you said Desmond wanted to see me."

Montoya sighed and muttered a curse. Yanking painfully on her arm, he said, "Come." She kept her face calm and didn't let him see that his actions hurt her.

They marched to Desmond's tent, and Montoya thrust aside the canvas flap over the opening. "Here she is," he snapped, pushing Rose inside.

Desmond stood up from the chair that he had placed beside a folding table. "Thank you, Paco," he said. "That will be all."

Montoya grunted at the tone of dismissal in Desmond's voice but didn't say anything. Compliantly, he dropped the flap and disappeared, but as he left the thought came to Rose that Desmond was eventually going to push the bandit leader too far. The possibility of someday receiving that promised ransom payment was going to wear thin—and Rose had a hunch the blowup was going to happen soon.

The sooner the better, she thought. If Montoya tried to kill Desmond, perhaps she could escape in the resulting confusion.

Or she might simply wind up Montoya's plaything. That might be even worse than being Desmond's prisoner. She had an idea that Montoya didn't worry too much about being gentle with his women.

Desmond clasped his hands behind his back and strolled toward her. "Well, Rose," he said with a smile, "have you changed your mind about paying that ransom? Surely you don't want to continue this existence the rest of your life, do you?"

"Maybe I like it," she said with a sarcastic smile of her own. "Maybe I like slaving away all day and being molested every night."

The smile disappeared from Desmond's lips as his mouth tightened into a grim line. "Things could be much better for you, you know. It doesn't have to be like this."

She stood there in stony silence.

Finally he sighed. "Very well. If you wish to continue being stubborn, that is your right. But I warn you, Paco is getting tired of waiting for the money I promised him. He may get angry."

"If he does, it will be directed at you, not me," Rose pointed out. "You are the one who promised him riches."

Desmond glowered and started to bring up one of his

hands, palm open, to slap her. Rose didn't flinch, and Desmond stopped the motion in midair. He sighed again. "I never dreamed you would be such an intractable bitch," he said gloomily. "You don't fight, but you never give an inch, either. What does it take to reach you, eh?"

She looked directly into his eyes and said softly, "More than you will ever be capable of."

Again she thought he was going to lose his temper, but he controlled his rage, the effort visible, and turned away. "Get out," he said in a choked voice. "Go back to your work. But tonight you will be sorry you have spoken to me this way. You will be *very* sorry."

Rose pushed the canvas aside and stepped out of the tent. Montoya was standing nearby, his massive arms folded across his chest. He grinned evilly at her, but she ignored him and headed back to the creek to resume her chore.

As she walked the short distance between the tent and the stream, her mind replayed the confrontation. Perhaps she shouldn't wait for Montoya to kill Desmond, she mused as she knelt on the creek bank and picked up a shirt to wash. It might be better to take care of him herself. Of course, if she did that, she would have to end her own life. She could not tolerate falling into the hands of Montoya and his men. Soon that would be her only option.

Over two weeks had passed since that awful, bloody night when she had been abducted from the estate of Wilbur MacInnes. At first she had thought that surely someone would come after her, the Army or perhaps even the Texas Rangers. And that would mean Sam Cody . . .

His rugged face drifted through her mind now, and she drew strength from the memory of it. She didn't know Cody well, but she was sure he wouldn't want her to give up.

For Cody's sake, she would hold out—a little longer.

Cody gripped Alonso Martinez's arm tightly and said in a low voice, "You go charging in there now, son, you won't do anything but get Rose and Estrella killed."

Alonso drew a deep, ragged breath, then blew it out in a sigh. "I suppose you are right, Cody," he said, his voice full of anger and despair. "But it is all I can stand to see my beautiful Yellow Rose being so ill-treated."

"You and me both, kid," Barney Gellman agreed. "At least she's alive, though. We didn't know if we'd even find her or not."

"This is true," Diego Alvarez put in. "Do not worry, *mi amigo*. With four such champions as ourselves, the lady will soon be freed."

"Can't be too soon for me," Cody muttered. The warning he had given Alonso had been as much for his own benefit as for the young man's. Like Alonso, Cody wanted to charge down into the valley with guns blazing.

The four men were stretched out at the crest of a rise behind and above one of the ridges that formed the valley where Montoya had his hideout. They were at least half a mile from the valley, but they were up high enough in the foothills that they could look down into the camp with the aid of the field glasses Cody always carried in his saddlebags. From this distance, however, it was very unlikely that any of Montoya's sentries would spot them, since they had edged their heads up just enough to see over the top of the rise.

They had watched Montoya yank Rose to her feet and lead her from the stream over to a large tent. When Montoya emerged a moment later, Cody speculated that inside the tent was the man who had hired the bandits to kidnap Rose. He wondered again who that mysterious mastermind was and what his motives were—but neither of those questions really mattered now. The only truly important thing was getting Rose out of there safe and sound.

Two days had passed since the four men had left Alvarez's camp, and the bandit leader had led them to this valley without much trouble. They had stopped along the way to ask questions at the small farms they passed, and none of the peasants they talked to had been willing to lie to the infamous Diego Alvarez.

But finding Montoya's camp and freeing the Yellow Rose were two very different things.

With a jerk of his head, Cody motioned for the others to pull back from the rim. All four men slid down the far side of the slope to the place where they had left their horses. Cody got his canteen from the dun's saddle, took a swig of water, and then said, "We've got to work out a plan of some sort. If we go in there wild, we won't accomplish a damn thing."

"A plan, *sí*, this is advisable," Alvarez agreed. "There are only four of us and many of them. We must do something to change the odds."

"My thinking exactly," Cody said.

Gellman frowned. "But what?" he asked. "A distraction of some kind?"

Cody nodded and said, "That's a good idea." He lifted his gaze and studied the foothills surrounding them. His eyes fastened on a nearby peak. The steep slope leading up to the pinnacle was dotted with large rocks. "You know," Cody mused, "if somebody could climb up the far side of that hill, he could start quite an avalanche on this side just by pushing over a couple of boulders."

Alvarez's dark eyes followed Cody's gaze, and after studying the scene for a few seconds, he nodded. "This is true," he said. "Such a rockslide would be very loud and raise much dust. But I do not think it would reach down to Montoya's camp."

"I hope not," Cody said. "I don't want to bury the place under a few tons of rock. We just need something to draw the attention of Montoya's men."

"An avalanche ought to do it," Gellman said, and Alonso nodded. Gellman went on, "The question is, who's going to make the climb and start the rocks falling?"

"That'll be your job," Cody said without hesitation. "Yours and Alonso's."

Immediately both men began protesting. Cody had expected as much. He held up his hands to forestall their complaints and went on, "While you're doing that, Alvarez and I will be slipping into Montoya's camp to get

Rose out of there. I reckon he and I have both done things like that before, so that part of the job will be up to us."

"Señor Silver Spurs is right," Alvarez added. "If anyone can free the woman, it is the two of us."

Cody wished he felt as confident as Alvarez sounded. The bandit had convinced Gellman and Alonso, however, and Gellman asked, "When will we make our move?"

"At dawn," Cody decided. "That'll give you plenty of time to make the climb to the top of that peak. The bad thing is you'll have to do it in the dark. But most of Montoya's men will be asleep then, and the darkness will also give Alvarez and me plenty of cover while we're getting close to the camp."

"We can make the climb now," Alonso suggested, "before the day's light is gone. That way, all we will have to do is wait until morning."

Cody nodded. "Good thinking. Just be careful not to start the rocks tumbling too soon, or you'll warn Montoya that somebody's around. It's liable to be a cold, uncomfortable night up there, too."

"I don't give a damn about that," Gellman rasped. "I've baked in the sun, been out of my head with fever, and ridden until my backside hurts night and day. I don't mind sitting on top of a hill all night if it means we'll have a better chance of getting Rose out of there."

"All right," Cody said, unable to suppress a grin. "Let's work out a signal." He looked around, then pointed out a sharp peak to the east. "As soon as the sun touches the top of that mountain in the morning, you start the slide. Alvarez and I will be ready to move when we hear the rumble."

Gellman and Alonso agreed. Cody knew he was placing a great deal of faith in them, but there was no way to avoid it. Rescuing Rose would require all four of them to do the jobs he'd laid out. If the plan went off without a hitch, at least they stood a chance of getting her safely away from the *bandidos*.

But staying ahead of the inevitable pursuit would be even harder. While Alvarez divided up the few supplies they had remaining, Cody turned his attention to that problem.

"We need some way to slow Montoya and his men down and keep them from coming after us right away," he said to Alvarez a little later when the bandit leader again joined him at the top of the hill. Cody had his field glasses focused on the valley, and his attention was concentrated on the gorge that provided the only real entrance and exit from the place.

Alvarez took the glasses from the Ranger and studied the layout himself for a few moments. "We should leave our horses outside the mouth of the gorge," he finally suggested. "You and I could climb down the slope on this side, but we would never make it on horseback. Once we have the women, we leave through the gorge and pick up the horses."

"That'll mean killing any sentries Montoya has out when we picket the horses," Cody pointed out.

Alvarez shrugged. "We shall take care of them quietly, and there will be fewer to deal with later, no?"

"Makes sense," Cody agreed, nodding. "Wish I had a few sticks of dynamite. We could blow up the sides of that gorge and block it off after we've made it through. Montoya would really be bottled up then."

"*Sí*. But do you have this dynamite?"

Cody shook his head glumly.

"Nor do I. So there is no point in wishing for it, eh?"

"Reckon you're right. Next best thing'd be to stampede Montoya's horses through the gorge and out onto the flat. They'd scatter, and it'd take him a while to catch enough of them to chase us."

"*Sí*, that would work. Give me a few hours' head start, and I promise you, that stupid dog Montoya will never catch me! Never!"

Cody thought Alvarez was underrating Montoya a little; after all, Montoya couldn't have built up a reputation rivaling Alvarez's own if he was as inept as Alvarez made him out to be. Still, if they struck quick and hard and luck broke their way, he thought they could pull this off.

But if they were unsuccessful, he and Alvarez, along

with Rose and Estrella, would almost certainly die. Gellman and Alonso might survive, at least for a while, but Montoya would probably figure out that someone had started the avalanche and would hunt them down.

All or nothing . . . Well, this wasn't the first time he had faced such a situation, Cody thought. And he was still here, still alive. Luck and daring and skill had always pulled him through before.

He put those thoughts out of his head as he and Alvarez rejoined Gelman and Alonso. It was time for the group to split up. Cody shook hands with the easterner and the musician and cautioned them, "Remember, take it slow and easy. You've got plenty of time, and if you get in a hurry, you're liable to make a mistake that could ruin everything."

"We'll be careful," Gellman promised. "Just you and Alvarez be ready in the morning to get in there and grab Rose away from those bastards."

"We will be," Cody assured him. He lifted his hand in a wave of farewell as Gellman and Alonso rode off, following a narrow, twisting trail that would take them deeper into the foothills to a place where they could begin their ascent.

Alvarez, too, watched the two riders go. When they were out of earshot, he asked Cody, "Do you think they will do as they were told, Silver Spurs?"

"I think they'll try, but I don't know if they'll succeed," Cody replied bluntly. "When you come right down to it, Alvarez, it's really up to you and me to get that girl out of there."

Alvarez grinned at him. "You must love her very much."

Cody didn't say anything. He wasn't even sure how to answer Alvarez. He wasn't in love with Rose, other than the way any man can fall in love when he first sees such a beautiful woman. But he felt a genuine liking and admiration for her, in addition to the potent desire she aroused in him.

With his logic and emotions both in a turmoil, he said curtly, "Come on. Let's go keep an eye on things until it gets dark." He started up the slope to the spot where they could spy on the valley.

A grin on his face, Alvarez followed.

Early in the evening, while the *bandidos* were eating supper down below and Cody and Alvarez were making do with some cold biscuits, the Ranger spotted a man in the bandit camp he hadn't seen before. The tall, slender, European-looking man emerged from the tent where Rose had been taken earlier and sauntered across the camp toward Montoya. Cody put the field glasses on him right away and studied the lean, saturnine features.

"You know that gringo?" Alvarez asked beside him.

Cody gave a little shake of his head. "Never saw him before. But I reckon he's the one who hired Montoya to grab Rose. There's no other reason for a man like him to be down there with Montoya."

"*Sí*, I agree with you, Silver Spurs. That is the man with whom you have a debt of honor to settle, just as I do with that dog Montoya."

Cody lowered the glasses and looked intently at Alvarez. "But both of us can forget about that if it means getting Rose away safely, right?" he asked sharply.

Alvarez shrugged. "Montoya must pay for sullying the name of Diego Alvarez. But if that day must wait, then it must."

Cody nodded, hoping that Alvarez meant what he said. Using the field glasses again, he focused them in on the man who was now talking to Montoya. As he studied the man's face, Cody thought about Al O'Neil and the Mexican serving girl, both of them cut to ribbons. The hard-faced, cold-eyed man who filled the lenses of the field glasses appeared capable of such an atrocity, all right. That thought made Cody wonder what Rose had been going through. When he'd looked at her earlier, she had seemed to be unharmed. But sometimes the worst wounds were the ones you couldn't see.

He glanced toward the peak towering above them and wondered how Gellman and Alonso were getting along.

They ought to be more than halfway to the summit by now, he thought. He almost envied them. At least they were doing something. All he and Alvarez could do right now was sit here and wait.

A woman in a bright skirt caught Cody's attention, and he used the glasses to examine her more closely. He wasn't surprised to recognize her as Estrella, Rose's maid. Since she had disappeared at the same time as Rose, they'd all assumed that the bandits had kidnapped her as well.

If that was the case, Estrella had adjusted well to her captivity, Cody saw. She had emerged from behind a clump of boulders, straightening her clothes as she walked across the camp. Immediately out behind her swaggered one of the bandits, a satisfied smirk on his face.

Well, people usually did whatever they had to do to survive, Cody thought grimly.

The hours dragged by. The sun sank behind the crags to the west, its departure throwing the blackness of night over the landscape like a blanket. Cody dozed a little on the hard ground, waking up stiff and sore. He and Alvarez talked in quiet voices, recalling the battle they'd fought side by side against renegade Comanches. Alvarez seemed to bear no grudge against the Ranger for capturing him in the first place. If anything, he found it amusing that Cody had snared him in a whorehouse, in the middle of conducting "business."

"That lady, she will never forgive you for interrupting at such a moment," he chuckled.

"I don't figure she was much of a lady," Cody replied dryly, "and as soon as I clouted you over the head with the barrel of my Colt, she started eyeing me pretty plain."

"No!" Alvarez exclaimed in a mock-pained voice. "Such disloyalty!"

Cody laughed quietly. "Sorry I had to be the one to break it to you."

"So, did you stay there for a time . . . ?"

"Nope. I slung you over the back of your horse and started for Del Rio. You know what happened after that."

"Sí. We encountered those savages chasing that wagon. But what happened in the town those men were from? I was, ah, busy after we reached Del Rio."

"Yeah, busy breaking out of jail." Cody reminisced for a few minutes about the assignment that had taken him out of town while Alvarez made his escape, and when he had wrapped up his tale, he looked up at the stars glittering overhead in the black velvet sky and noted, "It's after midnight now. We'll wait a while longer, then start working our way around toward that gorge."

The past was quickly forgotten. Danger—and plenty of it—was facing them in the present.

A half moon had been making its way through the sky, and when it was low to the horizon, Cody and Alvarez left their hiding place and rode slowly and carefully toward the mouth of the gorge that led into Montoya's stronghold. These foothills were rugged, harsh, and desolate, and each time their horses put a hoof down, there was a chance of noise that might reach the ears of Montoya's sentries. It took all the skill that Cody and Alvarez possessed to make their approach almost soundless.

Finally they neared the gorge, and Cody reined in. Alvarez followed his example. Both men swung down from their saddles and tied their horses' reins to a scrubby mesquite tree. From here they'd proceed on foot.

Alvarez led the way, his Indian heritage helping him to blend into the shadows so completely that Cody sometimes lost sight of him even though Alvarez was less than a yard away. Then they entered the stygian blackness inside the gorge.

Suddenly Cody heard the noise of a scuffle in front of him and knew that Alvarez had encountered one of Montoya's guards. A stray beam of starlight penetrated the shadows and reflected off a knife blade. Cody slid his own bowie from its sheath and crouched, ready in case Alvarez needed help. Silence was the most important thing now. If the guard managed to yell or get off a shot, they were lost.

Cody heard a faint, hideous gurgle nearby and knew that a blade had found someone's throat. Had that death rattle come from Alvarez or the guard? Cody tensed, and then a hand came out of the darkness and rested on his arm. "Silver Spurs," Alvarez hissed, using the nickname he had given the Ranger so that Cody would know who he was and not strike with his own knife. "Come. The man is dead."

They moved on, Cody stumbling a little as one of his feet struck the sprawled corpse. His other foot skidded on the rocky ground, and he knew it was because there was a pool of blood around the dead guard.

From his left came a startled, low-voiced curse. Cody whirled in that direction. His bowie was still in his hand, and without even thinking he brought his arm up and back. Aiming at the sound, he threw the heavy knife.

Luck and instinct guided the throw. There was the unmistakable thud of the blade sinking into flesh, followed a second later by a clatter of metal against rock. Cody ran silently across the gorge and knelt beside the feebly struggling second guard. The man was gasping for air. If he managed to gulp down enough to let out a cry for help—

Cody's fingers found the handle of the bowie protruding from the man's chest. He jerked the blade free and whipped it down, feeling it snag for a moment and then sink through the guard's throat to grate on his spinal column. The body underneath Cody shuddered and then was still. The Ranger felt around and found the rifle the man had dropped. He picked it up, wiped the bowie as best he could on the corpse's serape, then rejoined Alvarez.

"Another one?" whispered the bandit.

"Another one," Cody confirmed. "You reckon that's all?"

"Montoya probably feels so secure in this stronghold that two guards would seem sufficient to him. Still, we must be careful."

Cody couldn't have agreed more with that. With Alvarez still leading the way, they cat-footed through the rest of the gorge and finally emerged from it. The journey had taken only a few minutes, even with the pause to kill the two guards, but to Cody it seemed as if they had been in the depths of the gorge for an hour or more. The faint light in the valley from the moon and stars seemed to the Ranger almost as bright as daylight after his eyes had adjusted to the thick shadows he and Alvarez had just passed through.

They found a suitable hiding place in a cluster of small boulders near the edge of the gorge and settled down to wait for dawn. When they judged that sunrise was close, they'd begin moving deeper into the valley, getting as close to the large tent as they could. That was where Rose would be, with the man responsible for her captivity.

Cody glanced again at the peak where Gellman and Alonso were supposed to be waiting. Even if they failed to provide the distraction with the rockslide, Cody and Alvarez would try to rescue the Yellow Rose anyway. After coming this far, they had no other choice.

He was not going to leave this valley without her, Cody vowed.

CHAPTER
11

Cody wouldn't have thought it possible, but he had dozed off again, huddled there in the rocks with Alvarez. He awoke with a start, not knowing how long he'd been asleep, and heard Alvarez's deep, regular breathing beside him. The bandit was asleep, too. Biting back a curse, Cody reached over to poke Alvarez's shoulder. He glanced up at the sky and saw a faint line of gray to the east.

"Eh?" Alvarez exclaimed groggily, his hand grasping the butt of his pistol. He apparently quickly remembered where he was and whom he was with, and he sullenly said to Cody, "You should not awaken Diego Alvarez in such a manner, Silver Spurs. I am like the great cat, ready to strike out and kill the instant my eyes are open."

Cody ignored the grandiose boasting and whispered, "Come on. We've still got time to get ready before dawn, but we can't wait any longer."

With a nod Alvarez came up in a crouch and started out of the rocks toward the red, winking embers left in the ashes of the burned-down campfire. It was the only sign of life in the valley. Everyone in the encampment was asleep.

Cody grimaced as he thought about the way he'd nodded off. Of course, Alvarez had done the same thing. He supposed it came from growing up on the frontier and living in danger most of the time. A man learned to snatch what sleep he could, even if it was only a few minutes at a time.

No harm done, Cody told himself. Once again they'd been lucky. But he couldn't help but wonder when that luck was going to run out.

Alvarez *did* move a little like a big cat, Cody saw as he followed the bandit closer to Montoya's camp. The sky continued to lighten, and it was bright enough now for Cody to see the large tent in the center of the camp. Nearby was another tent, probably Montoya's. Everyone else—bandits and camp followers—slept outdoors in bedrolls. Cody could see the figures scattered haphazardly around the camp.

He and Alvarez headed for the rear of the main tent. When the avalanche began, they would cut an opening in the canvas with their knives and go in through the back as quickly as possible. Then it was just a matter of rescuing Rose, killing whoever was in the tent with her, finding out where Estrella was being held and grabbing her, and then getting the hell out while everybody else in camp was watching the rockslide. Simple, Cody thought wryly.

He had already located the band's horses; the animals were held in a rope corral not far from the tents. A couple of swipes from his bowie would free them, and the half-wild mstangs would be easy to stampede. Then a dash through the gorge, a pause to get their own mounts, and they would ride north as hard as they could for several miles before swinging east to rendezvous with Gellman and Alonso. It was a plan that should be successful . . . if everything went exactly as it was supposed to.

"Paco!"

The shout floating along the canyon froze both Cody and Alvarez. It was repeated, and then a man called in Spanish, "Look what we have found, Paco!"

Cody and Alvarez went to ground in a little hollow as the bandits rolled out of their blankets and sat up clutching rifles and pistols in response to the shouts. Cursing bitterly to himself, Cody watched as the men got to their feet and hurried to meet a small procession making its way down the canyon. Suddenly a ray of sunlight pierced the gloom, and Cody glanced back at the peak to the east. The sun had topped its spirelike height—the signal for

Gellman and Alonso to start the avalanche. But that was obviously not going to happen.

Gellman and Alonso were prisoners, being herded toward the camp at rifle point by several of the bandits.

"Madre de Dios!" Alvarez exclaimed through clenched teeth. "Where did they come from? How did they—?"

"Must be a foot trail down that cliff at the end of the canyon," Cody cut in with a strained whisper. "Montoya must've had some sentries posted up there, too, and they grabbed Gellman and Alonso."

"On the other side of that mountain?"

Cody shrugged a little. "Those two are city boys. They must've gotten turned around and started up the wrong slope. Doesn't really matter how they got caught. We still have to get Rose out of here."

"And those two?"

The quick glance Cody gave Alvarez was grim. "We'll do what we can," he said.

In the meantime Paco Montoya had emerged from his tent in response to the shouts from one of the men prodding Gellman and Alonso toward the camp. The bandit chieftain had a pistol in his hand and was scowling fiercely. Cody and Alvarez were about a hundred yards away from him and were looking at him from the side, but Cody could still tell how furious the bandit leader was to be disturbed this early. Montoya stalked out to meet the newcomers, trailed by several more men.

Cody saw movement at the entrance of the larger tent, and then Alvarez's hand closed over his arm. "The gringo," Alvarez hissed.

The tall, slender man stepped out of the tent. He wore what seemed to be a silk dressing gown, which looked completely out of place here in a bandit camp in the middle of these Mexican badlands. Like Montoya, he held a pistol in one hand and was watching curiously to see what was going on.

There was more movement behind him, and Cody caught his breath as the Yellow Rose stepped out of the tent. She wore a long skirt and a low-cut blouse that had probably been borrowed from one of the other women in the camp, but even from this distance Cody knew immediately it was her. There was no mistaking that slender but sensuous figure, the cascade of raven hair, the face that was lovely even after the ordeal she had gone through. She moved up behind the European, who had stopped some ten feet away from the tent's entrance to watch the confrontation between Montoya and the two prisoners.

That was when Rose lifted her arm, and Cody saw the morning sun reflect brightly off the blade she held in her hand—the blade she was about to plunge into the back of her captor.

Gellman must have noticed her at the same moment, because he shouted, "Rose!"

"Damn!" Cody said.

The Ranger surged to his feet as the European spun around to find Rose lunging at him, the knife sweeping down toward his chest. Cody broke into a run, not waiting to see if Alvarez was following or not. The plan was all shot to hell now anyway. All they could do was plunge ahead and hope for the best.

Cody's boots weren't made for running, but he covered a lot of ground in the space of a few seconds, bringing him within the outer limits of pistol range. He saw Rose's knife hand knocked aside by her intended victim. The man then caught her wrist and wrenched savagely, disarming her. At the same time Montoya howled a curse and lifted his pistol toward the onrushing Cody.

The Ranger had drawn his own Colt without even being aware of it. The six-gun was in his hand, an extension of his arm, as he triggered off a couple of shots. The bullets didn't hit anything, but they came close enough to make Montoya and his men dive for cover. Just behind Cody and to one side, Alvarez was rushing forward, too, and he opened up with his revolver. The booming gunshots rolled back in echoes from the surrounding hills.

Alonso whirled around and leapt at the nearest of his captors, tackling the outlaw around the waist and driving him to the ground. Gellman was also fighting back, grabbing the barrel of a rifle and wrenching it out of the hands of its owner. The burly easterner didn't bother to reverse the weapon. He swung it like a club at the guard, smashing the stock against the side of the man's head. Rifle stock and skull both shattered.

Rose was still struggling with the European. Cody was close enough to them now to hear her angry cries and the curses of the man, who was slapping her back and forth, the blows rocking her head and making her sag to her knees. Cody was tempted to snap a shot at him, but Rose was too close to her captor and there was too big a chance of hitting her. Instead the Ranger veered toward Montoya.

The bandit leader was down on one knee. The gun in his hand boomed, and Cody felt the wind of a slug passing close by his ear. He fired back, and Montoya pitched to the side. He couldn't tell if Montoya was hit or had simply dived out of the way of the bullet.

Alonso smashed a couple of punches to the jaw of the man he was struggling with, and the bandit went limp. As he rolled off the fallen guard, Alonso snatched the man's rifle out of his hands and came up looking for a target. But before he could fire, one of the other bandits threw a shot at him, and the slug clipped his shoulder. Alonso staggered and cried out in pain as the rifle slipped from his hands.

A few feet away Gellman was surrounded. He was in the middle of a knot of men who were slashing at him with rifle butts and pistol barrels. The blows thudded against his head and shoulders, and he sank to the ground despite his obvious determination to keep fighting. The odds were just too much. He was overwhelmed in a matter of moments and left stretched out on the ground, bloodied and battered, perhaps alive, perhaps dead.

Cody came to an abrupt stop when he saw the European shove Rose to the ground. The man lined his pistol on her, his hand quivering with rage and making the barrel of the gun tremble. Flicking a glance at Cody, the man cried out hoarsely, "Drop your gun or I'll kill her! I swear I will! Your friend, too!"

"Alvarez!" Cody barked. "Do as he says." Bending, he laid his own gun on the ground, and nearby a glowering Alvarez did the same.

"This is a bad mistake, Silver Spurs," Alvarez muttered under his breath so that only Cody could hear in the noisy confusion gripping the camp. "We should have made them kill us. That would have been simpler and less painful."

Cody had a hunch Alvarez was right. And yet he couldn't stand by and watch Rose murdered. As long as there was a chance he could turn things around, he had to hang on to life for all of them.

Montoya's men quickly surrounded Cody and Alvarez, and Montoya himself climbed to his feet. As the bandit leader approached them, Cody could tell that he was unharmed. None of the Ranger's bullets had found him. Montoya came to a stop in front of them and glowered at the rival *bandido*. "You are Alvarez," he said harshly. "You are even more ugly and insignificant than I thought you would be."

"And you bear with you the stench and the countenance of a hog," Alvarez replied.

Montoya snarled and brought his gun up, but he didn't fire. Instead, after a moment of trading glares with Alvarez, he swung toward Cody and demanded, "Who are you? Why does a *gringo* attack me in company with this pathetic excuse for a *bandido*?"

Before the Ranger could answer, the European spoke up. He had regained some of his composure, and he said, "I'd venture to guess his name is Cody. A Texas Ranger from Del Rio."

"A Ranger? One of Los Diablos Tejanos?" Montoya cocked the hammer of his Colt and lined its muzzle between Cody's eyes. "Gladly will I kill you, gringo dog."

"Wait!" The European spoke sharply, in a tone that said he was accustomed to being obeyed. He turned to Rose, who was lifting herself off the ground. Grasping her arm, he shoved her toward Cody. "Is this the man you thought would rescue you?"

"Cody," she gasped. "I am so sorry—"

"Don't worry about it," he told her with a faint smile. Looking back at Montoya and the other man, he went on,

"Just so you'll know, I'm not here as a Ranger. I came as a friend to the Yellow Rose, that's all."

"And I came to avenge the insult paid to my good name when I was impersonated by Montoya," Alvarez added.

The European smiled. "Oh, so the two of you figured that out, did you? Well, I must say, this is an unlikely alliance you formed. Too bad it was doomed to failure."

Gellman and Alonso had both been hauled to their feet, and now they were shoved forward to join Cody and Alvarez. Alonso was clutching his wounded shoulder, and his face was washed out from pain and loss of blood. Gellman stumbled along next to him, clearly still partly stunned by the beating he had received. When all four of the would-be rescuers were lined up together, Montoya smiled and asked, "We kill them now, no?"

"No," the European said without hesitation. "Your problem, Paco, is that you lack the flair necessary for true evil. You can kill those two if you wish"—he indicated Gellman and Alonso—"but the other two should be saved for something special."

Montoya nodded slowly. "*Sí*, I like the sound of that." He gestured curtly to his men. "Take those two away. Do with them as you will."

The *bandidos* laughed and crowded around Gellman and Alonso. Cody felt a ball of sickness form in his stomach as his two companions were jerked away. Many of the bandits had Yaqui blood in them, and he hated to think about the grisly fate that might be in store for the easterner and the musician.

Of course, he and Alvarez were in just as bad a fix. Whatever their captors had in mind for them, it would not be anything good.

The European strolled over to stand in front of Cody. Rose watched anxiously, her even white teeth catching her lower lip. "So you are the famous Cody," the man said smoothly. "I heard a great deal about you back in Del Rio from a man named Al O'Neil."

"Just before you killed him, I reckon."

The man sniffed and shrugged. "He had outlived his

usefulness, and leaving him alive behind me would not have been wise. By the way, my name is Pierre Desmond. You are probably wondering why I am here and what my interest is in the Yellow Rose."

"Not particularly," Cody told him.

A muscle in Desmond's jaw twitched, but he controlled his anger. "Very well. Be that way if you wish, but know that you hard-boiled frontiersmen are quite boring to me." He gestured to a couple of Montoya's men who stood nearby. "Take this man and the girl to my tent. I'm sure they would like some time alone before they are forever separated," he said melodramatically. "But stay nearby, and do not let them escape."

Cody glanced at Rose, and then the two of them were prodded toward the largest tent. Cody didn't know why Desmond was throwing him together with Rose, but at the moment he was just grateful for the opportunity to be with her again.

They stepped into the tent, and the flap dropped shut behind them. Instantly, Rose was in Cody's arms, burying her face against his chest and holding him tightly around the waist. She didn't cry, but a few shudders passed through her body.

"I won't tell you it's all right," Cody said softly as he stroked her hair, "because we both know it's not. But at least we're together again."

She nodded, then lifted her head to look up at him. "I dreamed you would come for me," she said. "There is a connection between you and me, a bond that can never be broken."

Cody tightened his embrace around her. She had put into words what he'd been feeling ever since that first morning when he'd seen her come into the lobby of the Rio Grande Hotel. He couldn't put a name on the bond she had spoken of, but it was there nonetheless, an almost mystical intertwining of their destinies. Cody had sensed it right away. There was no way of knowing what it might develop into in the future—and unless their luck changed, there wasn't to be a future.

A sudden shriek from outside made Rose press her face

against Cody again, and another shudder wracked her. Both of them knew that the scream had come from either Gellman or Alonso. Montoya's men would be getting to work on them. Rose whispered, "Desmond is the most evil man in the world."

"Who is he?" Cody asked, wanting to divert her attention from the terrible sounds outside. "Why is he doing all this?"

Quickly, Rose gave him an abbreviated account of her life and the reasons for Desmond's twisted hatred. She touched only lightly on the ordeal she had endured since being kidnapped in El Paso, but Cody didn't have any trouble filling in the blanks she left. Finally she concluded by saying, "When the shouting started and Desmond left the tent, he let his guard down for the first time by leaving his knife behind. I didn't think, I just picked it up and went after him. When I came out, I didn't see you and the others at first. I was concentrating on killing Desmond."

"That would have left you at the mercy of Montoya," Cody pointed out.

She shook her head and smiled ruefully. "No. Because once I had killed Desmond, I intended to plunge the blade into my own breast." She took a deep breath. "I should have done that long ago. At least if I had, you and poor Barney and Alonso would not be in such danger now."

Cody didn't waste time arguing with her. He said, "At least we're together," and rested his hand under her chin, cupping it and tilting her head back. He kissed her, and the sensation they had felt back in Del Rio crackled through them again.

"How very touching."

The unexpected intrusion startled Cody and Rose, and they broke off their kiss and turned toward the voice. Pierre Desmond was standing in the entrance of the tent holding back the flap, a smirk on his face.

"I'm sorry to interrupt," the Frenchman continued in the same ironic tone, "but there's something out here I want you to see."

Cody knew there was nothing outside the tent that Rose

needed to see, but there was nothing he could do to prevent it. Desmond had his pistol in his hand, and he motioned impatiently with the barrel. Keeping one hand firmly on Rose's arm, Cody led her out of the tent and back into the bright morning sunshine.

That sunshine illuminated a gruesome scene. Two boulders had been rolled up to the edge of the camp, and Gellman and Alonso were lashed to the rocks with cords that stretched their arms and legs painfully behind them. Both men had been stripped to the waist, and their faces and torsos shone with fresh blood from the myriad cuts inflicted on them. Their heads sagged forward, lolling loosely on their shoulders, but both of them were still alive and apparently conscious, their chests heaving as they gulped down air. The torture had paused for a moment, no doubt on orders from either Desmond or Montoya.

Casually, Desmond waved an elegantly slim hand at the two victims. "This is what is in store for you, Cody. I wanted you to see the results so that you can look forward to them yourself."

Cody stood stoically, but Rose gasped, "No! You cannot do this awful thing!"

Desmond smiled at her. "My dear, I can do anything I please," he said. "Except, it appears, bend your will to mine. But perhaps that will change."

Cody understood now. Desmond hoped to break Rose's spirit by threatening him with an agonizing death. Cody looked over at her and said firmly, "Don't let him stampede you. He doesn't scare me."

"Oh, but I should, Cody," Desmond said before she could reply. "You should be very afraid right now."

Montoya strode over, squared his shoulders, and inclined his head toward Gellman and Alonso. "We can finish off those two later," he said. "I want to get started on Alvarez now."

"By all means, my friend," Desmond said. "Do whatever you wish with Señor Alvarez."

Standing nearby with his arms folded casually across his chest, Alvarez stared haughtily at Montoya and said,

"You had better kill me quick, Montoya, before you wet your pants in fear of the great Diego Alvarez."

"Fear?" Montoya echoed with a snort of contempt. "Not even a baby mewling in its blanket would fear the likes of you, Alvarez."

"If this is so, then you will not hesitate to settle the score between us." Alvarez spoke quickly, not giving Montoya a chance to hesitate. "I challenge you to defend your honor, dog! I challenge you to fight me—face to face, knife to knife . . . *mano a mano!*"

Alvarez's voice rang out, and everyone in the camp heard it. Montoya's face darkend with rage. "You doubt the honor and courage of Paco Montoya?" he shouted at Alvarez, who just smiled smugly and remained standing at his ease, regarding his enemy coolly. Montoya brought his revolver up and thrust it in Alvarez's face, but Alvarez didn't flinch. Abruptly, Montoya turned away with a growled curse.

Desmond spoke up hurriedly. "I don't know if you're taking this seriously or not, Paco, but don't let this gentleman trick you into anything you don't want to do."

"That's right, Montoya," Cody added dryly. "None of us cares if you're a coward."

Montoya jammed his gun back in its holster and turned to Alvarez. His voice shaking with emotion, he said, "It will be as you said—*mano a mano!*" He took off his gun belt and tossed it to one of his men, then slid a huge knife from the sash around his waist. "Give Alvarez a knife!"

One of the band pressed his own blade into Alvarez's hand and stepped back quickly. A circle formed around the two bandit chieftains, a circle that also included Cody, Rose, and Desmond in its center. Cody looked at Desmond and asked quietly, "You going to let a bandit show you up, mister?"

"What do you mean?" Desmond snapped.

"Montoya's going to defend his honor. What about you?"

Rose put a hand on the Ranger's arm and said, "No, Cody," while Desmond just stared at him in surprise for a moment. Finally the Frenchman broke into a smile and said, "You are quite the smooth one, aren't you, Texan? You think to goad me into a fight, hoping that you can kill me and then escape, eh?"

Cody laughed. "How the devil am I going to do that? Doesn't matter if I kill you or not, we're still going to be surrounded by a couple of dozen bandits. I'm not going anywhere and I know it, Desmond. But if I've got to die, I'd sure as hell like to go down fighting—and I want a chance to take you with me."

Desmond hesitated again, and Cody could see the struggle going on in the Frenchman's mind between logic and his offended sense of honor. Not surprisingly, honor won, and Desmond said abruptly, "Very well. But I do not have one of those incredibly ugly knives you Texans carry, nor do I have any experience fighting with one." A sly look appeared on his face. "I am, however, willing to match my saber—one of the few reminders I have left of my military career—against your bowie."

Cody had not seen Desmond's saber, but he knew it would give the man quite an advantage in reach. Still, a mismatch was better than no chance at all. "Agreed," the Ranger said grimly.

"Can we get on with this?" Montoya demanded impatiently. "I have a dog to kill."

Alvarez just laughed.

"Any formal combat must have rules," Desmond insisted. "Paco, have your men draw back so there will be room for all four of us to do battle."

Montoya nodded and motioned his men back.

"Each man will face only his own opponent," Desmond went on. "If a man is killed, the victor will withdraw until the other contest is decided."

Cody, Alvarez, and Montoya all nodded in understanding.

Desmond took hold of Rose's arm and drew her away from Cody. He turned her over to one of Montoya's men with the instructions, "Keep her here and make sure she has her eyes open. I want her to see this."

He sent another man to his tent for the saber. The bandit quickly returned with a long leather scabbard, and

Desmond lovingly withdrew the tempered-steel blade. It was a classic cavalry saber, Cody saw, heavy, with a slight curve to it, and a thick brass guard around the hilt. In the hands of an experienced man, it would be a deadly weapon.

But so was a bowie knife. Cody's was handed to him by one of Montoya's men. Facing Desmond across the circle, the Ranger waited for the battle to begin. Alvarez and Montoya stood to their left, also ready.

Desmond took off the dressing gown and faced Cody wearing only his boots and a pair of trousers. He lifted the saber in a mock salute and said, *"En garde."*

"Whenever you're ready, mister," replied the Ranger.

Desmond and Montoya lunged forward at the same time. The Frenchman lifted the saber high and slashed downward with it, while Montoya came in low with his blade. Both Cody and Alvarez were ready for the attacks. Cody heard Alvarez's blade clang against Montoya's as Alvarez parried the blow, but then the Ranger was too busy defending himself to give any heed to the other fight.

He had to admit that Desmond handled the sword well. The flurry of thrusts and parries from the Frenchman was almost too fast for the eye to follow. But all of Cody's senses and reflexes were operating at the highest possible level, and everywhere Desmond's saber went, Cody's bowie was there to block it. The whole valley rang with the sound of steel against steel, counterpointed by the shouts of encouragement from Montoya's men.

Cody launched an offensive of his own to see how Desmond would handle it, even though he was risking a great deal by moving even closer. The Frenchman blocked Cody's moves and then cut at the Ranger's legs with the saber, forcing Cody to dodge backward desperately. Moving on the offensive again, Desmond came after him.

For long moments the two men moved around the circle, the flow of battle ebbing back and forth. From time to time Cody caught a glimpse of Alvarez and Montoya from the corner of his eye, but he didn't have a chance to track the progress of their combat. He was too concerned with keeping Desmond at bay. Neither was there time to look at Rose and see how she was holding up under the strain.

Desmond drove toward him again, slashing furiously with the saber. Cody ducked under the blows, throwing himself to one side and catching himself with his free hand as he landed. Suddenly a memory flashed through his mind. He recalled a prizefight he had seen once in New Orleans between a burly keelboater and a much more slender Creole. The smaller man had used a form of fighting called *la savate,* one of the spectators had explained to Cody, a method of combat that was very popular in France.

That was damned appropriate, Cody thought now as he drove both feet into the stomach of the onrushing Desmond and kicked him clear across the circle.

Cody sprang back upright and started to rush after Desmond, eager to press his advantage, but suddenly someone crashed into him, knocking him off balance. Cody twisted away as he caught himself and saw that he had run into Montoya. The collision had delayed him long enough so that Desmond was able to scramble back to his feet. Desmond came at him again, his face flushed with rage as he swung the saber.

Flinging up the bowie knife, Cody blocked the slashing cavalry blade. Sparks flew as the bowie slid down the saber until it grated to a stop against the hilt. Cody and Desmond strained against each other, each trying to turn aside the other's weapon, and then Desmond launched a blow at Cody's face with his left hand. The Ranger shifted so that Desmond's fist only grazed his ear, and at the same time he twisted his knife so that part of its S-shaped guard caught inside the guard of the saber. With the leverage provided once the knives were locked together, another sharp twist of Cody's bowie cleanly snapped the lighter, more brittle blade of the saber. The Frenchman cried out as if in physical pain as his weapon broke.

Cody drove a fist into Desmond's stomach, doubling him over, then smashed the hilt of the bowie into his jaw. Desmond was knocked sprawling on the ground, and Cody was on him in a flash, holding the razor-sharp tip of the big knife at his throat. Desmond stared up at him with wide, terrified eyes and screamed at Montoya's men, "Kill him! Shoot him, you dolts!" All thoughts of honor were forgotten.

On the verge of cutting Desmond's throat, Cody stopped himself at the last instant and raised his head, blinking away the sweat that had dripped into his eyes during the fight. Several feet away, the battle between Alvarez and Montoya had come to a conclusion as well, with the positions reversed. Alvarez was on the ground with Montoya's blade at his throat. Cody had just time enough to be a little startled by that outcome before Montoya barked at his men, "Do as Desmond says! Kill the *Tejano*!"

Rifles and pistols came up, ready to blast Cody into oblivion, but before any of Montoya's band could fire, gunfire rang out from the hills surrounding the valley. A deadly hail of lead swept the camp, tumbling several of the bandits lifelessly to the ground, and shouts came from the gorge leading into the valley. Cody jerked his head in that direction and saw a large group of men on horseback come galloping into view. All of them carried rifles, and they opened fire with devastating accuracy from the backs of their speeding mounts.

In a matter of instants the camp was turned into a scene of bloody chaos as Montoya's men tried to defend themselves from the unexpected attack. Montoya gaped at the onrushing riders, taking his attention off Alvarez. The rival bandit leader seized the opportunity, arching his back and heaving Montoya off him. As Montoya cursed and sprawled on the ground, Alvarez rolled over quickly, snatched up his fallen knife, and lunged at his hated enemy. With both hands gripping the hilt and an inarticulate cry of rage coming from his throat, Alvarez plunged the blade deep into Montoya's heart.

For a second Cody considered going ahead and slitting Desmond's throat, but he was no murderer. Besides, he had recognized Alvarez's men and knew that now there was a chance he and his companions might win this fight yet. He surged to his feet, dragging the stunned Desmond with him.

"You're going back to Texas, you son of a bitch," Cody growled. "You'll hang for what you've done."

Desmond moaned, all the fight gone out of him. Cody dragged him over to the boulders where Gellman and Alonso were tied, keeping his head down as he went in an effort to avoid stray bullets. A few slashes of the keen-edged bowie freed the two prisoners, who had regained some of their strength during the respite from torture.

Over the roar of gunfire Cody asked them, "Can you keep hold of Desmond?" When both Gellman and Alonso nodded, Cody thrust the Frenchman at them. "I've got to find Rose!"

He had lost track of her during the confusion of the attack by Alvarez's men on the camp. Whirling around, Cody tried to peer through the clouds of dust that had been kicked up by running men and galloping horses. The haze of powder smoke in the air stung his eyes, too.

Finally he spotted the singer stumbling along on the other side of the camp. The man who had been told to guard her was no longer with her, and Cody figured he had released her in order to fight back against the raiders. Cody shouted, "Rose!" Her head turned toward him, and she began making her way through the chaos and carnage.

Suddenly a figure loomed up behind her. Cody started to shout a warning, then saw the form was female. Not only that, but he recognized with relief that the other woman was Estrella, Rose's maid. With everything that had been going on, he hadn't had a chance to locate the girl before now. Cody watched, anxious for their safety, as Estrella ran up behind Rose.

He wasn't expecting what happened next.

Estrella tackled Rose, and the two women fell heavily to the ground and began to struggle. Confused, Cody started toward them, but before he had taken more than a couple of steps, Estrella wound up on top. Suddenly her arm lifted in the air, and Cody saw the knife clutched in her fist, ready to sweep downward and pierce the breast of the Yellow Rose.

He was too far away to reach them, and the only weapon he had was the bowie in his hand. Could he throw it in time, and with enough accuracy? The blade in Estrella's hand was already plummeting toward Rose.

A wild shot caught Estrella in the forehead. The bullet bored through her brain and flung her backward off her stunned victim. Cody grimaced and raced forward. He bent and caught Rose's arm, pulling her to her feet and folding her into his arms. A few feet away Estrella lay sprawled on her back, sightless eyes staring up at the sky.

The firing around them was only sporadic now, and Cody stood there holding Rose for a long moment as the sounds of battle died away. He wasn't sure exactly what had happened in the last few minutes, but the important thing was that both of them were still alive and relatively unharmed. Slowly, they turned away from Estrella's body and started toward Gellman and Alonso. The young Mexican, Cody saw, had picked up a six-gun that one of the fallen bandits had dropped. He had the pistol pointed in the general direction of Pierre Desmond, but when he saw Rose, Alonso's attention was diverted from the Frenchman.

Desmond lurched forward, apparently shaking off the stunned attitude that had gripped him ever since his defeat at Cody's hands. He grabbed the gun with one hand while the other fist cracked into Alonso's jaw. Staggered by the blow, the Mexican loosened his grip on the weapon enough for Desmond to tear it free.

"No!" Cody shouted, seeing what was about to happen.

The gun boomed, and Alonso was thrown backward by the slug. Gellman lunged at Desmond, but the Frenchman slashed at his head with the gun, cracking the barrel across Gellman's skull. As Gellman went down, Desmond whipped around to face Cody and Rose again.

"You'll both die!" he shrieked, fairly shaking with rage as he brought up the gun for the final shots.

There was no time to make an overhand throw with the knife. Cody shoved Rose to the side and at the same instant hurled the bowie with an upward flick of his wrist. The heavy blade smacked into Desmond's bare chest and knocked him back a step, but he stayed on his feet. The gun wavered in front of him as he tried to line it up on Cody. The Ranger stood there, watching as pain contorted Desmond's face. After a few seconds that seemed much longer the muzzle of the gun drooped toward the ground. The weapon blasted, but the bullet went harmlessly into the dirt.

Desmond followed it, flopping facedown in the dust and not moving again.

Silence settled down over the camp, a silence that was punctuated occasionally by moans of pain. Cody helped Rose back to her feet, then stalked over to Desmond's body. He kicked away the fallen gun, then hooked a booted toe under Desmond's shoulder and rolled him over. The Frenchman was dead, his eyes already turning glassy.

Diego Alvarez loomed up out of a cloud of dust, a pistol in each hand, blood dripping down one cheek from a deep gash, and a broad grin on his face. He tucked one of the guns behind his sash and used that hand to clap Cody on the back. "Good fight, eh?" he asked boomingly.

"If you say so," Cody grunted. "We're still alive, so I reckon you're right."

He turned and saw that Rose was kneeling beside Alonso. She had torn a piece off her skirt and was pressing it to the wound in the musician's side. Beside her stood Barney Gellman, who was rubbing the freshest lump on his head. The easterner seemed to be on the verge of collapse, but as he looked around, his gaze a menacing glare, it was obvious that sheer willpower and his determination to protect Rose were keeping him on his feet.

Several of Alvarez's men trotted up on their horses and grinned at their leader. "Montoya's men are all dead except for one who calls himself Esteban," one of them reported. "He claims he was not a member of the band, but a prisoner instead. I do not believe him."

"And you are wise not to," Alvarez agreed. "I will talk to him later—and he will not enjoy the conversation. What were our losses?"

"Three men killed, seven wounded."

"Bueno," Alvarez said, nodding soberly. "I mourn for the three dead. We will sing songs to their honor." He turned back to Cody. "You thought you were a dead man, no?"

"Looked like it at the time," Cody admitted.

Alvarez tapped his temple with a blunt finger. "Always, Diego Alvarez has a plan. You should know that about me by this time, Silver Spurs. Never underestimate the brain of Alvarez. . . ."

"I'll remember that," Cody said over his shoulder. Rose was on her feet now, leaving Gellman to care for Alonso, and she was waiting for him.

He went to her, reaching out to take her hands and leaving Alvarez to sing his own praises. The bandit chieftain didn't seem to mind.

CHAPTER

||||||||||||||||||||||||| 12 |||||||||||||||||||||||||

"**T**here is no law saying that an honorable man cannot be a prudent one as well," Diego Alvarez said several hours later as he puffed on a cigar he had liberated from Montoya's tent. "During a moment when you were otherwise occupied, Señor Silver Spurs, I simply instructed my men to follow at a discreet distance when we went looking for Montoya. If we did not need their assistance, they were not to interfere. Thankfully, my followers can be trusted to act according to the needs of the situation."

"So when they saw you about to get your gullet carved open by Montoya, they figured they'd better take a hand," Cody said with a smile.

Alvarez's teeth clamped down tightly on the cigar. "The dog was lucky," he growled. "Never again would he be able to best Diego Alvarez in fair combat."

"Well, never again is for damn sure. That knife you stuck through him came clear out his back."

"Please, gentlemen," the Yellow Rose murmured. "There has been enough death. Must we keep talking about it?"

"Rose is right," Cody said. "Time for the dead to stay dead."

They were sitting around a fresh campfire well removed from the scene of battle. Alvarez's men had disposed of the bodies of the slain *bandidos*—and Pierre Desmond—by dumping them in a ravine they'd found near the head of the valley. The only one who had received an actual burial in the rocky ground was Estrella. Despite the servant's betrayal, Rose could not bear for the girl's body to be tossed into the ravine with the bandits.

Now Cody, Rose, Alvarez, Gellman, and Alonso were recovering from the battle before preparing to leave this place. Alvarez had found some smoked meat and dried corn. It wasn't much of a meal, but washed down by the wine he had also found in Montoya's tent, the fare wasn't too bad.

"I'm just sorry we nearly ruined everything," Barney Gellman said. His wounds had been cleaned and bandaged, but there were so many of them that his entire torso had bindings wrapped around it. However, most of his strength had come back. Alonso, with a deep bullet crease on his side from the shot fired by Desmond, was weaker, but Cody had patched up enough such wounds to believe that the musician would be all right. Gellman went on, "Alonso told me I was taking the wrong trail on that peak, but I was convinced I was right. That'll teach me to be so damned stubborn. We stumbled right into those guards Montoya had out."

Alvarez lifted one of the wine bottles and let the liquid gurgle into his throat for several seconds before lowering it and saying, "Hey, we'll make a *bandido* out of you yet, Bernardo. Don't worry about it."

Gellman chuckled. "I don't think so. Soon as I get back across the border, I'm heading home to New York. A guy doesn't get in as much trouble there."

Cody had never been to the city in question, so he couldn't judge Gellman's statement. Instead, he said, "I can't believe Estrella sold you out like that, Rose. She must've really hated you."

Rose sighed. "I will never understand that. I always treated her well. I thought we were friends. But I guess I never really knew her." She looked meaningfully again at Cody. "You're still talking about it."

He grinned tiredly. "You're right." He came to his feet and held out his hand to her. "Why don't we take a walk and get our minds off it?"

"An excellent idea, sir." She managed a weary smile to match his own and took his hand.

While they strolled toward the mouth of the gorge, the others got ready to travel. Cody's dun and Alvarez's horse had been brought into the canyon and watered and fed along with the other animals. No one wanted to stay here in this vale of death tonight. They would start back toward Alvarez's stronghold and cover as much ground as possible by nightfall, being careful not to make the pace too difficult for the wounded.

Rose squeezed Cody's hand as they walked along. "I never gave up, you know," she told him. "I was sure you would come for me."

"And I knew you were still alive."

"But not unharmed," she went on. "Desmond . . . he was a terrible man. . . . He molested me—"

"There's no need to talk about it, like you said." Cody stopped and turned to face her. "It's over, and Desmond has paid for what he did. I reckon all of us have to put that behind us now."

Rose nodded, and Cody saw the faint sheen of tears in her eyes. In a soft voice she said, "I already knew there were bad men in the world, Cody, very bad men. But now I am glad to know there are good men, too."

She moved closer and rested her head against his chest, and the fragrance of her hair filled his senses. They both had a lot of pain to forget, he thought. And they would do that forgetting together, on the way back to El Paso.

"El Paso del Norte," Alvarez said, pointing as the group reined in on top of a small hill overlooking the Rio Grande and the city beyond.

The journey north from the mountains had taken nearly a week, and they had first paused for several days at the *jacal* of Dr. Cyril Mortimer. The expatriate physician had examined Gellman and Alonso, treated them with some of his herbs and poultices, and made them rest for a few days before pronouncing them fit to travel on to the border. Both men were now well on their way to recovery.

They wore clothes given to them by Alvarez's men, and Gellman looked particularly ludicrous in sombrero, serape, baggy pants, and rope-soled sandals. Still, Cody suspected—even if the easterner would never admit it—that Gellman was a damn sight more comfortable than he'd been in his suit.

Alvarez and several of his men had accompanied them to the Rio Grande, though the prevailing attitude among the bandits was that it was foolish to aid a Texas Ranger, despite having been on the same side for a while. Alvarez's word was law, however, and he had decreed that they'd furnish an escort for the travelers.

Now he signaled his men to fall back. "You will be all right from here," he told Cody and the others. "No one will dare bother you, knowing that you have been under the protection of Diego Alvarez." The stocky bandit spurred his horse alongside Rose's and bent to take her hand and lift it to his lips. "Farewell, Señorita Yellow Rose. I will never forget you. Your songs will echo through all the nights of my life."

"Good-bye, Señor Alvarez," Rose replied. "And thank you for everything."

"De nada." Alvarez shook hands with Gellman and Alonso, and then the two of them, along with Rose, started down the hill toward the river.

Alvarez had motioned for Cody to wait, and the Ranger now brought his dun over next to him. "Something you want to say, Alvarez?" Cody asked.

"Just that the next time we meet, the circumstances may be very different, Silver Spurs." Alvarez held out his hand. "But until then . . . *vaya con Dios.*"

Cody took his hand and said quietly, *"Vaya con Dios, Diego."* He knew exactly what Alvarez meant. They might respect each other and even consider each other friends, but they were still on opposite sides of the law. The day might come when one of them would have to die. Yet, as Alvarez had said, until then . . .

"Go with God," Cody repeated in English as he watched the bandit ride away. Then he hurried to catch up with Rose and the others.

"Are you still planning to go ahead with that concert tour?" he asked as he came up beside the singer moments later.

"Why not?" Rose asked. "Desmond is dead, and he was the source of all the trouble. Still, I have to admit I would feel better"—she looked over at him pointedly—"if a certain Ranger would consent to accompany me."

"Still can't do it," Cody said. "As soon as we cross that river, I'm a Ranger again."

Rose laughed, and the sound had the same thrilling sound as her singing. "Badge or no badge, my darling," she said, "across the border or not, you were *always* a Ranger."

Cody reckoned she was right.

THE PATRIOTS

Book I
SONS OF LIBERTY
by Adam Rutledge

★ ★ ★

1773-1775. The birth pangs of freedom are shaking a nation. The British have passed the Intolerable Acts, and the angry citizens of Boston are ready to rebel. Among the spokesmen for the insurrectionists are Samuel Adams, Paul Revere, and John Hancock, all members of the inner circle of the Committee of Safety.

Daniel and Quincy Reed, brothers from Virginia, arrive in the city at a time when everyone is being asked to choose sides in the coming conflict. Quincy, with the exuberance of youth, decides immediately, eagerly participating in the Boston Tea Party, but Daniel is slower to declare his sympathies for the rebel cause. When Daniel is recruited by the lovely and literate spy, Roxanne Darragh, he casts his lot with hers, and together they gather information for the Committee of Safety—until it becomes clear that there is a traitor in their midst.

As the first shots are fired at Lexington and Concord the brothers' suspicions escalate. Can this traitor sabotage the outcome of the early battles of the War for Independence? Will he interfere with the new-found love Daniel and Roxanne feel for each other?

**Turn the page for a preview of SONS OF LIBERTY,
on sale June 1992
wherever Bantam paperbacks are sold.**

The young man on the big bay horse was thirsty. He had been riding since early morning and, anxious to get to his destination, had not stopped for food or drink. Now as he spotted a tavern up ahead at a little crossroads, a grin broke out across his tanned face. Surely it would not hurt to stop for a quick mug of ale on a hot day.

In this summer of 1773, Daniel Reed was twenty years old, and much of that twenty years had been spent on the plantation of his parents, Geoffrey and Pamela Reed. It had not been idle time. Daniel had hunted and fished and spent every possible moment outdoors. His skin had acquired a healthy brown sheen, and the sun had also lightened his curly, naturally dark brown hair. Even relaxing in the saddle of the horse he had ridden from Virginia, he appeared unusually tall, lean, and muscular. He wore high-topped boots, dark brown whipcord pants, a lightweight linen shirt, and a black tricorn hat canted to the back of his head.

His brown eyes were intelligent. Despite his outdoor activities, his academic education had not been neglected. He had been to the best academy in Virginia and then to Yale College in the colony of Connecticut, and he had excelled in his studies at both places. He had done well enough that his parents had decided he should continue his schooling near Boston.

A long-barreled flintlock rifle, powder horn, and shot pouch were slung on one side of the saddle. Another bag filled with food and other supplies hung from the opposite side. To some people, a journey on horseback from Virginia to Massachusetts might be a daunting prospect. Daniel, however, had thoroughly enjoyed the trip, even dawdling along the way to do some hunting.

As he reined the bay to a halt in front of the tavern, he heard loud voices coming from within the building. Several horses were tied up at the front rail. This was farming country, and no doubt the tavern served as a gathering place for the people who lived hereabouts. Daniel was not surprised to find it doing a brisk business, even at this time of day.

He walked in and went directly across the room to the long bar behind which the white-aproned proprietor held court. The man was saying to several patrons lined up at the bar, "The British were begging for trouble, if you ask me. That damned Dudington put a lot o' good men in jail."

"A lot of smugglers, you mean," countered one of the men. "Common criminals, that's what they are."

"For bringing in tea that ain't taxed half to death?" the bartender asked. "That's no crime as far as I'm concerned."

Another man spoke up. "Those Rhode Islanders went too far when they burned the *Gaspee*, though. Wanton destruction's not going to solve anything."

Daniel leaned on the bar and, as he listened to the discussion, tried to catch the eye of the proprietor. The men's voices were loud and angry on both sides of the argument. Daniel frowned in concentration and finally remembered the incident about which they were talking. The year before, one of the British ships assigned to patrol the coast off Rhode Island had gone aground, and several boatloads of colonists, angry with the Crown's policies on the importing of tea, had rowed out to the vessel, taken it over from its crew, and set it on fire. The British authorities had been furious over the matter, but they had never been able to track down the men responsible. Daniel had read about it in the Virginia newspapers, as well as having heard his father and other men discuss it.

But all that had happened over a year earlier. Why were these Massachusetts men still arguing about it?

He finally got the attention of the bartender and asked, "Could I have a mug of ale, please?"

The man sauntered down the bar, leaned his big palms on the hardwood, and gave Daniel a dubious stare. "Be ye a patriot or a Tory?" he demanded.

Daniel blinked, taken aback by the question. "I . . . I don't suppose I know," he finally replied.

Men from both sides of the discussion seized on that. They gathered around him, hammering sharp questions at him, demanding to know his allegiances. He yearned to shout out that all he really wanted was to get to Boston.

"Forget about the ale," he told the bartender, turning and trying to push his way out of the knot of men that had formed around him. "I'll just water my horse and be gone."

"Not so quick, lad." A hard hand fell on his shoulder, stopping him. "Ye haven't answered our questions. Nobody's neutral in this anymore. Yer either a patriot or a damned loyalist!"

"Damned loyalist, is it?" snapped one of the men. "Better that than a treasonous, treacherous rebel!"

"Ye'd best take that back, Finn!"

"I'll do no such. And I'll not kowtow to the likes of you, either!"

Nervously licking his lips, Daniel watched both

sides surge toward each other, with him in the middle. "Excuse me . . ." he began.

Then the punches started to fly.

Daniel ducked under them, intending to head for the floor and get out of this ludicrous predicament any way he could. On the way down, though, someone shoved him hard, and he lost his balance. He fell heavily, and someone stepped on him. Above him, the argument had degenerated into a brawl. Men shouted curses and grunted in pain as blows fell.

Rolling over desperately, Daniel got clear of the melee and sprang to his feet. Everyone else in the place seemed to have forgotten about him. They were too busy swinging fists and trying to smash mugs over one another's heads. Regretting that he had ever stopped, Daniel scrambled for his hat, which had come off during the confusion, brushed himself off, and headed for the door.

Outside, he watered the bay at the trough, swung up into the saddle, and decided he was willing to stay thirsty until he got to Boston.

It was amazing, he thought as he sent the horse cantering down the road, that men would come to blows over something that had happened somewhere else over a year earlier. They had to hold strong views about the situation if they were willing to fight about it now.

He would have to think about that, he told himself, but later. Right now, he had the last leg of his journey to complete. With any luck he would be in Boston before the day was over.

Daniel felt excitement surge through him as he drew rein and brought his horse to a stop on a hill overlooking the city of Boston, its blue harbor to the east and the Charles River to the west. He had been to this bustling Atlantic coast city before, but the sight of it never failed to thrill him.

"Bound for town, are ye?"

Daniel turned to locate the source of the question. An old man in a floppy hat was at the reins of a mule-drawn wagon loaded with produce from one of the area's outlying farms. As he passed slowly he grinned at Daniel, revealing a large gap in his front teeth.

"That's right," Daniel said. "I'm going to Boston."

The old man gave him a little wave and moved on. Daniel stayed where he was, wanting to enjoy the sensation of looking out over the city for a few more minutes.

Arrangements had been made for Daniel to stay with his aunt and uncle during the summer, before finding a place of his own in the fall when he entered Harvard to read for the law. He was eager to see his cousin Elliot again. Putting his horse into a trot, he headed down the hill toward the Shawmut peninsula.

The road led to Boston Neck, a narrow spit of land where the Charles and the harbor just about met. On the other side of Boston Neck, past the public gallows, the peninsula widened rapidly, its confines filled by the sprawling community. Daniel followed Orange Street for several blocks, then cut over to Common Street, which ran along the east side of Boston Common. Traffic was heavy. He made his way among carriages, wagons, men on horseback like himself, and many pedestrians. On this sunny day the large, open, park-like green was busy. Couples strolled hand in hand on the soft grass; children trailed by barking dogs ran and played; old-timers, enjoying the youngsters' antics, sat under the double row of trees that bounded the common.

Under other circumstances, Daniel might have considered stopping for a few moments. Benjamin and Polly Markham, his uncle and aunt, knew he was coming, but considering the distance between Virginia and Massachusetts, it had been impossible to predict to the day when he would arrive. However, he felt sure his relatives would not be sitting around waiting for him. If he knew his mother's brother, Uncle Benjamin would be hard at work as usual, furthering the interests of the shipping company in which he was a partner.

Though no one would object if he stayed to enjoy the common for a while, Daniel pushed on, unwilling to delay his arrival any longer. The road cut across the northeast corner of the common and then ran straight through the fashionable residential district of Beacon Hill, where the first house in Boston had been built a hundred and fifty years earlier by William Blackstone, a settler from Charlestown, across the river to the north. The pace was more sedate here, with fewer people on the streets.

The Markham family owned a large house on one of Beacon Hill's cobblestone lanes. To someone accustomed to the open spaces of Virginia, the houses in Boston seemed to be crammed too close together, but Daniel knew that he would soon get used to the crowded living conditions of the city. With water surrounding it on both sides, he thought, Boston had grown about as much as it ever could.

He rode up the hill and drew rein in front of the elegant three-story home owned by his aunt and uncle. It was constructed of red brick and sat behind a flagstone sidewalk. As he swung down from his saddle and fastened the horse's reins to a wrought-iron pole that supported an oil lamp, the front door of the house burst open and a young man came running out.

"Daniel!" he called. "Is that you?"

"It's been less than a year since you saw me in Virginia, Elliot," Daniel replied with a grin, turning to greet his cousin. "You ought to recognize me."

Elliot Markham came to a stop in front of Daniel. "Yes, I think I do recall that ugly countenance," he gibed. Suddenly, he grabbed Daniel's hand and pumped it up and down in an enthusiastic handshake. "How are you, Cousin?"

"Slightly saddlesore but fine." Smiling broadly and still shaking Elliot's hand, Daniel threw his other arm around his cousin and thumped him heartily on the back. "What about you?"

"Never better, now that you're here."

Elliot Markham was a year younger than Daniel, an inch shorter, and had blue eyes to go with his blond hair and fair skin. He was also hopeless when it came to woodcraft, Daniel remembered from Elliot's visits to the Reed plantation. They had gone hunting together often but rarely bagged anything—since hunting with Elliot was like tramping through the woods with a squad of militia. He made enough noise for twelve men—more, if they were Virginians.

But Daniel supposed he was just as much out of place here in the city. There was no denying that Elliot was more worldly and sophisticated, even though he was a year younger. Daniel did not consider himself a bumpkin, and he was certainly not an embarrassment in a social setting . . . but he had his cousin to thank for refining his manners to meet the stringent standards of Boston. He had learned a great deal from Elliot.

"Come on inside," Elliot said, linking arms with Daniel to steer him toward the door. "I'm sure Mother and Father will be very glad to see you. We didn't know when you'd get here, but I've been keeping my eyes open for you. I just happened to be passing by the front window when I saw you ride up."

The door was still open. Elliot took Daniel through it into the foyer. The walls were papered in a rich brocade pattern, and to one side sat a small table with elaborately carved legs. Covering it was a linen cloth, and an oil lamp with a crystal mantle was set in the middle. On the opposite wall were hung two paintings, both landscapes of pastoral English scenes. At least Daniel had always supposed they were English; he had never been to England and possessed no desire to go there. The colonies were plenty big enough for him.

The parlor opened to the left of the foyer, and a hallway led straight ahead. Elliot started down this corridor, saying, "Father's in his study. He has some of his associates with him, but I'm sure he won't mind being interrupted. He said to let him know as soon as you got here."

Before they reached the heavy oak door of his uncle's study, Daniel heard Benjamin Markham's booming voice. He could not make out all the words in the tirade, but he caught "damnable insurrectionists," "high treason against the Crown," and "put a stop to it any way we have to!"

Elliot grinned and said, "You'll have to excuse Father. There was another meeting at Faneuil Hall last night, and when he heard about it, he got incensed, as usual."

Daniel shook his head. "Meeting? What sort of meeting?"

"Oh, the usual arguing about the king's taxes. People get together and talk about how awful the levies are, but it's just a bunch of hot air, in my opinion. I mean, you can't really do anything about what the king decrees, can you?"

"I suppose not. There was a mighty brawl at a tavern I visited on my trip north about the same sort of thing, though," Daniel said with a shrug. Down in Virginia, there had been ill feelings about some of the Crown's policies, but Daniel had never taken a great deal of interest in the discussions.

"At any rate, Father thinks there shouldn't be any talk against the king, and he despises Samuel Adams and that bunch," Elliot went on casually. "I just thought I should warn you, in case you've developed any so-called insurrectionist leanings."

Daniel laughed shortly. "Not likely. I have other things on my mind these days, such as going to Harvard College this fall."

"It's going to be good to have you around," Elliot said, his grin widening. "Come on. Let's beard the lion in its den, shall we?" He knocked quickly, then opened the door of the study and swept his arm around, gesturing for Daniel to precede him.

Daniel stepped into the gloomy room, which was paneled with dark wood and had thick curtains over its single window. When he had visited as a boy, he had never liked his uncle's study, except for the bookcases full of Benjamin Markham's intriguing leather-bound volumes. The books had always held a great attraction for Daniel, and he had managed to read quite a few of them during his stays.

Now the air was full of pipe smoke, and the room was as shadowy as he remembered. Daniel could tell by Benjamin Markham's stance in the center of the room that he had been pacing back and forth in front of his desk. He clutched an old briar pipe in his blunt fingers. Still straight and sturdily built in middle age, Benjamin had a strong jaw, piercing blue eyes, and a fringe of gray hair around a bald pate. He wore a black coat and breeches and a gray vest that were elegant and expensive despite their simplicity.

"Sorry to interrupt, Father," said Elliot, entering the room behind Daniel, "but look who's here."

"Hello, Daniel," Benjamin said cordially but without an excess of warmth. He stepped forward to greet his nephew. "How was your journey?"

"Just fine, Uncle Benjamin," Daniel replied as he shook the hand the older man thrust toward him.

"Well, it's good to see you. Your aunt and I have been looking forward to your visit." Benjamin gestured toward a trio of occupied armchairs arranged in a half circle in front of the desk. "Are you acquainted with these gentlemen?"

"Only Mr. Cummings, sir." Daniel nodded to one of the men, a thin, balding individual with rather pinched features. Daniel knew Theophilus Cummings was Benjamin Markham's business partner. The other two men were undoubtedly associates of theirs.

Benjamin confirmed that guess by saying, "This is Mr. Satterwaite and Mr. Johnson, two of our finest local merchants. Gentlemen, my nephew Daniel Reed."

The two men nodded to Daniel, and one of them—Satterwaite, Daniel thought—asked, "Where are you from, lad? Your accent marks you as a southerner."

"My family settled in Virginia, sir," Daniel said.

The man nodded and might have been about to say something else, but Benjamin spoke up first. "We've just been discussing the intolerable behavior of that rabble down at Faneuil Hall. Are you aware of the situation, Daniel?"

"Vaguely, sir."

"And your opinion?" Benjamin snapped.

Daniel had to shrug. "I'm not sure I have one."

"You don't have an opinion?" Cummings said in a sour voice that matched his expression. "Those people are talking about rebellion! Surely you have an opinion on that, young man."

"Well, I'm not in favor of violence," Daniel ventured.

"That's what they're going to get," Benjamin said. "If this constant badgering of the authorities continues, mark my words, there'll be trouble again, just like back in seventy."

Daniel knew what his uncle was talking about. Three years earlier, he had been planning to visit Elliot in Boston during the summer, but that spring, the so-called Boston Massacre had taken place, resulting in the deaths of several colonists during a melee with British troops. Tensions had remained high during that summer, and Daniel's parents had decided that a trip to Boston would not be wise. Instead, Elliot's mother and father had sent him to Virginia that year.

"I certainly hope it doesn't come to that," Daniel offered. "There's been enough fighting."

"There'll be more. Goddamned rebels—"

Elliot closed his hand over Daniel's arm and broke in on his father's vitriolic comments by saying, "I'll show you your room, Daniel. I'm sure you must be tired after your journey."

"Yes, I am, a bit." Daniel nodded to Benjamin. "It's good to see you again, Uncle. Thank you for allowing me to visit."

"Always glad to have you," Benjamin said gruffly. He puffed on his pipe for a moment as Elliot took Daniel out into the hall. When Elliot was closing the door, Benjamin resumed, "The king ought to send more troops . . ."

The angry statement was cut off as the door clicked

shut. Elliot led Daniel to the wide staircase at the right of the foyer. "I'm sorry," he said quietly. "I really thought Father might stop talking politics long enough to give you a proper welcome. Instead he just tried to draw you into the argument."

Daniel waved off the apology. "That's all right," he assured his cousin. "I'm flattered they thought enough of me to ask my opinion. I was a bit embarrassed that I'm not more well versed in the controversy, though."

"Who can keep up with it? If you ask me, the whole thing is overblown."

"Well, I don't know," Daniel said slowly as they climbed the stairs. "It's an interesting situation. This conflict between England and the colonies has been growing for quite a while. I'm afraid your father may be right. There could be more trouble."

Elliot glanced over at him. "And which side will you be on, Cousin?"

Daniel had to pause at the second-floor landing and shake his head. "I honestly don't know. I haven't thought about it that much. As I said, I've had other things on my mind."

As they went down the hallway, Daniel found himself frowning. Perhaps he should have devoted more thought to the growing antagonism between England and the colonies. Somehow, down in Virginia on the plantation where he had grown up, all the troubles had seemed so far away. Daniel's parents were more concerned with making a home and a living for themselves and their children than they were with political intricacies, and Daniel supposed that attitude had rubbed off on him to a certain extent.

"Well, I haven't thought a lot about it either," Elliot said, "but I'm sure my father is right. The people who are complaining are just stirring up trouble for everyone. I mean, my God, what would they have us do? Revolt against the king? It's absurd. It's high treason, just as my father says."

Something about Elliot's statements did not quite ring true to Daniel's ears, but he supposed that was because Elliot was only repeating what he had heard his father say many times. That could make the words sound false, even though Elliot might agree whole-heartedly with the position he was taking. All Daniel knew was that he did not want to press the matter.

The door to one of the bedrooms opened, and a stout woman with graying brown hair stepped out. She stopped short at the sight of Daniel, and a smile brightened her pleasantly handsome face. "Daniel!" she exclaimed. "You're here! I just opened the window in your room to let it air out a bit."

Daniel stepped forward and leaned over to brush a kiss across the woman's cheek. "Hello, Aunt Polly," he said.

"Did you just get here?"

"A few minutes ago," Elliot supplied the answer. "I've already taken him in to say hello to Father and get his political indoctrination."

"I hope Benjamin and his friends didn't make you uncomfortable, Daniel," Polly Markham said. "They do go on about all this trouble with the government."

"It was fine," Daniel assured her. "I was interested in what they had to say."

"You may get tired of hearing about it before you leave us," Polly said, rolling her eyes. "All day and every evening it's the same thing—insurrectionists and rabble-rousers. I'd much rather talk about pleasant things . . . like your mother and father. How are they?"

"Both of them are quite well, thank you. They send their love, of course."

"And little Quincy?"

Daniel had to smile at hearing his younger brother described as little. Quincy had shot up in the last year, since turning fourteen, and he was almost as tall as Daniel. "He's doing very well, Aunt Polly. You'll be seeing him in a few weeks when the rest of the family comes up for a visit."

"Of course. I haven't forgotten. It's going to be so good to see everyone again." Polly stepped aside. "Well, you go on in. I'll have one of the servants bring in your things."

"There's just one bag tied to the saddle. And my rifle, of course. But if you could have someone bring that in and take my horse around to the stable . . . ?"

"Certainly." Polly smiled at him again, dimples appearing in her plump cheeks. "It's good to have you here with us, Daniel. I hope you'll enjoy your visit."

"I'm sure I will."

And with everything that is going on in Boston right now, Daniel mused, *it may indeed turn out to be a very interesting summer.*

CODY'S LAW BOOK 6:

RENEGADE TRAIL

by Matthew S. Hart

Texas Ranger Sam Cody's latest assignment is to track down an outlaw gang plaguing West Texas. While the assignment is hardly unusual, the circumstances are: the outlaw leader has been identified as Barry Whittingham, a noble Englishman who immigrated to America after Reconstruction and wound up in Texas—and a former Ranger.

Since he and Wittingham were once troopmates, Cody won't be able to go in and work undercover, as he often does. Instead, his commander has sent Seth Williams along on the mission, a young Ranger with some undercover experience who joined the force after Whittingham resigned. While Cody starts working with the local sheriff and the Army—the desperadoes have waylaid a couple of supply trains—Seth encounters a pair of young hardcases whose ambition is to ride with Whittingham's gang. Seth is soon in the thick of things, and the two Rangers find themselves on opposite sides, walking a fine line between not killing each other and maintaining Seth's cover.

The already-complicated assignment gets even knottier with the arrival of Leigh Gilmore, a beautiful young woman from Dallas who is searching for her sister, Sara—kidnapped by an outlaw rumored to be Barry Whittingham—and is determined to find her, with or without Cody's help. But appearances aren't necessarily what they seem—and a willing victim is also an unwitting linchpin in a deadly double-cross.

**Read on for an exciting preview of RENEGADE TRAIL,
on sale in summer 1992
wherever Bantam Books are sold.**

CHAPTER 1

There were days, Cody thought, when it was good to be alive, and you knew from the time you got up in the morning that everything was going to be just fine.

Then there were days like today.

His hat clamped on tight, his brown eyes squinted in concentration, and a frown tugging down his thick, dark mustache, he urged the rangy lineback dun beneath him on to greater speed, and as he leaned forward in the saddle, he slid the Winchester '73 from the sheath strapped under his right thigh. Guiding the dun with his knees, he worked the rifle's lever and jacked a shell into the chamber.

The horse was damn ugly standing still, but its ground-eating pace right now was a thing of beauty. Its deceptively easy stride carried it down a long, gentle slope toward the flatland, where the San Antonio-to-El-Paso stage road ran. Bucketing along that trail—and kicking up a huge cloud of dust with its hurried passage—was a Concord coach being pulled by a six-horse hitch. The stagecoach swayed and bounced on its thick leather thoroughbraces as the driver shouted curses and flailed at the backs of the horses with his whip. On the box beside the driver the guard was twisted around, firing his revolver back at the riders pursuing the coach.

Cody's keen senses had immediately taken in the entire scene when he'd topped the rise a few moments earlier. Not that there was a hell of a lot else out here to see or hear. To his right was the shallow, slow-moving Rio Grande, and beyond the river in Mexico were foothills rising into a low range of mountains. To the left was nothing but semiarid Texas prairie for as far as the eye could see. The stagecoach and the bandits chasing it easily stood out against the landscape, and the harsh crash and boom of gunfire shattered the hot stillness.

There was no doubt in Cody's mind that the men chasing the coach were outlaws. A holdup was the only reason for nearly a dozen riders to be racing after a stagecoach, firing their pistols as they rode. It didn't take a lot of experience as a lawman to recognize such a thing. As soon as Cody had realized what was going on, he'd heeled the dun out of its easy lope and into a gallop.

A saddle was the worst place in the world for shooting accurately, but Cody didn't really care if he hit anything. He triggered a couple of shots toward the outlaws, hoping that having somebody else take cards in this hand would spook the gang and they'd clear out.

The riders hesitated. They were close enough now that Cody could see they had their bandannas pulled up over their faces to form crude masks. The stagecoach came on toward him as he angled toward the trail.

Cody's day hadn't started out nearly so vigorously. He had left El Paso early that morning while the air still held a hint of coolness. The dun was well rested, and so was Cody. After riding out of the border city, he had meandered along the river instead of the road, content to take his time on the way back to Del Rio. It looked like it was going to be a quiet, easy ride. Then around midmorning he'd heard shooting, seen a haze of dust rising in the air ahead of him and to the left, and sent the dun up the rise to see what was happening.

Now he knew.

Cody pumped a couple more rounds at the bandits, making them falter even more. Chasing a stagecoach was one thing; going up against a man with a

Winchester who knew how to use it was another. They had him outnumbered, all right, but they might not want to pay the price he would extract from them before going down himself.

The outlaws hauled back on their reins, slowing their horses. They were going to turn and run; Cody sensed that with every instinct in his body—and then a good-sized rock at the edge of the stage road ruined everything.

The stage veered toward the shallow ditch at the left of the road. The driver recovered and jerked the team back toward the center of the trail, but not before the rear wheel clipped the rock that had apparently been thrown up when the ditch was dug. The wheel was jolted up, and with a crack that was audible even over the shooting and the pounding of hooves, the rear axle of the coach broke. The left wheel spun completely off, and that corner of the vehicle hit the ground, dragging a deep furrow in the hard-packed earth of the road for a few feet before the coach slewed around and started to tip over. The tongue snapped as the coach rolled, but the horses were still attached to it by their harness, and they were pulled down, too. A huge cloud of dust blossomed around the wreckage, hiding the coach and team for several seconds.

Cody cursed. The outlaws, who'd been on the verge of breaking off their attack, let out whoops of glee as they saw the stagecoach crash. It'd be easy pickings now, good reason to stay and dispose of him. After all, ten-to-one odds were enough for just about anybody. Putting the spurs to their horses, the highwaymen surged forward again.

Cody yanked the dun to a stop. He couldn't settle for scaring off the desperadoes any longer; his shooting had to be more accurate now. Bringing the Winchester to his shoulder, he laid his cheek on the smooth wooden stock and settled the blade of the front sight on the breast pocket of one of the lead riders. A squeeze of the trigger made the rifle buck against Cody's shoulder as it cracked.

"Damn!" he exclaimed as he peered through the dust. The outlaw hadn't gone down, so his bullet had missed.

Wheeling the dun toward the coach, Cody kicked it into a run again. The wrecked stagecoach was the only cover around here—and he was going to need some.

There wasn't much wind today, not enough to shred the dust and carry it off. It had to float away by itself, and that'd take some time. Cody plunged into the cloud, yanking the dun to a halt as he tried to locate the coach. His eyes smarted from the dust. After a second he saw the bulk of the overturned vehicle and swung down hurriedly from the saddle. A swat on the dun's rump sent it leaping away. The horse would run off out of range of the fighting, Cody knew, then turn and wait for him.

He sprinted toward the stagecoach, hearing bullets whine through the haze around him. Realizing that if the driver or the guard had survived the crash, they might think he was one of the outlaws and take a shot at him, he bellowed, "Ranger coming in! Texas Ranger!" Once he got close enough, they'd be able to see the badge on his vest, the already-famous silver star set within a silver circle, and they'd know he was telling the truth.

Muzzle flashes winked from behind the coach as Cody skirted the vehicle. The shots weren't directed at him, so he knew the defenders must have heard and understood him. He dropped into a crouch behind the wreckage, poked the barrel of his rifle over the coach, and fired three shots as fast as he could work the lever, aiming toward where the outlaws had been. The dust was beginning to thin out now, and he thought he could see shadowy forms on horseback.

A glance to his right showed Cody that three men were fighting along with him. One he recognized as the driver, so the other two must have been passengers in the stage. The guard was lying on the ground, conscious but grimacing in pain from a leg that was bent at a strange, severe angle. Cody thought he glimpsed the whiteness of bone poking out through a rip in the man's pants.

"Anybody hurt inside the coach?" Cody asked.

The driver shook his head. "We was mighty lucky," he said. "These two gents were the only passengers. Matt there's the only one got hurt, and his leg's busted bad."

Cody dropped to a knee beside the injured guard. "I can see that." He put a hand on the man's shoulder. "Hang on, friend. We'll drive those bandidos off, then see about fixing up that leg of yours."

"Give the . . . sonsabitches . . . a couple of slugs for me," the guard grated through clenched teeth.

Cody flashed him a grim smile, then stood up again and lifted the Winchester. He saw movement out of the corner of his eye to the left, wheeled in that direction, and held off on the trigger just long enough to recognize that one of the outlaws was swooping in close to the coach. The Ranger's rifle barked wickedly.

With a screech of pain, the figure on horseback plunged from the saddle and landed in a limp heap on the ground. A couple of riders were right behind him, but they threw on the brakes, spun their horses, and went back the other direction in a hurry.

"Good shootin', Ranger!" one of the passengers exclaimed.

The dust had cleared enough now for Cody to see that the remaining outlaws had pulled back and regrouped. He didn't try to fool himself into thinking they were going to pull out just because they'd lost one man. If anything, that would just make them more determined. The odds were all on their side, especially since, from the looks of things, the Ranger had the only Winchester. The other three men were using handguns.

"They'll be coming again in a minute," Cody said. "Better get some fresh cartridges in your guns while you've got the chance."

He followed his own advice, taking shells from the loops on the left side of his gun belt and sliding them into the rifle's loading gate until the magazine was full again. Then he stooped and picked up the empty casings that had been ejected from the Winchester and put them in his pocket. Might as well be optimistic and assume that he'd have a chance to reload them when he got back to Del Rio, he thought.

Turning to his companions, he asked, "Why are those boys so determined? No offense, gents, but from the looks of you, they wouldn't make that big of a haul."

The two passengers were both middle-aged men in well-worn range clothes. One of them grinned and said, "We ride for the 7X spread out close to El Paso. Our boss sent us to San Antone to pick up some money at his bank. He's goin' to use the cash to pay off a fella he's buyin' some new breedin' stock from."

"How much cash?"

"Twenty-two thousand dollars."

Cody let out a low whistle and nodded toward the outlaws. "I reckon that bunch got wind of the deal?"

"Must have, though I don't see how they did."

"Your boss ought to use a bank in El Paso," Cody said dryly. "That'd be closer."

"That's what we been tellin' him, but Elmer's been bankin' in San Antone for a long time, and he's a stubborn ol' feller."

Cody understood the situation better now. That much money was an irresistable lure for lawless men. The ranch hands carrying it were probably longtime employees of the owner of the 7X, men who could be trusted not only with money, but also with the life of a friend. But it was always possible for things to go wrong, just as they obviously had in this case.

"Here they come again!" the stage driver yelled.

Cody looked up to see the outlaws galloping toward them. The desperadoes weren't bunched up now. They were spreading out, veering to the sides. Cody grimaced. The outlaws were being smart. Instead of attacking head on, they were going to circle the wreckage and try to catch the defenders in a crossfire. Worse yet, they had pouched their sixes and brought out their long guns—which meant they were going to carry out the attack beyond pistol range.

"Keep your heads down," Cody warned his companions. "This is going to be bad."

Chances were they were all going to die.

Cody brought his Winchester to his shoulder again, set on bringing down a few of them. But before he could settle on a target and squeeze the trigger, one of the outlaws rolled from his saddle and thumped to the ground. A split second later Cody heard the far-distant sound of a shot.

Somebody else had taken a hand.

But he couldn't wonder about that now. With bullets thudding into the coach beside him, Cody took aim and pulled the trigger. The blast of the rifle was rewarded by another outlaw knocked off his horse.

The driver and the two passengers had gone to ground to present smaller targets. Cody followed their example, dropping to one knee as he shifted his aim. He took a deep breath to steady himself and touched off another shot. One of the outlaws swayed in the saddle, hit but not knocked down. Still, the wounded man swung his horse away from the fight, and that was almost as good.

Cody heard more gunfire, saw another man drop. The odds were getting cut in a hurry now. The Ranger glanced to the east, squinting through the shifting clouds of dust, and saw another rider approaching. The newcomer sent his horse dashing forward several yards as he levered his rifle. He then jerked the animal to a halt, raised himself in his stirrups, aimed, and fired again.

The Ranger kept up his own shooting, emptying half of the Winchester's magazine in a matter of minutes. The line of outlaws was ragged now, holes being shot in it from both directions. They had lost four men—maybe more; it was hard to tell—and they hadn't done a lick of damage since the coach had crashed.

Twenty-two grand just wasn't enough when you were caught in a crossfire between two men who could shave a gnat's whiskers at a hundred yards. Yelling curses, the survivors of the gang whirled their horses toward the south and the Rio Grande. All they wanted now was to get the border river between them and the two riflemen taking such a heavy toll on them.

Cody was more than willing to let them go.

He stood up and watched the fleeing bandits for a moment. The driver and the two passengers got to their feet, too, and brushed alkali dust from their clothes. Cody switched his attention to the man who had saved them by pitching in when he did. The stranger was cantering toward them now, still holding his rifle ready across his chest in case the outlaws decided to make one last try at the job.

There was something familiar about the man, and Cody suddenly realized he wasn't a stranger after all. As the newcomer rode closer, Cody recognized the young man wearing a flat-crowned brown hat, a buckskin shirt, whipcord pants, and boot-topped moccasins. He had a thatch of blond hair that hung almost to his shoulders and a ready grin that split his lean face. A badge was pinned to his buckskin shirt, not identical to the one Cody wore but shaped in the same pattern. Rangers usually made their own badges, so there were always subtle differences.

"Howdy, Cody," the youngster called as he reined in. "Looks like I came along just in time."

"I'd say so," Cody agreed, tucking his rifle under his left arm. "No offense, Seth—but what the hell are you doing here?"

Seth Williams kept grinning as he slid his rifle back into the saddle boot and then swung down from his horse. Like Cody, he was a member of Ranger Company C, headquartered far down the Rio Grande at Del Rio. "Well, that's a fine way to greet a fella who just saved your bacon," he groused. "Not even a 'Thanks, Seth. We'd'a been buzzard bait without you.'"

One of the passengers spoke up. "I'll say it. Thanks, young fella."

"You're welcome, mister. Just doing my duty as a Ranger."

"And you still haven't told me what you're doing here," Cody reminded him. "It's a long way to Del Rio."

Seth frowned. "Didn't you get Cap'n Vickery's wire?"

Cody leaned his rifle against the overturned coach and knelt beside the injured guard, who was only half-conscious now from loss of blood and the shock of his broken leg. While the driver went to cut loose the struggling horses in his team and find out how badly they were hurt, Cody examined the guard's leg, saying to Seth as he did so, "I don't know anything about a wire. I haven't even been in touch with headquarters since I got back to El Paso from Mexico. If the cap'n sent me a telegram, it must've gotten lost somewhere along the way."

Hunkering on the other side of the guard, Seth nodded. "Yeah, could be. How'd that job in Mexico wind up?"

"All right," the older Ranger grunted. Seth didn't need to know all the details; Cody would put them in his report to Captain Vickery when he got back to headquarters. "We've got to get this leg set. Find me something to use for a splint."

Seth and the two ranch hands from the 7X took on that chore. Out here in this largely treeless country, finding a piece of wood of a suitable length and thickness for a splint wasn't always easy. Seth solved the problem by bringing Cody a couple of pieces of the broken axle from the stagecoach.

"Wish I had some whiskey for you, friend," Cody said to the guard, not knowing if the man heard him or not. "This is going to hurt."

He had cut away the man's pant leg, exposing the gruesome injury. There was no way to get the pieces of bone back together without causing more damage to the tissue around them, but that couldn't be helped. Taking a deep breath, Cody grasped the man's leg and forced the bone sections back into place. The guard screamed in agony and tried to come up off the ground, but Seth and the two cowhands held him fast.

Once that was done, Cody tied the splints in place and then bound up the wound with strips torn from the guard's shirt. The man still needed a lot of medical attention, as soon as possible, but Cody had done all he could.

Seth looked up. "Somebody coming," he said.

Cody lifted his own gaze to the trail and saw a buckboard rattling and bouncing along it from the east, being drawn by a pair of old mules. At the reins was a swarthy, stocky man in the white cotton pants, faded serape, and broad-brimmed sombrero of a Mexican farmer. Beside him on the seat was a middle-aged woman wearing a dark dress and a shawl over her head—the farmer's wife, no doubt. Half a dozen children rode in the back of the wagon.

Cody stood up and raised a hand, gesturing for the peon to stop. The man hauled back on the reins and brought the mules to a halt. His dark face was impassive as he surveyed the wreckage of the stagecoach in the road. There was room for him to drive around it, but for the moment he was content to see what Cody wanted. The youngsters clustered at the front of the wagon bed, peering curiously over the shoulders of their parents.

"Howdy, folks," Cody said. "We've had some trouble here. Hope you can give us a hand."

The woman spoke in a low voice to her husband, the liquid Spanish coming fast and furious. The man nodded, then said to Cody, "What is it you require of us, señor?"

"Got a man hurt here," Cody replied, pointing to the guard, who had passed out. "We need to get him on to El Paso so that a doctor can take a look at him."

"I see his leg is broken," the farmer said. He glanced nervously at the bodies of the fallen outlaws, sprawled motionlessly on the ground some fifty yards away. "Those men, they are responsible?"

"They're bandits," Cody told him, nodding. "They tried to rob the stagecoach. My friend, here, and I are Texas Rangers, and we were lucky enough to run off the rest of them."

"*Sí*, lucky."

The stagecoach driver stepped up beside Cody and said impatiently, "Look here, Pancho, are you goin' to sit there and jaw all day? You know what the Ranger's tellin' you. We need your wagon."

"I was getting around to asking, not telling," Cody pointed out in a quiet voice. Only someone who knew him well would've heard the anger in it.

"We don't have time to waste on a bunch of long-winded talk," snapped the driver. "Matt's hurt, and I intend to get him to town as soon as those Mexes climb down from that wagon."

Cody bit back his own curt response. The man was worried about his partner, and the Ranger couldn't blame him for that. But Cody didn't intend to stand by and watch the Mexican family being taken advantage of, either.

Digging in the pocket of his denim pants, Cody brought out a ten dollar gold piece and flipped it to the farmer, who caught it deftly in midair. "We'd like to rent your wagon, señor, and hire your services as driver, too. Reckon there's room in the back for this injured man and the other folks, too?"

The man nodded eagerly, his eyes shining as he looked at the coin clutched in his callused hand. Likely it was more money than he'd seen in one place for quite a while. "*Sí,*" he said. "We go to visit my sister in El Paso del Norte, but as you can see, we have little in the way of belongings. Plenty of room in back."

The stage driver grumbled a little, but apparently even he could see that he had no right to commandeer the wagon and strand the farmer and his family out here in the middle of nowhere. They were damned lucky, in fact, that the buckboard had come along when it did. The injured man couldn't ride a horse, so they'd have been stuck out here in the hot sun all day while Cody and Seth rode back to El Paso and brought help. Of course, if the two Rangers hadn't happened along from opposite directions when they did, the occupants of the stagecoach probably wouldn't have survived the outlaw attack.

As the driver, the two cowhands, and the farmer carefully loaded the guard into the buckboard, Cody turned to Seth and asked, "Now, what was this about some telegram Cap'n Vickery sent me?"

Seth grinned. "The old mossback's got a job for us."

"Us?" repeated Cody. "And you wouldn't talk about the cap'n like that if he was here."

"Damn right I wouldn't! He'd skin me alive." Then

Seth's expression became more serious. "Anyway, I was on my way to meet you. We're supposed to join up and take a little detour into the Davis Mountains. Orders are to meet a fella at Fort Davis and take care of a small chore up there before heading back to Del Rio."

Cody frowned and rubbed his jaw in consternation. Riding all the way up to the Army post in the Davis Mountains of West Texas was hardly a "little detour." It'd mean several days of hard traveling. Whatever the assignment was, it had to be serious.

"Maybe we'd better ride back into El Paso so that I can wire the cap'n and get all the details," he said.

"No need to do that," Seth said quickly. "I can fill you in, Cody." He waved at the group of people clustered around the buckboard. "These folks don't need our help anymore. That bunch of owlhoots won't be back. And if you backtrack all the way to El Paso, that'll just delay things that much more. Better just to head on to Fort Davis."

Cody waited for Seth's protests to run down, then asked, "Are you sure you know what this is all about?"

The young Ranger nodded emphatically. "Alan and I were there when the cap'n was talking about it with Lieutenant Whitcomb. We even got a look at the letter from the sheriff at Fort Davis, asking for the Rangers to give him a hand. I can tell you all about it."

"All right, fair enough," Cody decided. "Besides, I've seen enough of El Paso to last me for a while. We'll head north as soon as these people are on their way."

"What about those dead outlaws?"

Cody just shrugged, and that was answer enough. It was too hot to be wasting sweat digging graves for owlhoots. The coyotes would take care of them.

Even with the injured guard stretched out in the back of the buckboard, there was room for the two worn carpetbags of the 7X cowhands. They took the bags from the stagecoach boot and piled them in the wagon while the driver retrieved the mail pouch from the box. That was all they had. The three men piled into the wagonbed with the Mexican youngsters while the farmer took his seat again and picked up the reins. As loaded down as it was, the buckboard wouldn't make very good time going into El Paso, but it sure beat nothing.

Cody whistled for his dun, which was still standing off about a hundred yards away, watching the goings-on. The horse came to him at a trot and stopped right in front of him, nuzzling the hand Cody held out. The Ranger patted the dun's nose, then stepped up into the saddle. Edging the horse over beside the wagon as Seth mounted up, Cody said to the stage driver, "You treat these folks right. Remember, they're the ones helping you."

The man nodded sheepishly. "I know, Ranger. Reckon I got a little worked up earlier 'cause I was worried about Matt. Won't happen again."

"Figured as much." Cody lifted a finger to the brim of his hat and nodded to the woman. "*Buenos días, señora.* And *gracias* to you and your husband."

The two Rangers sat, hands crossed on their saddle horns, and watched as the buckboard pulled away. They stayed there until it had dwindled to a speck in the heat and dust, and then Cody turned the dun's head toward the northeast.

"Let's go," he said. "You can tell me all about it on the way."

CODY'S LAW

Matthew S. Hart

❑ **GUNMETAL JUSTICE** 29030-4 $3.50/$4.50 in Canada
Texas Ranger justice is about to catch up with a ruthless land baron and his henchmen. A showdown's coming, and Cody will have to ride into hell to end the trail of tyranny.

❑ **DIE LONESOME** 29127-0 $3.50/$4.50 in Canada
Two hundred Winchester repeating rifles have been stolen from an army supply depot. Undercover and alone, Cody has the brains to set a dangerous trap, and the guts to use a beautiful saloonkeeper as bait. But someone is desperately waiting for a chance to plug this lawman full of lead.

❑ **BORDER SHOWDOWN** 29371-0 $3.50/$4.50 in Canada
A band of ruthless desperadoes is spreading a reign of bloody terror...and Cody comes up with an ingenious plan to bring these hard cases to justice. It will take every ounce of courage Cody possesses to bring the culprits to justice.

❑ **BOUNTY MAN** 29517-9 $3.50/$4.50 in Canada
All Cody wants is to get his uncle, a notoriously ruthless bounty hunter, out of Twin Creeks. But when a posse of hired killers shows up to spring his relative's prisoner, Cody and his uncle must join forces—or watch Twin Creeks drown in a sea of blood.

Elmer Kelton is "one of the best of a new breed of Western writers who have driven the genre into new territory."
—*The New York Times*

Winner of numerous awards, including the Western Heritage Award from the National Cowboy Hall of Fame for this novel, the Golden Spur and the Sadleman from the Western Writers of America, Elmer Kelton is a Western storyteller with a special talent for capturing the fiercely independent spirit of his native Texas.